The Snake's Pass

The Snake's Pass
Bram Stoker

MINT EDITIONS

The Snake's Pass was first published in 1890.

This edition published by Mint Editions 2021.

ISBN 9781513282039 | E-ISBN 9781513287058

Published by Mint Editions®

 MINT
EDITIONS

minteditionbooks.com

Publishing Director: Jennifer Newens
Design & Production: Rachel Lopez Metzger
Project Manager: Micaela Clark
Typesetting: Westchester Publishing Services

Contents

I

A Sudden Storm

Between two great mountains of grey and green, as the rock cropped out between the tufts of emerald verdure, the valley, almost as narrow as a gorge, ran due west towards the sea. There was just room for the roadway, half cut in the rock, beside the narrow strip of dark lake of seemingly unfathomable depth that lay far below between perpendicular walls of frowning rock. As the valley opened, the land dipped steeply, and the lake became a foam-fringed torrent, widening out into pools and miniature lakes as it reached the lower ground. In the wide terrace-like steps of the shelving mountain there were occasional glimpses of civilization emerging from the almost primal desolation which immediately surrounded us—clumps of trees, cottages, and the irregular outlines of stone-walled fields, with black stacks of turf for winter firing piled here and there. Far beyond was the sea—the great Atlantic—with a wildly irregular coast-line studded with a myriad of clustering rocky islands. A sea of deep dark blue, with the distant horizon tinged with a line of faint white light, and here and there, where its margin was visible through the breaks in the rocky coast, fringed with a line of foam as the waves broke on the rocks or swept in great rollers over the level expanse of sands.

The sky was a revelation to me, and seemed to almost obliterate memories of beautiful skies, although I had just come from the south and had felt the intoxication of the Italian night, where in the deep blue sky the nightingale's note seems to hang as though its sound and the colour were but different expressions of one common feeling.

The whole west was a gorgeous mass of violet and sulphur and gold—great masses of storm-cloud piling up and up till the very heavens seemed weighted with a burden too great to bear. Clouds of violet, whose centres were almost black and whose outer edges were tinged with living gold; great streaks and piled up clouds of palest yellow deepening into saffron and flame-colour which seemed to catch the coming sunset and to throw its radiance back to the eastern sky.

The view was the most beautiful that I had ever seen, and, accustomed as I had been only to the quiet pastoral beauty of a grass country, with occasional visits to my Great Aunt's well-wooded estate in the South of England, it was no wonder that it arrested my attention and absorbed my imagination. Even my brief half-a-year's travel in Europe, now just concluded, had shown me nothing of the same kind.

Earth, sea and air all evidenced the triumph of nature, and told of her wild majesty and beauty. The air was still—ominously still. So still was all, that through the silence, that seemed to hedge us in with a sense of oppression, came the booming of the distant sea, as the great Atlantic swell broke in surf on the rocks or stormed the hollow caverns of the shore.

Even Andy, the driver, was for the nonce awed into comparative silence. Hitherto, for nearly forty miles of a drive, he had been giving me his experiences—propounding his views—airing his opinions; in fact he had been making me acquainted with his store of knowledge touching the whole district and its people—including their names, histories, romances, hopes and fears—all that goes to make up the life and interest of a country-side.

No barber—taking this tradesman to illustrate the popular idea of loquacity *in excelsis*—is more consistently talkative than an Irish car-driver to whom has been granted the gift of speech. There is absolutely no limit to his capability, for every change of surrounding affords a new theme and brings on the tapis a host of matters requiring to be set forth.

I was rather glad of Andy's 'brilliant flash of silence' just at present, for not only did I wish to drink in and absorb the grand and novel beauty of the scene that opened out before me, but I wanted to understand as fully as I could some deep thought which it awoke within me. It may have been merely the grandeur and beauty of the scene—or perhaps it was the thunder which filled the air that July evening—but I felt exalted in a strange way, and impressed at the same time with a new sense of the reality of things. It almost seemed as if through that opening valley, with the mighty Atlantic beyond and the piling up of the storm-clouds overhead, I passed into a new and more real life.

Somehow I had of late seemed to myself to be waking up. My foreign tour had been gradually dissipating my old sleepy ideas, or perhaps overcoming the negative forces that had hitherto dominated my life; and now this glorious burst of wild natural beauty—the majesty of nature at its fullest—seemed to have completed my awakening, and I felt as though I looked for the first time with open eyes on the beauty and reality of the world.

Hitherto my life had been but an inert one, and I was younger in many ways and more deficient in knowledge of the world in all ways than other young men of my own age. I had stepped but lately from boyhood, with all boyhood's surroundings, into manhood, and as yet I was hardly at ease in my new position.

For the first time in my life I had had a holiday—a real holiday, as one can take it who can choose his own way of amusing himself.

I had been brought up in an exceedingly quiet way with an old clergyman and his wife in the west of England, and except my fellow pupils, of whom there was never at any time more than one other, I had had little companionship. Altogether I knew very few people. I was the ward of a Great Aunt, who was wealthy and eccentric and of a sternly uncompromising disposition. When my father and mother were lost at sea, leaving me, an only child, quite unprovided for, she undertook to pay for my schooling and to start me in a profession if I should show sufficient aptitude for any. My father had been pretty well cut off by his family on account of his marriage with what they considered his inferior, and times had been, I was always told, pretty hard for them both. I was only a very small boy when they were lost in a fog when crossing the Channel; and the blank that their loss caused me made me, I dare say, seem even a duller boy than I was. As I did not get into much trouble and did not exhibit any special restlessness of disposition, my Great Aunt took it, I suppose, for granted that I was very well off where I was; and when, through growing years, the fiction of my being a schoolboy could be no longer supported, the old clergyman was called "guardian" instead of "tutor," and I passed with him the years that young men of the better class usually spend in College life. The nominal change of position made little difference to me, except that I was taught to ride and shoot, and was generally given the rudiments of an education which was to fit me for being a country gentleman. I dare say that my tutor had some secret understanding with my Great Aunt, but he never gave me any hint whatever of her feelings towards me. A part of my holidays each year was spent in her place, a beautiful country seat. Here I was always treated by the old lady with rigid severity but with the best of good manners, and by the servants with affection as well as respect. There were a host of cousins, both male and female, who came to the house; but I can honestly say that by not one of them was I ever treated with cordiality. It may have been my fault, or the misfortune of my shyness; but I never met one of them without being made to feel that I was an "outsider."

I can understand now the cause of this treatment as arising from their suspicions when I remember that the old lady, who had been so severe with me all my life, sent for me when she lay on her deathbed, and, taking my hand in hers and holding it tight, said, between her gasps:—

"Arthur, I hope I have not done wrong, but I have reared you so that the world may for you have good as well as bad—happiness as well as unhappiness; that you may find many pleasures where you thought there were but few. Your youth, I know, my dear boy, has not been a happy one; but it was because I, who loved your dear father as if he had been my own son—and from whom I unhappily allowed myself to be estranged until it was too late—wanted you to have a good and happy manhood."

She did not say any more, but closed her eyes and still held my hand. I feared to take it away lest I should disturb her; but presently the clasp seemed to relax, and I found that she was dead.

I had never seen a dead person, much less anyone die, and the event made a great impression on me. But youth is elastic, and the old lady had never been much in my heart.

When the will was read, it was found that I had been left heir to all her property, and that I would be called upon to take a place among the magnates of the county. I could not fall at once into the position and, as I was of a shy nature, resolved to spend at least a few months in travel. This I did, and when I had returned, after a six months' tour, I accepted the cordial invitation of some friends, made on my travels, to pay them a visit at their place in the County of Clare.

As my time was my own, and as I had a week or two to spare, I had determined to improve my knowledge of Irish affairs by making a detour through some of the counties in the west on my way to Clare.

By this time I was just beginning to realize that life has many pleasures. Each day a new world of interest seemed to open before me. The experiment of my Great Aunt might yet be crowned with success.

And now the consciousness of the change in myself had come home to me—come with the unexpected suddenness of the first streak of the dawn through the morning mists. The moment was to be to me a notable one; and as I wished to remember it to the full, I tried to take in all the scene where such a revelation first dawned upon me. I had fixed in my mind, as the central point for my memory to rest on, a promontory right under the direct line of the sun, when I was interrupted by a remark made, not to me but seemingly to the universe in general:—

"Musha! but it's comin' quick."

"What is coming?" I asked.

"The shtorm! Don't ye see the way thim clouds is dhriftin'? Faix! but it's fine times the ducks 'll be afther havin' before many minutes is past."

I did not heed his words much, for my thoughts were intent on the scene. We were rapidly descending the valley, and, as we got lower, the promontory seemed to take bolder shape, and was beginning to stand out as a round-topped hill of somewhat noble proportions.

"Tell me, Andy," I said, "what do they call the hill beyond?"

"The hill beyant there is it? Well, now, they call the place Shleenanaher."

"Then that is Shleenanaher mountain?"

"Begor it's not. The mountain is called Knockcallte-crore. It's Irish."

"And what does it mean?"

"Faix, I believe it's a short name for the Hill iv the Lost Goolden Crown."

"And what is Shleenanaher, Andy?"

"Throth, it's a bit iv a gap in the rocks beyant that they call Shleenanaher."

"And what does that mean? It is Irish, I suppose?"

"Thrue for ye! Irish it is, an' it manes 'The Shnake's Pass.'"

"Indeed! And can you tell me why it is so called?"

"Begor, there's a power iv raysons guv for callin' it that. Wait till we get Jerry Scanlan or Bat Moynahan, beyant in Carnaclif! Sure they knows every laygend and shtory in the bar'ny, an'll tell them all, av ye like. Whew! Musha! here it comes."

Surely enough it did come. The storm seemed to sweep through the valley in a single instant—the stillness changed to a roar, the air became dark with the clouds of drifting rain. It was like the bursting of a waterspout in volume, and came so quickly that I was drenched to the skin before I could throw my mackintosh round me. The mare seemed frightened at first, but Andy held her in with a steady hand and with comforting words, and after the first rush of the tempest she went on as calmly and steadily as hitherto, only shrinking a little at the lightning and the thunder.

The grandeur of that storm was something to remember. The lightning came in brilliant sheets that seemed to cleave the sky, and threw weird lights amongst the hills, now strange with black sweeping shadows. The thunder broke with startling violence right over our heads, and flapped and buffeted from hillside to hillside, rolling and reverberating away into the distance, its farther voices being lost in the crash of each succeeding peal.

On we went, through the driving storm, faster and faster; but the storm abated not a jot. Andy was too much occupied with his work to speak, and as for me it took all my time to keep on the rocking and swaying car, and to hold my hat and mackintosh so as to shield myself, as well as I could, from the pelting storm. Andy seemed to be above all considerations of personal comfort. He turned up his coat collar, that was all; and soon he was as shiny as my own waterproof rug. Indeed, altogether, he seemed quite as well off as I was, or even better, for we were both as wet as we could be, and whilst I was painfully endeavouring to keep off the rain he was free from all responsibility and anxiety of endeavour whatever.

At length, as we entered on a long straight stretch of level road, he turned to me and said:—

"Yer 'an'r it's no kind iv use dhrivin' like this all the way to Carnaclif. This shtorm 'll go on for hours. I know thim well up in these mountains, wid' a nor'-aist wind blowin'. Wouldn't it be betther for us to get shelther for a bit?"

"Of course it would," said I. "Try it at once! Where can you go?"

"There's a place nigh at hand, yer 'an'r, the Widdy Kelligan's sheebeen, at the cross-roads of Glennashaughlin. It's quite contagious. Gee-up! ye ould corn-crake! hurry up to Widdy Kelligan's."

It seemed almost as if the mare understood him and shared his wishes, for she started with increased speed down a laneway that opened out a little on our left. In a few minutes we reached the cross-roads, and also the sheebeen of Widow Kelligan, a low whitewashed thatched house, in a deep hollow between high banks in the south-western corner of the cross. Andy jumped down and hurried to the door.

"Here's a sthrange gintleman, Widdy. Take care iv him," he called out, as I entered.

Before I had succeeded in closing the door behind me he was unharnessing the mare, preparatory to placing her in the lean-to stable, built behind the house against the high bank.

Already the storm seemed to have sent quite an assemblage to Mrs. Kelligan's hospitable shelter. A great fire of turf roared up the chimney, and round it stood, and sat, and lay a steaming mass of nearly a dozen people, men and women. The room was a large one, and the inglenook so roomy that nearly all those present found a place in it. The roof was black, rafters and thatch alike; quite a number of cocks and hens found shelter in the rafters at the end of the room. Over the fire was a large pot, suspended on a wire, and there was a savoury and inexpressibly appetizing smell of marked volume throughout the room of roasted herrings and whisky punch.

As I came in all rose up, and I found myself placed in a warm seat close to the fire, whilst various salutations of welcome buzzed all around me. The warmth was most grateful, and I was trying to convey my thanks for the shelter and the welcome, and feeling very awkward over it, when, with a "God save all here!" Andy entered the room through the back door.

He was evidently a popular favourite, for there was a perfect rain of hearty expressions to him. He, too, was placed close to the fire, and a steaming jorum of punch placed in his hands—a similar one to that which had been already placed in my own. Andy lost no time in sampling that punch. Neither did I; and I can honestly say that if he enjoyed his more than I did mine he must have had a very happy few minutes. He lost no time in making himself and all the rest comfortable.

"Hurroo!" said he. "Musha! but we're just in time. Mother, is the herrins done? Up with the creel, and turn out the pitaties; they're done, or me senses desaves me. Yer 'an'r, we're in the hoight iv good luck! Herrins, it is, and it might have been only pitaties an' point."

"What is that?" I asked.

"Oh, that is whin there is only wan herrin' amongst a crowd—too little to give aich a taste, and so they put it in the middle and point the pitaties at it to give them a flaviour."

All lent a hand with the preparation of supper. A great potato basket, which would hold some two hundredweight, was turned bottom up—the pot was taken off the fire, and the contents turned out on it in a great steaming mass of potatoes. A handful of coarse salt was taken from a box and put on one side of the basket, and another on the other side. The herrings were cut in pieces, and a piece given to each.—The dinner was served.

There were no plates, no knives, forks or spoons—no ceremony—no precedence—nor was there any heartburning, jealousy or greed. A happier meal I never took a part in—nor did I ever enjoy food more.

Such as it was it was perfect. The potatoes were fine and cooked to perfection; we took them in our fingers, peeled them how we could, dipped them in the salt—and ate till we were satisfied.

During the meal several more strangers dropped in and all reported the storm as showing no signs of abating. Indeed, little such assurance was wanting, for the fierce lash of the rain and the howling of the storm as it beat on the face of the house, told the tale well enough for the meanest comprehension.

When dinner was over and the basket removed, we drew around the fire again—pipes were lit—a great steaming jug of punch made its appearance, and conversation became general. Of course, as a stranger, I came in for a good share of attention.

Andy helped to make things interesting for me, and his statement, made by my request, that I hoped to be allowed to provide the punch for the evening, even increased his popularity, whilst it established mine. After calling attention to several matters which evoked local stories and jokes and anecdotes, he remarked:—

"His 'an'r was axin' me just afore the shtorm kem on as to why the Shleenanaher was called so. I tould him that none could tell him like Jerry Scanlan or Bat Moynahan, an' here is the both of them, sure enough. Now, boys, won't ye oblige the sthrange gintleman an tell him what yez know iv the shtories anent the hill?"

"Wid all the plisure in life," said Jerry Scanlan, a tall man of middle age, with a long, thin, clean shaven face, a humorous eye, and a shirt collar whose points in front came up almost to his eyes, whilst the back part disappeared into the depths of his frieze coat collar behind.

"Begor yer 'an'r I'll tell ye all I iver heerd. Sure there's a laygend, and there's a shtory—musha! but there's a wheen o' both laygends and shtories—but there's wan laygend beyant all—Here! Mother Kelligan, fill up me glass, fur sorra one o' me is a good dhry shpaker—Tell me, now, sor, do they allow punch to the Mimbers iv Parlymint whin they're spakin'?" I shook my head.

"Musha! thin, but its meself they'll niver git as a mimber till they alther that law. Thank ye, Mrs. Kelligan, this is just my shtyle. But now for the laygend that they tell of Shleenanaher:—"

II

The Lost Crown of Gold

Well, in the ould ancient times, before St. Patrick banished the shnakes from out iv Ireland, the hill beyant was a mighty important place intirely. For more betoken, none other lived in it than the King iv the Shnakes himself. In thim times there was up at the top iv the hill a wee bit iv a lake wid threes and sedges and the like growin' round it; and 'twas there that the King iv the Shnakes made his nist—or whativer it is that shnakes calls their home. Glory be to God! but none us of knows anythin' of them at all, at all, since Saint Patrick tuk them in hand."

Here an old man in the chimney corner struck in:—

"Thrue for ye, Acushla; sure the bit lake is there still, though more belike its dhry now it is, and the threes is all gone."

"Well," went on Jerry, not ill-pleased with this corroboration of his story, "the King iv the Shnakes was mighty important intirely. He was more nor tin times as big as any shnake as any man's eyes had iver saw; an' he had a goolden crown on to the top iv his head, wid a big jool in it that tuk the colour iv the light, whether that same was from the sun or the moon; an' all the shnakes had to take it in turns to bring food, and lave it for him in the cool iv the evenin', whin he would come out and ate it up and go back to his own place. An' they do say that whiniver two shnakes had a quarr'll they had to come to the King, an' he decided betune them; an' he tould aich iv them where he was to live, and what he was to do. An' wanst in ivery year there had to be brought to him a live baby; and they do say that he would wait until the moon was at the full, an' thin would be heerd one wild wail that made every sowl widin miles shuddher, an' thin there would be black silence, and clouds would come over the moon, and for three days it would never be seen agin."

"Oh, Glory be to God!" murmured one of the women, "but it was a terrible thing!" and she rocked herself to and fro, moaning, all the motherhood in her awake.

"But did none of the min do nothin'?" said a powerful-looking young fellow in the orange and green jersey of the Gaelic Athletic Club, with his eyes flashing; and he clenched his teeth.

"Musha! how could they? Sure, no man ever seen the King iv the Shnakes!"

"Thin how did they know about him?" he queried doubtfully.

"Sure, wasn't one of their childher tuk away iv'ry year? But, anyhow, it's all over now! an' so it was that none iv the min iver wint. They do say that one woman what lost her child, run up to the top of the hill; but what she seen, none could tell, for, whin they found her she was a ravin' lunatic, wid white hair an eyes like a corpse—an' the mornin' afther they found her dead in her bed wid a black mark round her neck as if she had been choked, an' the mark was in the shape iv a shnake. Well! there was much sorra and much fear, and whin St. Pathrick tuk the shnakes in hand the bonfires was lit all over the counthry. Never was such a flittin' seen as whin the shnakes came from all parts wrigglin' and crawlin' an shkwirmin'."

Here the narrator dramatically threw himself into an attitude, and with the skill of a true improvisatore, suggested in every pose and with every limb and in every motion the serpentine movements.

"They all came away to the West, and seemed to come to this wan mountain. From the North and the South and the East they came be millions an' thousands an' hundhreds—for whin St. Patrick ordhered them out he only tould them to go, but he did'nt name the place—an there was he up on top of Brandon mountain wid his vistments on to him an' his crozier in his hand, and the shnakes movin' below him, all goin up North, an', sez he to himself:—

"'I must see about this.' An' he got down from aff iv the mountain, and he folly'd the shnakes, and he see them move along to the hill beyant that they call Knockcalltecrore. An' be this time they wor all come from all over Ireland, and they wor all round the mountain—exceptin' on the say side—an' they all had their heads pointed up the hill, and their tails pointed to the Saint, so that they didn't see him, an' they all gave wan great hiss, an' then another, an' another, like wan, two, three! An' at the third hiss the King of the Shnakes rose up out of the wee fen at the top of the hill, wid his gold crown gleamin'—an' more betoken it was harvest time, an' the moon was up, an' the sun was settin', so the big jool in the crown had the light of both the sun an' the moon, an' it shone so bright that right away in Lensther the people thought the whole counthry was afire. But whin the Saint seen him, his whole forrum seemed to swell out an' get bigger an' bigger, an' he lifted his crozier, an' he pointed West, an' sez he, in a voice like a shtorm, 'To the say all ye shnakes! At wanst! to the say!'

"An' in the instant, wid wan movement, an' wid a hiss that made the air seem full iv watherfalls the whole iv the shnakes that was round the hill wriggled away into the say as if the fire was at their tails. There was so many iv them that they filled up the say out beyant to Cusheen Island, and them that was behind, had to shlide over their bodies. An' the say piled up till it sent a wave mountains high rollin' away across the Atlantic till it sthruck upon the shore iv America—though more betoken it wasn't America thin, for it wasn't discovered till long afther. An' there was so many shnakes that they do say that all the white sand that dhrifts up on the coast from the Blaskets to Achill Head is made from their bones." Here Andy cut in:—

"But, Jerry, you haven't tould us if the King iv the Shnakes wint too."

"Musha! but it's in a hurry ye are. How can I tell ye the whole laygend at wanst; an', moreover, when me mouth is that dhry I can hardly spake at all—an' me punch is all dhrunk——"

He turned his glass face down on the table, with an air of comic resignation. Mrs. Kelligan took the hint and refilled his glass whilst he went on:—

"Well! whin the shnakes tuk to say-bathin' an' forgot to come in to dhry themselves, the ould King iv thim sunk down agin into the lake, an' Saint Pathrick rowls his eyes, an' sez he to himself:—

"'Musha! is it dhramin' I am, or what? or is it laughin' at me he is? Does he mane to defy me?' An' seein' that no notice was tuk iv him at all, he lifts his crozier, and calls out:—

"'Hi! Here! You! Come here! I want ye!'—As he spoke, Jerry went through all the pantomime of the occasion, exemplifying by every movement the speech of both the Saint and the Snake.

"Well! thin the King iv the Shnakes puts up his head, out iv the lake, an' sez he:—

"'Who calls?'

"'I do,' says Saint Pathrick, an' he was so much mulvathered at the Shnake presumin' to sthay, afther he tould thim all to go, that for a while he didn't think it quare that he could sphake at all.

"'Well, what do ye want wid me?' sez the Shnake.

"'I want to know why you didn't lave Irish soil wid all th' other Shnakes,' sez the Saint.

"'Ye tould the Shnakes to go,' sez the King, 'an' I am their King, so I am; and your wurrds didn't apply to me!' an' with that he dhrops like a flash of lightnin' into the lake agin.

"Well! St. Patrick was so tuk back wid his impidence that he had to think for a minit, an' then he calls again:—

"'Hi! here! you!'

"'What do you want now?' sez the King iv the Shnakes, again poppin' up his head.

"'I want to know why you didn't obey me ordhers?' sez the Saint. An' the King luked at him an' laughed; and he looked mighty evil, I can tell ye—for be this time the sun was down and the moon up, and the jool in his crown threw out a pale cold light that would make you shuddher to see. 'An',' says he, as slow an' as hard as an attorney (saving your prisence) when he has a bad case:—

"'I didn't obey,' sez he, 'because I thraverse the jurisdiction.'

"'How do ye mane?' asks St. Pathrick.

"'Because,' sez he, 'this is my own houldin',' sez he, 'be perscriptive right,' sez he. 'I'm the whole govermint here, and I put a nexeat on meself not to lave widout me own permission,' and he ducks down agin into the pond.

"Well, the Saint began to get mighty angry, an' he raises his crozier, and he calls him agin:—

"'Hi! here! you!' and the Shnake pops up.

"'Well! Saint, what do you want now? Amn't I to be quit iv ye at all?'

"'Are ye goin', or are ye not?' sez the Saint.

"'I'm king here; an' I'm not goin'.'

"'Thin,' says the Saint, 'I depose ye!'

"'You can't,' sez the Shnake, 'whilst I have me crown.'

"'Then I'll take it from ye,' sez St. Pathrick.

"'Catch me first!' sez the Shnake; an' wid that he pops undher the wather, what began to bubble up and boil. Well thin! the good Saint stood bewildhered, for as he was lukin' the wather began to disappear out of the wee lake—and then the ground iv the hill began to be shaken as if the big Shnake was rushin' round and round it down deep down undher the ground.

"So the Saint stood on the edge of the empty lake an' held up his crozier, and called on the Shnake to come forth. And when he luked down, lo! an' behold ye! there lay the King iv the Shnakes coiled round the bottom iv the lake—though how he had got there the Saint could niver tell, for he hadn't been there when he began to summons him. Then the Shnake raised his head, and, lo! and behold ye! there was no crown on to it.

"'Where is your crown?' sez the Saint.

"'It's hid,' sez the Shnake, leerin' at him.

"'Where is it hid?'

"'It's hid in the mountain! Buried where you nor the likes iv you can't touch it in a thousand years!' an' he leered agin.

"'Tell me where it may be found?' sez the Saint starnly. An' thin the Shnake leers at him again wid an eviller smile than before; an' sez he:—

"'Did ye see the wather what was in the lake?'

"'I did,' sez Saint Pathrick.

"'Thin, when ye find that wather ye may find me jool'd crown, too,' sez he; an' before the Saint could say a word, he wint on:—

"'An' till ye git me crown I'm king here still, though ye banish me. An' mayhap, I'll come in some forrum what ye don't suspect, for I must watch me crown. An' now I go away—iv me own accorrd.' An' widout one word more, good or bad, he shlid right away into the say, dhrivin' through the rock an' makin' the clift that they call the Shleenanaher—an' that's Irish for the Shnake's Pass—until this day."

"An' now, sir, if Mrs. Kelligan hasn't dhrunk up the whole bar'l, I'd like a dhrop iv punch, for talkin' is dhry wurrk," and he buried his head in the steaming jorum, which the hostess had already prepared.

The company then began to discuss the legend. Said one of the women:—

"I wondher what forrum he tuk when he kem back!" Jerry answered:—

"Sure, they do say that the shiftin' bog wor the forrum he tuk. The mountain wid the lake on top used to be the fertilest shpot in the whole counthry; but iver since the bog began to shift this was niver the same."

Here a hard-faced man named McGlown, who had been silent, struck in with a question:—

"But who knows when the bog did begin to shift?"

"Musha! Sorra one of me knows; but it was whin th' ould Shnake druv the wather iv the lake into the hill!"—There was a twinkle in the eyes of the storyteller, which made one doubt his own belief in his story.

"Well, for ma own part," said McGlown, "A don't believe a sengle word of it."

"An' for why not?" said one of the women. "Isn't the mountain called 'Knockcalltecrore,' or 'The Hill of the Lost Crown iv Gold,' till this day?" Said another:—

"Musha! how could Misther McGlown believe anythin', an' him a Protestan'."

"A'll tell ye that A much prefer the facs," said McGlown. "Ef hestory es till be believed, A much prefer the story told till me by yon old man. Damn me! but A believe he's old enough till remember the theng itself."

He pointed as he spoke to old Moynahan, who, shrivelled up and white-haired, crouched in a corner of the ingle-nook, holding close to the fire his wrinkled shaky hands.

"What is the story that Mr. Moynahan has, may I ask?" said I. "Pray oblige, me, won't you? I am anxious to hear all I can of the mountain, for it has taken my fancy strangely."

The old man took the glass of punch, which Mrs. Kelligan handed him as the necessary condition antecedent to a story, and began:—

"Oh, sorra one of me knows anythin' except what I've heerd from me father. But I oft heerd him say that he was tould, that it was said, that in the Frinch invasion that didn't come off undher Gineral Humbert, whin the attimpt was over an' all hope was gone, the English sodgers made sure of great prize-money whin they should git hould of the threasure chist. For it was known that there was much money goin' an' that they had brought a lot more than iver they wanted for pay and expinses in ordher to help to bribe some of the people that was houldin' off to be bought by wan side or the other—if they couldn't manage to git bought be both. But sure enough they wor all sould, bad cess to thim! and the divil a bit of money could they lay their hands on at all."

Here the old man took a pull at his jug of punch, with so transparent a wish to be further interrogated that a smile flashed round the company. One of the old crones remarked, in an audible *sotto voce:*—

"Musha! But Bat is the cute story-teller intirely. Ye have to dhrag it out iv him! Go on, Bat! Go on! Tell us what become iv the money."

"Oh, what become iv the money? So ye would like to hear! Well, I'll tell ye.—Just one more fill of the jug, Mrs. Kelligan, as the gintleman wishes to know all about it.—Well! they did say that the officer what had charge of the money got well away with some five or six others. The chist was a heavy wan—an iron chist bang full up iv goold! Oh, my! but it was fine! A big chist—that high, an' as long as the table, an' full up to the led wid goolden money an' paper money, an' divil a piece of white money in it at all! All goold, every pound note iv it."

He paused, and glanced anxiously at Mrs. Kelligan, who was engaged in the new brew.

"Not too much wather if ye love me, Katty. You know me wakeness!— Well, they do say that it tuk hard work to lift the chist into the boat; an' thin they put in a gun carriage to carry it on, an' tuk out two horses, an' whin the shmoke was all round an' the darkness of night was on they got on shore, an' made away down South from where the landin' was made at Killala. But, anyhow, they say that none of them was ever heerd of agin. But they was thraced through Ardnaree an' Lough Conn, an' through Castlebar Lake an' Lough Carra, an' through Lough Mask an' Lough Corrib. But they niver kem out through Galway, for the river was watched for thim day an' night be the sodgers; and how they got along God knows! for 'twas said they suffered quare hardships. They tuk the chist an' the gun carriage an' the horses in the boat, an' whin they couldn't go no further they dhragged the boat over the land to the next lake, an' so on. Sure one dhry sayson, when the wathers iv Corrib was down feet lower nor they was iver known afore, a boat was found up at the Bealanabrack end that had lay there for years; but the min nor the horses nor the treasure was never heerd of from that day to this—so they say," he added, in a mysterious way, and he renewed his attention to the punch, as if his tale was ended.

"But, man alive!" said McGlown, "that's only a part. Go on, man dear! an' fenesh the punch after."

"Oh, oh! Yes, of course, you want to know the end. Well! no wan knows the end. But they used to say that whin the min lift the boat they wint due west, till one night they sthruck the mountain beyant; an' that there they buried the chist an' killed the horses, or rode away on them. But anyhow, they wor niver seen again; an' as sure as you're alive, the money is there in the hill! For luk at the name iv it! Why did any wan iver call it 'Knockcalltore'—an' that's Irish for 'the Hill of the Lost Gold'—if the money isn't there?"

"Thrue for ye!" murmured an old woman with a cutty pipe. "For why, indeed? There's some people what won't believe nothin' altho' it's undher their eyes!" and she puffed away in silent rebuke to the spirit of scepticism— which, by the way, had not been manifested by any person present.

There was a long pause, broken only by one of the old women, who occasionally gave a sort of half-grunt, half-sigh, as though unconsciously to fill up the hiatus in the talk. She was a 'keener' by profession, and was evidently well fitted to, and well drilled in, her work. Presently old Moynahan broke the silence:—

"Well! it's a mighty quare thing anyhow that the hill beyant has been singled out for laygends and sthories and gossip iv all kinds consarnin' shnakes an' the like. An' I'm not so sure, naythur, that some iv thim isn't there shtill—for mind ye! it's a mighty curious thin' that the bog beyant keeps shiftin' till this day. And I'm not so sure, naythur, that the shnakes has all left the hill yit!"

There was a chorus of "Thrue for ye!"

"Aye, an' it's a black shnake too!" said one.

"An' wid side-whishkers!" said another.

"Begorra! we want Saint Pathrick to luk in here agin!" said a third.

I whispered to Andy the driver:—

"Who is it they mean?"

"Whisht!" he answered, but without moving his lips; "but don't let on I tould ye! Sure an' it's Black Murdock they mane."

"Who or what is Murdock?" I queried.

"Sure an' he is the Gombeen Man."

"What is that? What is a gombeen man?"

"Whisper me now!" said Andy; "ax some iv the others. They'll larn it ye more betther nor I can."

"What is a gombeen man?" I asked to the company generally.

"A gombeen man is it? Well! I'll tell ye," said an old, shrewd-looking man at the other side of the hearth. "He's a man that linds you a few shillin's or a few pounds whin ye want it bad, and then niver laves ye till he has tuk all ye've got—yer land an' yer shanty an' yer holdin' an' yer money an' yer craps; an' he would take the blood out of yer body if he could sell it or use it anyhow!"

"Oh, I see, a sort of usurer."

"Ushurer? aye that's it; but a ushurer lives in the city an' has laws to hould him in. But the gombeen has nayther law nor the fear iv law. He's like wan that the Scriptures says 'grinds the faces iv the poor.' Begor! it's him that'd do little for God's sake if the divil was dead!"

"Then I suppose this man Murdock is a man of means—a rich man in his way?"

"Rich is it? Sure an' it's him as has plinty. He could lave this place if he chose an' settle in Galway—aye or in Dublin itself if he liked betther, and lind money to big min—landlords an' the like—instead iv playin' wid poor min here an' swallyin' them up, wan be wan.—But he can't go! He can't go!" This he said with a vengeful light in his eyes; I turned to Andy for explanation.

"Can't go! How does he mean? What does he mean?"

"Whisht! Don't ax me. Ax Dan, there. He doesn't owe him any money!"

"Which is Dan?"

"The ould man there be the settle what has just spoke, Dan Moriarty. He's a warrum man, wid money in bank an' what owns his houldin'; an' he's not afeerd to have his say about Murdock."

"Can any of you tell me why Murdock can't leave the Hill?" I spoke out.

"Begor' I can," said Dan, quickly. "He can't lave it because the Hill houlds him!"

"What on earth do you mean? How can the Hill hold him?"

"It can hould tight enough! There may be raysons that a man gives— sometimes wan thing, an' sometimes another; but the Hill houlds—an' houlds tight all the same!"

Here the door was opened suddenly, and the fire blazed up with the rush of wind that entered. All stood up suddenly, for the new comer was a priest. He was a sturdy man of middle age, with a cheerful countenance. Sturdy as he was, however, it took him all his strength to shut the door, but he succeeded before any of the men could get near enough to help him. Then he turned and saluted all the company:—

"God save all here."

All present tried to do him some service. One took his wet great coat, another his dripping hat, and a third pressed him into the warmest seat in the chimney corner, where, in a very few seconds, Mrs. Kelligan handed him a steaming glass of punch, saying, "Dhrink that up, yer Riv'rence. 'Twill help to kape ye from catchin' cowld."

"Thank ye, kindly," he answered, as he took it. When he had half emptied the glass, he said:—

"What was it I heard as I came in about the Hill holding some one?" Dan answered:—

"'Twas me, yer Riverence, I said that the Hill had hould of Black Murdock, and could hould him tight."

"Pooh! pooh! man; don't talk such nonsense. The fact is, sir," said he, turning to me after throwing a searching glance round the company, "the people here have all sorts of stories about that unlucky Hill—why, God knows; and this man Murdock, that they call Black Murdock, is a money-lender as well as a farmer, and none of them like him, for he is a hard man and has done some cruel things among them. When they say the Hill holds him, they mean that he doesn't like to leave it because he hopes to find a treasure that is said to be buried in it. I'm not sure but that the blame is to be thrown on the different names given to the Hill. That most commonly given is Knockcalltecrore, which is a corruption of the Irish phrase Knock-na-callte-crōin-ōir, meaning, 'The Hill of the Lost Golden Crown;' but it has been sometimes called Knockcalltore—short for the Irish words Knock-na-callte-ōir, or 'The Hill of the Lost Gold.' It is said that in some old past time it was called Knocknanaher, or 'The Hill of the Snake;' and, indeed, there's one place on it they call Shleenanaher, meaning the 'Snake's Pass.' I dare say, now, that they have been giving you the legends and stories and all the rubbish of that kind. I suppose you know, sir, that in most places the local fancy has run riot at some period and has left a good crop of absurdities and impossibilities behind it?"

I acquiesced warmly, for I felt touched by the good priest's desire to explain matters, and to hold his own people blameless for crude ideas which he did not share. He went on:—

"It is a queer thing that men must be always putting abstract ideas into concrete shape. No doubt there have been some strange matters regarding this mountain that they've been talking about—the Shifting Bog, for instance; and as the people could not account for it in any way that they can understand, they knocked up a legend about it. Indeed, to be just to them, the legend is a very old one, and is mentioned in a manuscript of the twelfth century. But somehow it was lost sight of till about a hundred years ago, when the loss of the treasure-chest from the French invasion at Killala set all the imaginations of the people at work, from Donegal to Cork, and they fixed the Hill of the Lost Gold as the spot where the money was to be found. There is not a word of fact in the story from beginning to end, and"—here he gave a somewhat stern glance round the room—"I'm a little ashamed to hear so much chat and nonsense given to a strange gentleman like as if it was so much gospel. However, you mustn't be too hard in your thoughts on the poor people here, sir, for they're good people—none better in all Ireland—in all the world for that—but they talk too free to do themselves justice."

All those present were silent for awhile. Old Moynahan was the first to speak.

"Well, Father Pether, I don't say nothin' about Saint Pathrick an the shnakes, meself, because I don't know nothin' about them; but I know that me own father tould me that he seen the Frinchmin wid his own eyes crossin' the sthrame below, an' facin' up the mountain. The moon was risin' in the west, an' the hill threw a big shadda. There was two min an' two horses, an' they had a big box on a gun carriage. Me father seen them cross the sthrame. The load was so heavy that the wheels sunk in the clay, an' the min had to pull at them to git them up again. An' didn't he see the marks iv the wheels in the ground the very nixt day?"

"Bartholomew Moynahan, are you telling the truth?" interrupted the priest, speaking sternly.

"Throth an I am, Father Pether; divil a word iv a lie in all I've said."

"Then how is it you've never told a word of this before?"

"But I have tould it, Father Pether. There's more nor wan here now what has heered me tell it; but they wor tould as a saycret!"

"Thrue for ye!" came the chorus of almost every person in the room. The unanimity was somewhat comic and caused amongst them a shamefaced silence, which lasted quite several seconds. The pause was not wasted, for by this time Mrs. Kelligan had brewed another jug of punch, and glasses were replenished. This interested the little crowd and they entered afresh into the subject. As for myself, however, I felt strangely uncomfortable. I could not quite account for it in any reasonable way.

I suppose there must be an instinct in men as well as in the lower orders of animal creation—I felt as though there were a strange presence near me.

I quietly looked round. Close to where I sat, on the sheltered side of the house, was a little window built in the deep recess of the wall, and, further, almost obliterated by the shadow of the priest as he sat close to the fire. Pressed against the empty lattice, where the glass had once been, I saw the face of a man—a dark, forbidding face it seemed in the slight glimpse I caught of it. The profile was towards me, for he was evidently listening intently, and he did not see me. Old Moynahan went on with his story:—

"Me father hid behind a whin bush, an' lay as close as a hare in his forrum. The min seemed suspicious of bein' seen and they looked carefully all round for the sign of anywan. Thin they started up the side of the hill; an' a cloud came over the moon so that for a bit me father could see nothin'. But prisintly he seen the two min up on the side of the hill at the south, near Joyce's mearin'. Thin they disappeared agin, an' prisintly he seen the horses an' the gun carriage an' all up in the same place, an' the moonlight sthruck thim as they wint out iv the shadda; and men an' horses an' gun carriage an' chist an' all wint round to the back iv the hill at the west an' disappeared. Me father waited a minute or two to make sure, an' thin he run round as hard as he could an' hid behind the projectin' rock at the enthrance iv the Shleenanaher, an' there foreninst him! right up the hill side he seen two min carryin' the chist, an' it nigh weighed thim down. But the horses an' the gun carriage was nowhere to be seen. Well! me father was stealin' out to folly thim, when he loosened a sthone an' it clattered down through the rocks at the Shnake's Pass wid a noise like a dhrum, an' the two min sot down the chist an' they turned; an' whin they seen me father one of them runs at him, and he turned an' run. An' thin another black cloud crossed the moon; but me father knew ivery foot of the mountain side, and he run on through the dark. He heerd the footsteps behind him for a bit, but they seemed to get fainter an' fainter; but he niver stopped runnin' till he got to his own cabin.—An' that was the last he iver see iv the men or the horses or the chist. Maybe they wint into the air or the say, or the mountain; but anyhow they vanished, and from that day to this no sight or sound or word iv them was ever known!"

There was a universal, 'Oh!' of relief as he concluded, whilst he drained his glass.

I looked round again at the little window—but the dark face was gone.

Then there arose a perfect bable of sounds. All commented on the story, some in Irish, some in English, and some in a speech, English indeed, but so purely and locally idiomatic that I could only guess at what was intended to be conveyed. The comment generally took the form that two men were to be envied, one of them, the gombeen man, Murdock, who owned a portion of the western side of the hill, the other one, Joyce, who owned another section of the same aspect.

In the midst of the buzz of conversation the clattering of hoofs was heard. There was a shout, and the door opened again and admitted a stalwart stranger of some fifty years of age, with a strong, determined face, with kindly eyes, well dressed but wringing wet, and haggard, and seemingly disturbed in mind. One arm hung useless by his side.

"Here's one of them!" said Father Peter.

III

The Gombeen Man

God save all here," said the man as he entered.

Room was made for him at the fire. He no sooner came near it and tasted the heat than a cloud of steam arose from him.

"Man! but ye're wet," said Mrs. Kelligan. "One'd think ye'd been in the lake beyant!"

"So I have," he answered, "worse luck! I rid all the way from Galway this blessed day to be here in time, but the mare slipped coming down Curragh Hill and threw me over the bank into the lake. I wor in the wather nigh three hours before I could get out, for I was foreninst the Curragh Rock an' only got a foothold in a chink, an' had to hold on wid me one arm for I fear the other is broke."

"Dear! dear! dear!" interrupted the woman. "Sthrip yer coat off, acushla, an' let us see if we can do anythin'."

He shook his head, as he answered:—

"Not now, there's not a minute to spare. I must get up the Hill at once. I should have been there be six o'clock. But I mayn't be too late yit. The mare has broke down entirely. Can any one here lend me a horse?"

There was no answer till Andy spoke:—

"Me mare is in the shtable, but this gintleman has me an' her for the day, an' I have to lave him at Carnaclif tonight."

Here I struck in:—

"Never mind me, Andy! If you can help this gentleman, do so: I'm better off here than driving through the storm. He wouldn't want to go on, with a broken arm, if he hadn't good reason!"

The man looked at me with grateful eagerness:—

"Thank yer honour, kindly. It's a rale gintleman ye are! An' I hope ye'll never be sorry for helpin' a poor fellow in sore throuble."

"What's wrong, Phelim?" asked the priest. "Is there anything troubling you that any one here can get rid of?"

"Nothin', Father Pether, thank ye kindly. The throuble is me own intirely, an' no wan here could help me. But I must see Murdock tonight."

There was a general sigh of commiseration; all understood the situation.

"Musha!" said old Dan Moriarty, *sotto voce.* "An' is that the way of it! An' is he too in the clutches iv that wolf? Him that we all thought was so warrum. Glory be to God! but it's a quare wurrld it is; an' it's few there is in it that is what they seems. Me poor frind! is there any way I can help ye? I have a bit iv money by me that yer welkim to the lend iv av ye want it."

The other shook his head gratefully:—

"Thank ye kindly, Dan, but I have the money all right; it's only the time I'm in trouble about!"

"Only the time! me poor chap! It's be time that the divil helps Black Murdock an' the likes iv him, the most iv all! God be good to ye if he has got his clutch on yer back, an' has time on his side, for ye'll want it!"

"Well! anyhow, I must be goin' now. Thank ye kindly, neighbours all. When a man's in throuble, sure the goodwill of his frinds is the greatest comfort he can have."

"All but one, remember that! all but one!" said the priest.

"Thank ye kindly, Father, I shan't forget. Thank ye Andy: an' you, too, young sir, I'm much beholden to ye. I hope, some day, I may have it to do a good turn for ye in return. Thank ye kindly again, and good night." He shook my hand warmly, and was going to the door, when old Dan said:—

"An' as for that black-jawed ruffian, Murdock—" He paused, for the door suddenly opened, and a harsh voice said:—

"Murtagh Murdock is here to answer for himself!"—It was my man at the window.

There was a sort of paralyzed silence in the room, through which came the whisper of one of the old women:—

"Musha! talk iv the divil!"

Joyce's face grew very white; one hand instinctively grasped his riding switch, the other hung uselessly by his side. Murdock spoke:—

"I kem here expectin' to meet Phelim Joyce. I thought I'd save him the throuble of comin' wid the money." Joyce said in a husky voice:—

"What do ye mane? I have the money right enough here. I'm sorry I'm a bit late, but I had a bad accident—bruk me arrum, an' was nigh dhrownded in the Curragh Lake. But I was goin' up to ye at once, bad as I am, to pay ye yer money, Murdock." The Gombeen Man interrupted him:—

"But it isn't to me ye'd have to come, me good man. Sure, it's the sheriff, himself, that was waitin' for ye', an' whin ye didn't come"—here Joyce winced; the speaker smiled—"he done his work."

"What wurrk, acushla?" asked one of the women. Murdock answered slowly:—

"He sould the lease iv the farrum known as the Shleenanaher in open sale, in accordance wid the terrums of his notice, duly posted, and wid warnin' given to the houldher iv the lease."

There was a long pause. Joyce was the first to speak:—

"Ye're jokin', Murdock. For God's sake say ye're jokin'! Ye tould me yerself that I might have time to git the money. An' ye tould me that the puttin' me farrum up for sale was only a matther iv forrum to let me pay ye back in me own way. Nay! more, ye asked me not to te tell any iv the neighbours, for fear some iv them might want to buy some iv me land. An' it's niver so, that whin ye got me aff to Galway to rise the money, ye went on wid the sale, behind me back—wid not a soul by to spake for me or mine—an' sould up all I have! No! Murtagh Murdock, ye're a hard man I know, but ye wouldn't do that! Ye wouldn't do that!"

Murdock made no direct reply to him, but said seemingly to the company generally:—

"I ixpected to see Phelim Joyce at the sale today, but as I had some business in which he was consarned, I kem here where I knew there'd be neighbours—an' sure so there is."

He took out his pocket-book and wrote names, "Father Pether Ryan, Daniel Moriarty, Bartholomew Moynahan, Andhrew McGlown, Mrs. Katty Kelligan—that's enough! I want ye all to see what I done. There's nothin' undherhand about me! Phelim Joyce, I give ye formial notice that yer land was sould an' bought be me, for ye broke yer word to repay me the money lint ye before the time fixed. Here's the Sheriff's assignmint, an' I tell ye before all these witnesses that I'll proceed with ejectment on title at wanst."

All in the room were as still as statues. Joyce was fearfully still and pale, but when Murdock spoke the word "ejectment" he seemed to wake in a moment to frenzied life. The blood flushed up in his face and he seemed about to do something rash; but with a great effort he controlled himself and said:—

"Mr. Murdock, ye won't be too hard. I got the money today—it's here—but I had an accident that delayed me. I was thrown into the Curragh Lake and nigh drownded an' me arrum is bruk. Don't be so close as an hour or two—ye'll never be sorry for it. I'll pay ye all, and more, and thank ye into the bargain all me life; ye'll take back the paper, won't ye, for me childhren's sake—for Norah's sake?"

He faltered; the other answered with an evil smile:—

"Phelim Joyce, I've waited years for this moment—don't ye know me betther nor to think I would go back on meself whin I have shtarted on a road? I wouldn't take yer money, not if ivery pound note was spread into an acre and cut up in tin-pound notes. I want yer land—I have waited for it, an' I mane to have it!—Now don't beg me any more, for I won't go back—an' tho' its many a grudge I owe ye, I square them all before the neighbours be refusin' yer prayer. The land is mine, bought be open sale; an' all the judges an' coorts in Ireland can't take it from me! An' what do ye say to that now, Phelim Joyce?"

The tortured man had been clutching the ash sapling which he had used as a riding whip, and from the nervous twitching of his fingers I knew that something was coming. And it came; for, without a word, he struck the evil face before him—struck as quick as a flash of lightning— such a blow that the blood seemed to leap out round the stick, and a vivid welt rose in an instant. With a wild, savage cry the Gombeen Man jumped at him; but there were others in the room as quick, and before another blow could be struck on either side both men were grasped by strong hands and held back.

Murdock's rage was tragic. He yelled, like a wild beast, to be let get at his opponent. He cursed and blasphemed so outrageously that all were silent, and only the stern voice of the priest was heard:—

"Be silent Murtagh Murdock! Aren't you afraid that the God overhead will strike you dead? With such a storm as is raging as a sign of His power, you are a foolish man to tempt Him."

The man stopped suddenly, and a stern dogged sullenness took the place of his passion. The priest went on:—

"As for you, Phelim Joyce, you ought to be ashamed of yourself; ye're not one of my people, but I speak as your own clergyman would if he were here. Only this day has the Lord seen fit to spare you from a terrible death; and yet you dare to go back of His mercy with your angry passion. You had cause for anger—or temptation to it, I know—but you must learn to kiss the chastening rod, not spurn it. The Lord knows what He is doing for you as for others, and it may be that you will look back on this day in gratitude for His doing, and in shame for your own anger. Men, hold off your hands—let those two men go; they'll quarrel no more—before me at any rate, I hope."

The men drew back. Joyce held his head down, and a more despairing figure or a sadder one I never saw. He turned slowly away, and leaning against the wall put his face between his hands and sobbed. Murdock scowled, and the scowl gave place to an evil smile as looking all around he said:—

"Well, now that me work is done, I must be gettin' home."

"An' get some wan to iron that mark out iv yer face," said Dan. Murdock turned again and glared around him savagely as he hissed out:—

"There'll be iron for some one before I'm done. Mark me well! I've never gone back or wakened yit whin I promised to have me own turn. There's thim here what'll rue this day yit! If I am the shnake on the hill—thin beware the shnake. An' for him what shtruck me, he'll be in bitther sorra for it yit—him an' his!" He turned his back and went to the door.

"Stop!" said the priest. "Murtagh Murdock, I have a word to say to you—a solemn word of warning. Ye have today acted the part of Ahab towards Naboth the Jezreelite; beware of his fate! You have coveted your neighbour's goods—you have used your power without mercy; you have made the law an engine of oppression. Mark me! It was said of old that what measure men meted should be meted out to them again. God is very just. 'Be not deceived, God is not mocked. For what things a man shall sow, those also shall he reap.' Ye have sowed the wind this day—beware lest you reap the whirlwind! Even as God visited his sin upon Ahab the Samarian, and as He has visited similar sins on others in His own way—so shall He visit yours on you. You are worse than the land-grabber—worse than the man who only covets. Saintough is a virtue compared with your act! Remember the story of Naboth's vineyard, and the dreadful end of it. Don't answer me! Go and repent if you can, and leave sorrow and misery to be comforted by others—unless you wish to undo your wrong yourself. If you don't—then remember the curse that may come upon you yet!"

Without a word Murdock opened the door and went out, and a little later we heard the clattering of his horse's feet on the rocky road to Shleenanaher.

When it was apparent to all that he was really gone a torrent of commiseration, sympathy and pity broke over Joyce. The Irish nature is essentially emotional, and a more genuine and stronger feeling I never saw. Not a few had tears in their eyes, and one and all were manifestly deeply touched. The least moved was, to all appearance, poor Joyce himself. He seemed to have pulled himself together, and his sterling manhood and courage and pride stood by him. He seemed, however, to yield to the kindly wishes of his friends; and when we suggested that his hurt should be looked to, he acquiesced:—

"Yes, if you will. Betther not go home to poor Norah and distress her with it. Poor child! she'll have enough to bear without that."

His coat was taken off, and between us we managed to bandage the wound. The priest, who had some surgical knowledge, came to the conclusion that there was only a simple fracture. He splinted and bandaged the arm, and we all agreed that it would be better for Joyce to wait until the storm was over before starting for home. Andy said he could take him on the car, as he knew the road well, and that, as it was partly on the road to Carnaclif, we should only have to make a short detour and would pass the house of the doctor, by whom the arm could be properly attended to.

So we sat around the fire again, whilst, without, the storm howled and the fierce gusts which swept the valley seemed at times as if they would break in the door, lift off the roof, or in some way annihilate the time-worn cabin which gave us shelter.

There could, of course, be only one subject of conversation now, and old Dan simply interpreted the public wish, when he said:—

"Tell us, Phelim, sure we're all friends here! how Black Murdock got ye in his clutches? Sure any wan of us would get you out of thim if he could."

There was a general acquiescence. Joyce yielded himself, and said:—

"Let me thank ye, neighbours all, for yer kindness to me and mine this sorraful night. Well! I'll say no more about that; but I'll tell ye how it was that Murdock got me into his power. Ye know that boy of mine, Eugene?"

"Oh! and he's the fine lad, God bless him! an' the good lad too!"—this from the women.

"Well! ye know too that he got on so well whin I sint him to school that Dr. Walsh recommended me to make an ingineer of him. He said he had such promise that it was a pity not to see him get the right start in life, and he gave me, himself, a letther to Sir George Henshaw, the great ingineer. I wint and seen him, and he said he would take the boy. He tould me that there was a big fee to be paid, but I was not to throuble about that—at any rate, that he himself didn't want any fee, and he would ask his partner if he would give up his share too. But the latther was hard up for money. He said he couldn't give up all fee, but that he would take half the fee, provided it was paid down in dhry money. Well! the regular fee to the firm was five hundhred pounds, and as Sir George had giv up half an' only half th' other half was to be paid, that was possible. I hadn't got more'n a few pounds by me—for what wid dhrainin' and plantin' and fencin' and the payin' the boy's schoolin', and the girl's at the Nuns' in Galway, it had put me to the pin iv me collar to find the money up to now. But I didn't like to let the boy lose his chance in life for want of an effort, an' I put me pride in me pocket an' kem an' asked Murdock for the money. He was very smooth an' nice wid me—I know why now—an' promised he would give it at wanst if I would give him security on me land. Sure he joked an' laughed wid me, an' was that cheerful that I didn't misthrust him. He tould me it was only forrums I was signin' that'd never be used"—Here Dan Moriarty interrupted him:—

"What did ye sign, Phelim?"

"There wor two papers. Wan was a writin' iv some kind, that in considheration iv the money lent an' his own land—which I was to take over if the money wasn't paid at the time appointed—he was to get me lease from me: an' the other was a power of attorney to Enther Judgment for the amount if the money wasn't paid at the right time. I thought I was all safe as I could repay him in the time named, an' if the worst kem to the worst I might borry the money from some wan else—for the lease is worth the sum tin times over—an' repay him. Well! what's the use of lookin' back, anyhow! I signed the papers—that was a year ago, an' one week. An' a week ago the time was up!" He gulped down a sob, and went on:—

"Well! ye all know the year gone has been a terrible bad wan, an' as for me it was all I could do to hould on—to make up the money was impossible. Thrue the lad cost me next to nothin', for he arned his keep be exthra work, an' the girl, Norah, kem home from school and laboured wid me, an' we saved every penny we could. But it was all no use!—we couldn't get the money together anyhow. Thin we had the misfortin wid the cattle that ye all know of; an' three horses, that I sould in Dublin, up an' died before the time I guaranteed them free from sickness." Here Andy struck in:—

"Thrue for ye! Sure there was some dhreadful disordher in Dublin among the horse cattle, intirely; an' even Misther Docther Perfesshinal Ferguson himself couldn't git undher it!" Joyce went on:—

"An' as the time grew nigh I began to fear, but Murdock came down to see me whin I was alone, an' tould me not to throuble about the money an' not to mind about the sheriff, for he had to give him notice. 'An',' says he, 'I wouldn't, if I was you, tell Norah anythin' about it, for it might frighten the girl—for weemin is apt to take to heart things like that that's only small things to min like us.' An' so, God forgive me, I believed him; an' I niver tould me child anything about it—even whin I got the notice from the sheriff. An' whin the Notice tellin' of the sale was posted up on me land, I tuk it down meself so that the poor child wouldn't be frightened—God help me!" He broke down for a bit, but then went on:—

"But somehow I wasn't asy in me mind, an' whin the time iv the sale dhrew nigh I couldn't keep it to meself any longer, an' I tould Norah. That was only yesterday, and look at me today! Norah agreed wid me that we shouldn't trust the Gombeen, an' she sent me off to the Galway Bank to borry the money. She said I was an honest man an' farmed me own land, and that the bank might lind the money on it. An' sure enough whin I wint there this mornin' be appointment, wid the Coadjuthor himself to inthroduce me, though he didn't know why I wanted the money—that was Norah's idea, and the Mother Superior settled it for her—the manager, who is a nice gintleman, tould me at wanst that I might have the money on me own note iv hand. I only gave him a formal writin', an' I took away the money. Here it is in me pocket in good notes; they're wet wid the lake, but I'm thankful to say all safe. But it's too late, God help me!" Here he broke down for a minute, but recovered himself with an effort:—

"Anyhow the bank that thrusted me musn't be wronged. Back the money goes to Galway as soon as iver I can get it there. If I am a ruined man I need'nt be a dishonest wan! But poor Norah! God help her! it will break her poor heart."

There was a spell of silence only broken by sympathetic moans. The first to speak was the priest.

"Phelim Joyce, I told you a while ago, in the midst of your passion, that God knows what He is doin', and works in His own way. You're an honest man, Phelim, and God knows it, and, mark me, He won't let you nor yours suffer. 'I have been young,' said the Psalmist, 'and now am old; and I have not seen the just forsaken, nor his seed seeking bread.' Think of that, Phelim!—may it comfort you and poor Norah. God bless her! but she's the good girl. You have much to be thankful for, with a daughter like her to comfort you at home and take the place of her poor mother, who was the best of women; and with such a boy as Eugene, winnin' name and credit, and perhaps fame to come, even in England itself. Thank God for His many mercies, Phelim, and trust Him."

There was a dead slience in the room. The stern man rose, and coming over took the priest's hand.

"God bless ye, Father!" he said, "it's the true comforter ye are."

The scene was a most touching one; I shall never forget it. The worst of the poor man's trouble seemed now past. He had faced the darkest hour; he had told his trouble, and was now prepared to make the best of everything—for the time at least—for I could not reconcile to my mind the idea that that proud, stern man, would not take the blow to heart for many a long day, that it might even embitter his life.

Old Dan tried comfort in a practical way by thinking of what was to be done. Said he:—

"Iv course, Phelim, it's a mighty throuble to give up yer own foine land an' take Murdock's bleak shpot instead, but I daresay ye will be able to work it well enough. Tell me, have ye signed away all the land, or only the lower farm? I mane, is the Cliff Fields yours or his?"

Here was a gleam of comfort evidently to the poor man. His face lightened as he replied:—

"Only the lower farm, thank God! Indeed, I couldn't part wid the Cliff Fields, for they don't belong to me—they are Norah's, that her poor mother left her—they wor settled on her, whin we married, be her father, and whin he died we got them. But, indeed, I fear they're but small use be themselves; shure there's no wather in them at all, savin' what runs off me ould land; an' if we have to carry wather all the way down the hill from—from me new land"—this was said with a smile, which was a sturdy effort at cheerfulness—"it will be but poor work to raise anythin' there—ayther shtock or craps. No doubt but Murdock will take away the sthrame iv wather that runs there now. He'll want to get the cliff lands, too, I suppose."

I ventured to ask a question:—

"How do your lands lie compared with Mr. Murdock's?"

There was bitterness in his tone as he answered, in true Irish fashion: "Do you mane me ould land, or me new?"

"The lands that were—that ought still to be yours," I answered.

He was pleased at the reply, and his face softened as he replied:—

"Well, the way of it is this. We two owns the West side of the hill between us. Murdock's land—I'm spakin' iv them as they are, till he gets possession iv mine—lies at the top iv the hill; mine lies below. My land is the best bit on the mountain, while the Gombeen's is poor soil, with only a few good patches here and there. Moreover, there is another thing. There is a bog which is high up the hill, mostly on his houldin', but my land is free from bog, except one end of the big bog, an' a stretch of dry turf, the best in the counthry, an' wid' enough turf to last for a hundhred years, it's that deep."

Old Dan joined in:—

"Thrue enough! that bog of the Gombeen's isn't much use anyhow. It's rank and rotten wid wather. Whin it made up its mind to sthay, it might have done betther!"

"The bog? Made up its mind to stay! What on earth do you mean?" I asked. I was fairly puzzled.

"Didn't ye hear talk already," said Dan, "of the shiftin' bog on the mountain?"

"I did."

"Well, that's it! It moved an' moved an' moved longer than anywan can remimber. Me grandfather wanstould me that whin he was a gossoon it wasn't nigh so big as it was when he tould me. It hasn't shifted in my time, and I make bould to say that it has made up its mind to settle down where it is. Ye must only make the best of it, Phelim. I daresay ye will turn it to some account."

"I'll try what I can do, anyhow. I don't mane to fould me arms an' sit down op-pawsit me property an' ate it!" was the brave answer.

For myself, the whole idea was most interesting. I had never before even heard of a shifting bog, and I determined to visit it before I left this part of the country.

By this time the storm was beginning to abate. The rain had ceased, and Andy said we might proceed on our journey. So after a while we were on our way; the wounded man and I sitting on one side of the car, and Andy on the other. The whole company came out to wish us God-speed, and with such comfort as good counsel and good wishes could give we ventured into the inky darkness of the night.

Andy was certainly a born car-driver. Not even the darkness, the comparative strangeness of the road, or the amount of whisky-punch which he had on board could disturb his driving in the least; he went steadily on. The car rocked and swayed and bumped, for the road was a bye one, and in but poor condition—but Andy and the mare went on alike unmoved. Once or twice only, in a journey of some three miles of winding bye-lanes, crossed and crossed again by lanes or water-courses, did he ask the way. I could not tell which was roadway and which water-way, for they were all water-courses at present, and the darkness was profound. Still, both Andy and Joyce seemed to have a sense lacking in myself, for now and again they spoke of things which I could not see at all. As, for instance, when Andy asked:—

"Do we go up or down where the road branches beyant?" Or again: "I disremimber, but is that Micky Dolan's ould apple three, or didn't he cut it down? an' is it Tim's foment us on the lift?"

Presently we turned to the right, and drove up a short avenue towards a house. I knew it to be a house by the light in the windows, for shape it had none. Andy jumped down and knocked, and after a short colloquy, Joyce got down and went into the Doctor's house. I was asked to go too, but thought it better not to, as it would only have disturbed the Doctor in his work; and so Andy and I possessed our souls in patience until Joyce came out again, with his arm in a proper splint. And then we resumed our journey through the inky darkness.

However, after a while either there came more light into the sky, or my eyes became accustomed to the darkness, for I thought that now and again I beheld "men as trees walking."

Presently something dark and massive seemed outlined in the sky before us—a blackness projected on a darkness—and, said Andy, turning to me:—

"That's Knockcalltecrore; we're nigh the foot iv it now, and pretty shortly we'll be at the enthrance iv the boreen, where Misther Joyce'll git aff."

We plodded on for a while, and the hill before us seemed to overshadow whatever glimmer of light there was, for the darkness grew more profound than ever; then Andy turned to my companion:—

"Sure, isn't that Miss Norah I see sittin' on the sthyle beyant?" I looked eagerly in the direction in which he evidently pointed, but for the life of me I could see nothing.

"No! I hope not," said the father, hastily. "She's never come out in the shtorm. Yes! It is her, she sees us."

Just then there came a sweet sound down the lane:—

"Is that you, father?"

"Yes! my child; but I hope you've not been out in the shtorm."

"Only a bit, father; I was anxious about you. Is it all right, father; did you get what you wanted?" She had jumped off the stile and had drawn nearer to us, and she evidently saw me, and went on in a changed and shyer voice:—

"Oh! I beg your pardon, I did not see you had a stranger with you."

This was all bewildering to me; I could hear it all—and a sweeter voice I never heard—but yet I felt like a blind man, for not a thing could I see, whilst each of the three others was seemingly as much at ease as in the daylight.

"This gentleman has been very kind to me, Norah. He has given me a seat on his car, and indeed he's come out of his way to lave me here."

"I am sure we're all grateful to you, sir; but, father, where is your horse? Why are you on a car at all? Father, I hope you haven't met with any accident—I have been so fearful for you all the day." This was spoken in a fainter voice; had my eyes been of service, I was sure I would have seen her grow pale.

"Yes, my darlin', I got a fall on the Curragh Hill, but I'm all right. Norah dear! Quick, quick! catch her, she's faintin'!—my God! I can't stir!"

I jumped off the car in the direction of the voice, but my arms sought the empty air. However, I heard Andy's voice beside me:—

"All right! I have her. Hould up, Miss Norah; yer dada's all right, don't ye see him there, sittin' on me car. All right, sir, she's a brave girrul! she hasn't fainted."

"I am all right," she murmured, faintly; "but, father, I hope you are not hurt?"

"Only a little, my darlin', just enough for ye to nurse me a while; I daresay a few days will make me all right again. Thank ye, Andy; steady now, till I get down; I'm feelin' a wee bit stiff." Andy evidently helped him to the ground.

"Good night, Andy, and good night you too, sir, and thank you kindly for your goodness to me all this night. I hope I'll see you again." He took my hand in his uninjured one, and shook it warmly.

"Good night," I said, and "good-bye: I am sure I hope we shall meet again."

Another hand took mine as he relinquished it—a warm, strong one—and a sweet voice said, shyly:—

"Good night, sir, and thank you for your kindness to father."

I faltered "Good night," as I raised my hat; the aggravation of the darkness at such a moment was more than I could equably bear. We heard them pass up the boreen, and I climbed on the car again.

The night seemed darker than ever as we turned our steps towards Carnaclif, and the journey was the dreariest one I had ever taken. I had only one thought which gave me any pleasure, but that was a pretty constant one through the long miles of damp, sodden road—the warm hand and the sweet voice coming out of the darkness, and all in the shadow of that mysterious mountain, which seemed to have become a part of my life. The words of the old story-teller came back to me again and again:—

"The Hill can hould tight enough! A man has raysons—sometimes wan thing and sometimes another—but the Hill houlds him all the same!"

And a vague wonder grew upon me as to whether it could ever hold me, and how!

IV

The Secrets of the Bog

Some six weeks elapsed before my visits to Irish friends were completed, and I was about to return home. I had had everywhere a hearty welcome; the best of sport of all kinds, and an appetite beyond all praise—and one pretty well required to tackle with any show of success the excellent food and wine put before me. The west of Ireland not only produces good viands in plenty and of the highest excellence, but there is remaining a keen recollection, accompanied by tangible results, of the days when open house and its hospitable accompaniments made wine merchants prosperous—at the expense of their customers.

In the midst of all my pleasure, however, I could not shake from my mind—nor, indeed, did I want to—the interest which Shleenanaher and its surroundings had created in me. Nor did the experience of that strange night, with the sweet voice coming through the darkness in the shadow of the hill, become dim with the passing of the time. When I look back and try to analyse myself and my feelings with the aid of the knowledge and experience of life received since then, I think that I must have been in love. I do not know if philosophers have ever undertaken to say whether it is possible for a human being to be in love in the abstract—whether the something which the heart has a tendency to send forth needs a concrete objective point! It may be so; the swarm of bees goes from the parent hive with only the impulse of going—its settling is a matter of chance. At any rate I may say that no philosopher, logician, metaphysician, psychologist, or other thinker, of whatsoever shade of opinion, ever held that a man could be in love with a voice.

True that the unknown has a charm—*omne ignotum pro magnifico.* If my heart did not love, at least it had a tendency to worship. Here I am on solid ground; for which of us but can understand the feelings of those men of old in Athens, who devoted their altars "To The Unknown God?" I leave the philosophers to say how far apart, or how near, are love and worship; which is first in historical sequence, which is greatest or most sacred! Being human, I cannot see any grace or beauty in worship without love.

However, be the cause what it might, I made up my mind to return home viâ Carnaclif. To go from Clare to Dublin by way of Galway and Mayo is to challenge opinion as to one's motive. I did not challenge opinion, I distinctly avoided doing so, and I am inclined to think that there was more of Norah than of Shleenanaher in the cause of my reticence. I could bear to be "chaffed" about a superstitious feeling respecting a mountain, or I could endure the same process regarding a girl of whom I had no high ideal, no sweet illusive memory.

I would never complete the argument, even to myself—then; later on, the cause or subject of it varied!

It was not without a certain conflict of feelings that I approached Carnaclif, even though on this occasion I approached it from the South, whereas on my former visit I had come from the North. I felt that the time went miserably slowly, and yet nothing would have induced me to admit so much. I almost regretted that I had come, even whilst I was harrowed with thoughts that I might not be able to arrive at all at Knockcalltecrore. At times I felt as though the whole thing had been a dream; and again as though the romantic nimbus with which imagination had surrounded and hallowed all things must pass away and show that my unknown beings and my facts of delicate fantasy were but stern and vulgar realities.

The people at the little hotel made me welcome with the usual effusive hospitable intention of the West. Indeed, I was somewhat nettled at how well they remembered me, as for instance when the buxom landlady said:—

"I'm glad to be able to tell ye, sir, that yer carman, Andy Sullivan, is here now. He kem with a commercial from Westport to Roundwood, an' is on his way back, an' hopin' for a return job. I think ye'll be able to make a bargain with him if ye wish."

I made to this kindly speech a hasty and, I felt, an ill-conditioned reply, to the effect that I was going to stay in the neighbourhood for only a few days and would not require the car. I then went to my room, and locked my door muttering a malediction on officious people. I stayed there for some time, until I thought that probably Andy had gone on his way, and then ventured out.

I little knew Andy, however. When I came to the hall, the first person that I saw was the cheerful driver, who came forward to welcome me:—

"Musha! but it's glad I am to see yer 'an'r. An' it'll be the proud man I'll be to bhring ye back to Westport wid me."

"I'm sorry Andy," I began, "that I shall not want you, as I am going to stay in this neighbourhood for a few days."

"Sthay is it? Begor! but it's more gladerer shtill I am. Sure the mare wants a rist, an' it'll shute her an' me all to nothin'; an' thin whilst ye're here I can be dhrivin' yer 'an'r out to Shleenanaher. It isn't far enough to intherfere wid her rist."

I answered in, I thought, a dignified way—I certainly intended to be dignified:—

"I did not say, Sullivan, that I purposed going out to Shleenanaher or any other place in the neighbourhood."

"Shure no, yer 'an'r, but I remimber ye said ye'd like to see the Shiftin' Bog; an' thin Misther Joyce and Miss Norah is in throuble, and ye might be a comfort to thim."

"Mr. Joyce! Miss Norah! who are they?" I felt that I was getting red and that the tone of my voice was most unnatural.

Andy's sole answer was as comical a look as I ever saw, the central object in which was a wink which there was no mistaking. I could not face it, and had to say:

"Oh yes, I remember now! was not that the man we took on the car to a dark mountain?"

"Yes, surr—him and his daughther!"

"His daughter! I do not remember her. Surely we only took him on the car." Again I felt angry, and with the anger an inward determination not to have Andy or anyone else prying around me when I should choose to visit even such an uncompromising phenomenon as a shifting bog. Andy, like all humourists, understood human nature, and summed up the situation conclusively in his reply—inconsequential though it was:—

"Shure yer 'an'r can thrust me; its blind or deaf an' dumb I am, an' them as knows me knows I'm not the man to go back on a young gintleman goin' to luk at a bog. Sure doesn't all young min do that same? I've been there meself times out iv mind! There's nothin' in the wurrld foreninst it! Lukin' at bogs is the most intherestin' thin' I knows."

There was no arguing with Andy; and as he knew the place and the people, I, then and there, concluded an engagement with him. He was to stay in Carnaclif whilst I wanted him, and then drive me over to Westport.

As I was now fairly launched on the enterprise, I thought it better to lose no time, but arranged to visit the bog early the next morning.

As I was lighting my cigar after dinner that evening Mrs. Keating, my hostess, came in to ask me a favour. She said that there was staying in the house a gentleman who went over every day to Knockcalltecrore, and as she understood that I was going there in the morning, she made bold to ask if I would mind giving a seat on my car to him as he had turned his ancle that day and feared he would not be able to walk. Under the circumstances I could only say "yes," as it would have been a churlish thing to refuse. Accordingly I gave permission with seeming cheerfulness, but when I was alone my true feelings found vent in muttered grumbling:—"I ought to travel in an ambulance instead of a car." "I seem never to be able to get near this Shleenanaher without an invalid." "Once ought to be enough! but it has become the regulation thing now." "I wish to goodness Andy would hold his infernal tongue— I'd as lief have a detective after me all the time." "It's all very well to be a good Samaritan as a luxury—but as a profession it becomes monotonous." "Confound Andy! I wish I'd never seen him at all."

This last thought brought me up standing, and set me face to face with my baseless ill-humour. If I had never seen Andy I should never have heard at all of Shleenanaher. I should not have known the legend—I should not have heard Norah's voice.

"And so," said I to myself, "this ideal fantasy—this embodiment of a woman's voice, has a concrete name already. Aye! a concrete name, and a sweet one too."

And so I took another step on my way to the bog, and lost my ill-humour at the same time. When my cigar was half through and my feelings were proportionately soothed, I strolled into the bar and asked Mrs. Keating as to my companion of the morrow. She told me that he was a young engineer named Sutherland.

"What Sutherland?" I asked. Adding that I had been at school with a Dick Sutherland, who had, I believed, gone into the Irish College of Science.

"Perhaps it's the same gentleman, sir. This is Mr. Richard Sutherland, and I've heerd him say that he was at Stephen's Green."

"The same man!" said I, "this is jolly! "Tell me, Mrs. Keating, what brings him here?"

"He's doin' some work on Knockcalltecrore for Mr. Murdock, some quare thing or another. They do tell me, sir, that it's a most mystayrious thing, wid poles an' lines an' magnets an' all kinds of divilments. They say that Mr. Murdock is goin' from off of his head ever since he had the law of poor Phelim Joyce. My! but he's the decent man, that same Mr. Joyce, an' the Gombeen has been hard upon him."

"What was the law suit?" I asked.

"All about a sellin' his land on an agreement. Mr. Joyce borryed some money, an' promised if it wasn't paid back at a certain time that he would swop lands. Poor Joyce met wid an accident comin' home with the money from Galway an' was late, an' when he got home found that the Gombeen had got the sheriff to sell up his land on to him. Mr. Joyce thried it in the Coorts, but now Murdock has got a decree on to him an' the poor man 'll to give up his fat lands an' take the Gombeen's poor ones instead."

"That's bad! when has he to give up?"

"Well, I disremember meself exactly, but Mr. Sutherland will be able to tell ye all about it as ye drive over in the mornin."

"Where is he now? I should like to see him; it may be my old schoolfellow."

"Troth, it's in his bed he is; for he rises mighty arly, I can tell ye."

After a stroll through the town (so-called) to finish my cigar I went to bed also, for we started early. In the morning, when I came down to my breakfast I found Mr. Sutherland finishing his. It was my old schoolfellow; but from being a slight, pale boy, he had grown into a burly, hale, stalwart man, with keen eyes and a flowing brown beard. The only pallor noticeable was the whiteness of his brow, which was ample and lofty as of old.

We greeted each other cordially, and I felt as if old times had come again, for Dick and I had been great friends at school. When we were on our way I renewed my inquiries about Shleenanaher and its inhabitants. I began by asking Sutherland as to what brought him there. He answered:—

"I was just about to ask you the same question. 'What brings you here?'"

I felt a difficulty in answering as freely as I could have wished, for I knew that Andy's alert ears were close to us, so I said:—

"I have been paying some visits along the West Coast, and I thought I would take the opportunity on my way home of investigating a very curious phenomenon of whose existence I became casually acquainted on my way here—a shifting bog."

Andy here must strike in:—

"Shure the masther is mighty fond iv bogs, intirely. I don't know there's anything in the wurruld what intherests him so much."

Here he winked at me in a manner that said as plainly as if spoken in so many words, "All right, yer 'an'r, I'll back ye up!"

Sutherland laughed as he answered:—

"Well, you're in the right place here, Art; the difficulty they have in this part of the world is to find a place that is *not* bog. However, about the shifting bog on Knockcalltecrore, I can, perhaps, help you as much as any one. As you know, geology has been one of my favourite studies, and lately I have taken to investigate in my spare time the phenomena of this very subject. The bog at Shleenanaher is most interesting. As yet, however, my investigation can only be partial, but very soon I shall have the opportunity which I require."

"How is that?" I asked.

"The difficulty arises," he answered, "from a local feud between two men, one of them my employer, Murdock, and his neighbour, Joyce."

"Yes," I interrupted, "I know something of it. I was present when the sheriff's assignment was shown to Joyce, and saw the quarrel. But how does it affect you and your study?"

"This way; the bog is partly on Murdock's land and partly on Joyce's, and until I can investigate the whole extent I cannot come to a definite conclusion. The feud is so bitter at present that neither man will allow the other to set foot over his boundary—or the foot of any one to whom the other is friendly. However, tomorrow the exchange of lands is to be effected, and then I shall be able to continue my investigation. I have already gone nearly all over Murdock's present ground, and after tomorrow I shall be able to go over his new ground—up to now forbidden to me."

"How does Joyce take his defeat?"

"Badly, poor fellow, I am told; indeed, from what I see of him, I am sure of it. They tell me that up to lately he was a bright, happy fellow, but now he is a stern, hard-faced, scowling man; essentially a man with a grievance, which makes him take a jaundiced view of everything else. The only one who is not afraid to speak to him is his daughter, and they are inseparable. It certainly is cruelly hard on him. His farm is almost an ideal one for this part of the world; it has good soil, water, shelter, trees, everything that makes a farm pretty and comfortable, as well as being good for farming purposes; and he has to change it for a piece of land as irregular in shape as the other is compact; without shelter, and partly taken up with this very bog and the utter waste and chaos which, when it shifted in former times, it left behind."

"And how does the other, Murdock, act?"

"Shamefully; I feel so angry with him at times that I could strike him. There is not a thing he can say or do, or leave unsaid or undone, that is not aggravating and insulting to his neighbour. Only that he had the precaution to bind me to an agreement for a given time I'm blessed if I would work for him, or with him at all—interesting as the work is in itself, and valuable as is the opportunity it gives me of studying that strange phenomenon, the shifting bog."

"What is your work with him?" I asked: "mining or draining, or what?"

He seemed embarrassed at my question. He "hum'd and 'ha'd'—then with a smile he said quite frankly:—

"The fact is that I am not at liberty to say. The worthy Gombeen Man put a special clause in our agreement that I was not during the time of my engagement to mention to any one the object of my work. He wanted the clause to run that I was never to mention it; but I kicked at that, and only signed in the modified form."

I thought to myself "more mysteries at Shleenanaher!" Dick went on:—

"However, I have no doubt that you will very soon gather the object for yourself. You are yourself something of a scientist, if I remember?"

"Not me!" I answered. My Great Aunt took care of that when she sent me to our old tutor. Or, indeed, to do the old boy justice, he tried to teach me something of the kind; but I found out it wasn't my vogue. Anyhow, I haven't done anything lately."

"How do you mean?"

"I haven't got over being idle yet. It's not a year since I came into my fortune. Perhaps—indeed I hope—that I may settle down to work again."

"I'm sure I hope so, too, old fellow," he answered gravely. "When a man has once tasted the pleasure of real work, especially work that taxes the mind and the imagination, the world seems only a poor place without it."

"Like the wurrld widout girruls for me, or widout bog for his 'an'r!" said Andy, grinning as he turned round on his seat.

Dick Sutherland, I was glad to see, did not suspect the joke. He took Andy's remark quite seriously, and said to me:—

"My dear fellow, it is delightful to find you so interested in my own topic."

I could not allow him to think me a savant. In the first place he would very soon find me out, and would then suspect my motives ever after. And again, I had to accept Andy's statement, or let it appear that I had some other reason or motive—or what would seem even more suspicious still, none at all; so I answered:—

"My dear Dick, my zeal regarding bog is new; it is at present in its incipient stage in so far as erudition is concerned. The fact is, that although I would like to learn a lot about it, I am at the present moment profoundly ignorant on the subject."

"Like the rest of mankind!" said Dick. "You will hardly believe that although the subject is one of vital interest to thousands of persons in our own country—one in which national prosperity is mixed up to a large extent—one which touches deeply the happiness and material prosperity of a large section of Irish people, and so helps to mould their political action, there are hardly any works on the subject in existence."

"Surely you are mistaken," I answered.

"No! unfortunately, I am not. There is a Danish book, but it is geographically local; and some information can be derived from the Blue Book containing the report of the International Commission on turf-cutting, but the special authorities are scant indeed. Some day, when you want occupation, just you try to find in any library, in any city of the world, any works of a scientific character devoted to the subject. Nay more! try to find a fair share of chapters in scientific books devoted to it. You can imagine how devoid of knowledge we are, when I tell you that even the last edition of the 'Enclycopædia Britannica' does not contain the heading 'bog.'"

"You amaze me!" was all I could say.

Then as we bumped and jolted over the rough bye-road Dick Sutherland gave me a rapid but masterly survey of the condition of knowledge on the subject of bogs, with special application to Irish bogs, beginning with such records as those of Giraldus Cambrensis—of Dr. Boate—of Edmund Spenser—from the time of the first invasion when the state of the land was such that, as is recorded, when a spade was driven into the ground a pool of water gathered forthwith. He told me of the extent and nature of the bog-lands—of the means taken to reclaim them, and of his hopes of some heroic measures being ultimately taken by Government to reclaim the vast Bog of Allen which remains as a great evidence of official ineptitude.

"It will be something," he said, "to redeem the character for indifference to such matters so long established, as when Mr. King wrote two hundred years ago, 'We live in an Island almost infamous for bogs, and yet, I do not remember, that any one has attempted much concerning them.'" We were close to Knockcalltecrore when he finished his impromptu lecture thus:—

"In fine, we cure bog by both a surgical and a medical process. We drain it so that its mechanical action as a sponge may be stopped, and we put in lime to kill the vital principle of its growth. Without the other, neither process is sufficient; but together, scientific and executive man asserts his dominance."

"Hear! hear!" said Andy. "Musha, but Docther Wilde himself, Rest his sowl! couldn't have put it aisier to grip. It's a purfessionaler the young gintleman is intirely!"

We shortly arrived at the south side of the western slope of the hill, and as Andy took care to inform me, at the end of the boreen leading to the two farms, and close to the head of the Snake's Pass.

Accordingly, I let Sutherland start on his way to Murdock's, whilst I myself strolled away to the left, where Andy had pointed out to me, rising over the slope of the intervening spur of the hill, the top of one of the rocks which formed the Snake's Pass. After a few minutes of climbing up a steep slope, and down a steeper one, I arrived at the place itself.

From the first moment that my eyes lit on it, it seemed to me to be a very remarkable spot, and quite worthy of being taken as the scene of strange stories, for it certainly had something 'uncanny' about it.

I stood in a deep valley, or rather bowl, with behind me a remarkably steep slope of green sward, whilst on either hand the sides of the hollow rose steeply—that on the left, down which I had climbed, being by far the steeper and rockier of the two. In front was the Pass itself.

It was a gorge or cleft through a great wall of rock, which rose on the seaside of the promontory formed by the hill. This natural wall, except at the actual Pass itself, rose some fifty or sixty feet over the summit of the slope on either side of the little valley; but right and left of the Pass rose two great masses of rock, like the pillars of a giant gateway. Between these lay the narrow gorge, with its walls of rock rising sheer some two hundred feet. It was about three hundred feet long, and widened slightly outward, being shaped something funnel-wise, and on the inner side was about a hundred feet wide. The floor did not go so far as the flanking rocks, but, at about two-thirds of its length, there was a perpendicular descent, like a groove cut in the rock, running sheer down to the sea, some three hundred feet below, and as far under it as we could see. From the northern of the flanking rocks which formed the Pass the rocky wall ran northwards, completely sheltering the lower lands from the west, and running into a towering rock that rose on the extreme north, and which stood up in jagged peaks something like "The Needles" off the coast of the Isle of Wight.

There was no doubt that poor Joyce's farm, thus sheltered, was an exceptionally favoured spot, and I could well understand how loth he must be to leave it.

Murdock's land, even under the enchantment of its distance, seemed very different, and was just as bleak as Sutherland had told me. Its south-western end ran down towards the Snake's Pass. I mounted the wall of rock on the north of the Pass to look down, and was surprised to find that down below me was the end of a large plateau of some acres in extent which ran up northward, and was sheltered north and west by a somewhat similar formation of rock to that which protected Joyce's land. This, then, was evidently the place called the "Cliff Fields" of which mention had been made at Widow Kelligan's.

The view from where I stood was one of ravishing beauty. Westward in the deep sea, under grey clouds of endless variety, rose a myriad of clustering islets, some of them covered with grass and heather, where cattle and sheep grazed; others were mere rocks rising boldly from the depths of the sea, and surrounded by a myriad of screaming wild-fowl. As the birds dipped and swept and wheeled in endless circles, their white breasts and grey wings varying in infinite phase of motion—and as the long Atlantic swell, tempered by its rude shocks on the outer fringe of islets, broke in fleecy foam and sent living streams through the crevices of the rocks and sheets of white water over the boulders where the sea rack rose and fell, I thought that the earth could give nothing more lovely or more grand.

Andy's voice beside me grated on me unpleasantly:—

"Musha! but it's the fine sight it is entirely; it only wants wan thing."

"What does it want?" I asked, rather shortly.

"Begor, a bit of bog to put your arrum around while ye're lukin' at it," and he grinned at me knowingly.

He was incorrigible. I jumped down from the rock and scrambled into the boreen. My friend Sutherland had gone on his way to Murdock's, so calling to Andy to wait till I returned, I followed him.

I hurried up the boreen and caught up with him, for his progress was slow along the rough laneway. In reality I felt that it would be far less awkward having him with me; but I pretended that my only care was for his sprained ankle. Some emotions make hypocrites of us all!

With Dick on my arm limping along we passed up the boreen, leaving Joyce's house on our left. I looked out anxiously in case I should see Joyce—or his daughter; but there was no sign of anyone about. In a few minutes Dick, pausing for a moment, pointed out to me the shifting bog.

"You see," he said, "those two poles? the line between them marks the mearing of the two lands. We have worked along the bog down from there." He pointed as he spoke to some considerable distance up the hill to the north where the bog began to be dangerous, and where it curved around the base of a grassy mound, or shoulder of the mountain.

"Is it a dangerous bog?" I queried.

"Rather! It is just as bad a bit of soft bog as ever I saw. I wouldn't like to see anyone or anything that I cared for try to cross it!"

"Why not?"

"Because at any moment they might sink through it; and then, good-bye—no human strength or skill could ever save them."

"Is it a quagmire, then? or like a quicksand?"

"Like either, or both. Nay! it is more treacherous than either. You may call it, if you are poetically inclined, a 'carpet of death!' What you see is simply a film or skin of vegetation of a very low kind, mixed with the mould of decayed vegetable fibre and grit and rubbish of all kinds which have somehow got mixed into it, floating on a sea of ooze and slime—of something half liquid half solid, and of an unknown depth. It will bear up a certain weight, for there is a degree of cohesion in it; but it is not all of equal cohesive power, and if one were to step on the wrong spot—" He was silent.

"What then?"

"Only a matter of specific gravity! A body suddenly immersed would, when the air of the lungs had escaped and the *rigor mortis* had set in, probably sink a considerable distance; then it would rise after nine days, when decomposition began to generate gases, and make an effort to reach the top. Not succeeding in this, it would ultimately waste away, and the bones would become incorporated with the existing vegetation somewhere about the roots, or would lie among the slime at the bottom."

"Well," said I, "for real cold-blooded horror, commend me to your men of science."

This passage brought us to the door of Murdock's house—a plain, strongly-built cottage, standing on a knoll of rock that cropped up from the plateau round it. It was surrounded with a garden hedged in by a belt of pollard ash and stunted alders.

Murdock had evidently been peering surreptitiously through the window of his sitting-room, for as we passed in by the gate he came out to the porch. His salutation was not an encouraging one:—

"You're somethin' late this mornin', Mr. Sutherland. I hope ye didn't throuble to delay in ordher to bring up this sthrange gintleman. Ye know how particular I am about any wan knowin' aught of me affairs."

Dick flushed up to the roots of his hair, and, much to my surprise, burst out quite in a passionate way:—

"Look you here, Mr. Murdock, I'm not going to take any cheek from you, so don't you give any. Of course I don't expect a fellow of your stamp to understand a gentleman's feelings—damn it! how can you have a gentleman's understanding when you haven't even a man's? You ought to know right well that what I said I would do, I shall do. I despise you and your miserable secrets and your miserable trickery too much to take to myself anything in which they have a part; but when I bring with me a friend, but for whom I shouldn't have been here at all—for I couldn't have walked—I expect that neither he nor I shall be insulted. For two pins I'd not set foot on your dirty ground again!"

Here Murdock interrupted him:—

"Aisy now! ye're undher agreement to me; an' I hould ye to it."

"So you can, you miserable scoundrel, because you know I shall keep my word; but remember that I expect proper treatment; and remember, too, that if I want an assistant I am to have one."

Again Murdock interrupted—but this time much more soothingly:

"Aisy! Aisy! haven't I done every livin' thing ye wanted—and helped ye meself every time? Sure arn't I yer assistant?"

"Yes, because you—you wanted to get something, and couldn't do without me. And mind this! you can't do without me yet. But be so good as to remember that I choose my own assistant; and I shall not choose you unless I like. You can keep me here, and pay me for staying as we agreed; but don't you think that I could fool you if I would?"

"Ye wouldn't do that, I know—an' me thrusted ye!"

"You trusted me! you miserable wretch—yes! you trusted me by a deed, signed, sealed, and delivered. I don't owe you anything for that."

"Mr. Sutherland, sir! ye're too sharp wid me. Yer frind is very welkim. Do what you like—go where you choose—bring whom you will—only get on wid the worrk and kape it saycret."

"Aye!" sneered Dick, "you are ready to climb down because you want something done, and you know that this is the last day for work on this side of the hill. Well, let me tell you this—for you'll do anything for greed—that you and I together, doing all we can, shall not be able to cover all the ground. I haven't said a word to my friend—and I don't know how he will take any request from you after your impudence; but he is my friend, and a clever man, and if you ask him nicely, perhaps he will be good enough to stay and lend us a hand."

The man made me a low bow and asked me in suitable terms if I would kindly stop part of the day and help in the work. Needless to say I acquiesced. Murdock eyed me keenly, as though to make up his mind whether or no I recollected him—he evidently remembered me—but I affected ignorance, and he seemed satisfied. I was glad to notice that the blow of Joyce's riding switch still remained across his face as a livid scar. He went away to get the appliances ready for work, in obedience to a direction from Sutherland.

"One has to cut that hound's corns rather roughly," said the latter, with a nice confusion of metaphors, as soon as Murdock had disappeared.

Dick then told me that his work was to make magnetic experiments to ascertain, if possible, if there was any iron hidden in the ground.

"The idea," he said, "is Murdock's own, and I have neither lot nor part in it. My work is simply to carry out his ideas, with what mechanical skill I can command, and to invent or arrange such appliances as he may want. Where his theories are hopelessly wrong, I point this out to him, but he goes on or stops just as he chooses. You can imagine that a fellow of his low character is too suspicious to ever take a hint from any one! We have been working for three weeks past, and have been all over the solid ground, and are just finishing the bog."

"How did you first come across him?" I asked.

"Very nearly a month ago he called on me in Dublin, having been sent by old Gascoigne, of the College of Science. He wanted me to search for iron on his property. I asked if it was regarding opening mines? he said, 'no, just to see if there should be any old iron lying about.' As he offered me excellent terms for my time, I thought he must have some good—or rather I should say some strong motive. I know now, though he has never told me, that he is trying for the money that is said to have been lost and buried here by the French after Humbert's expedition to Killala."

"How do you work?" I asked.

"The simplest thing in the world; just carry about a strong magnet—only we have to do it systematically."

"And have you found anything as yet?"

"Only old scraps—horseshoes, nails, buckles, buttons; our most important find was the tire of a wheel. The old Gombeen thought he had it that time!" and Dick laughed.

"How did you manage the bog?"

"That is the only difficult part; we have poles on opposite sides of the bog with lines between them. The magnet is fixed, suspended from a free wheel, and I let it down to the centre from each side in turn. If there were any attraction I should feel it by the thread attached to the magnet which I hold in my hand."

"It is something like fishing?"

"Exactly."

Murdoch now returned and told us that he was ready, so we all went to work. I kept with Sutherland at the far side of the bog, Murdoch remaining on the near side. We planted or rather placed a short stake in the solid ground, as close as we could get it to the bog, and steadied it with a guy from the top; the latter I held, whilst Murdoch, on the other side, fulfilled a similar function. A thin wire connected the two stakes; on this Sutherland now fixed the wheel, from which the magnet depended. On each side we deflected the stake until the magnet almost touched the surface of the bog. After a few minutes' practice I got accustomed to the work, and acquired sufficient dexterity to be able to allow the magnet to run freely. Inch by inch we went over the surface of the bog, moving slightly to the south-west each time we shifted, following the edges of the bog. Every little while Dick had to change sides, so as to cover the whole extent of the bog, and when he came round again had to go back to where he had last stopped on the same side.

All this made the process very tedious, and the day was drawing to a close when we neared the posts set up to mark the bounds of the two lands. Several times during the day Joyce had come up from his cottage and inspected our work, standing at his own side of the post. He looked at me closely, but did not seem to recognize me. I nodded to him once, but he did not seem to see my salutation, and I did not repeat it.

All day long I never heard the sweet voice; and as we returned to Carnaclif after a blank day—blank in every sense of the word—the air seemed chiller and the sunset less beautiful than before. The last words I heard on the mountain were from Murdock:—

"Nothin' tomorrow, Mr. Sutherland! I've a flittin' to make, but I pay the day all the same; I hould ye to your conthract. An' remember, surr, we're in no hurry wid the wurrk now, so ye'll not need help any more."

Andy made no remark till we were well away from the hill, and then said, dryly:—

"I'm afeerd yer 'an'r has had but a poor day; ye luk as if ye hadn't seen a bit iv bog at all, at all. Gee up, ye ould Corncrake! the gintlemin does be hurryin' home fur their tay, an' fur more wurrk wid bogs tomorra!"

V

ON KNOCKNACAR

When Sutherland and I had finished dinner that evening we took up the subject of bogs where we had left it in the morning. This was rather a movement of my own making, for I felt an awkwardness about touching on the special subject of the domestic relations of the in-habitants of Knockcalltecrore. After several interesting remarks, Dick said:—

"There is one thing that I wish to investigate thoroughly, the correlation of bog and special geological formations."

"For instance?" said I.

"Well, specially with regard to limestone. Just at this part of the country I find it almost impossible to pursue the investigation any more than Van Troil could have pursued snake studies in Iceland."

"Is there no limestone at all in this part of the country?" I queried.

"Oh yes, in lots of places, but as yet I have not been able to find any about here. I say 'as yet' on purpose, because it seems to me that there must be some on Knockcalltecrore."

Needless to say the conversation here became to me much more interesting; Dick went on:—

"The main feature of the geological formation of all this part of the country is the vast amount of slate and granite, either in isolated patches or lying side by side. And as there are instances of limestone found in quaint ways, I am not without hopes that we may yet find the same phenomenon."

"Where do you find the instances of these limestone formations?" I queried, for I felt that as he was bound to come back to, or towards Shleenanaher, I could ease my own mind by pretending to divert his from it.

"Well, as one instance, I can give you the Corrib River—the stream that drains Lough Corrib into Galway Bay; in fact, the river on which the town of Galway is built. At one place one side of the stream all is granite, and the other is all limestone; I believe the river runs over the union of the two formations. Now, if there should happen to be a similar formation, even in the least degree, at Knockcalltecrore, it will be a great thing.

"Why will it be a great thing?" I asked.

"Because there is no lime near the place at all; because with limestone on the spot a hundred things could be done that, as things are at present, would not repay the effort. With limestone we could reclaim the bogs cheaply all over the neighbourhood—in fact a limekiln there would be worth a small fortune. We could build walls in the right places; I can see how a lovely little harbour could be made there at a small expense. And then beyond all else would be the certainty—which is at present in my mind only a hope or a dream—that we could fathom the secret of the shifting bog, and perhaps abolish or reclaim it."

"This is exceedingly interesting," said I, as I drew my chair closer. And I only spoke the exact truth, for at that moment I had no other thought in my mind. "Do you mind telling me more, Dick? I suppose you are not like Lamb's Scotchman that will not broach a half-formed idea!"

"Not the least in the world. It will be a real pleasure to have such a good listener. To begin at the beginning, I was much struck with that old cavity on the top of the hill. It is one of the oddest things I have ever seen or heard of. If it were in any other place or amongst any other geological formation I would think its origin must have been volcanic. But here such a thing is quite impossible. It was evidently once a lake."

"So goes the legend. I suppose you have heard it?"

"Yes! and it rather confirms my theory. Legends have always a base in fact; and whatever cause gave rise to the myth of St. Patrick and the King of the Snakes, the fact remains that the legend is correct in at least one particular—that at some distant time there was a lake or pond on the spot."

"Are you certain?"

"A very cursory glance satisfied me of that. I could not go into the matter thoroughly, for that old wolf of mine was so manifestly impatient that I should get to his wild-goose chase for the lost treasure-chest, that the time and opportunity were wanting. However, I saw quite enough to convince me."

"Well, how do you account for the change? What is your theory regarding the existence of limestone?"

"Simply this, that a lake or reservoir on the top of a mountain means the existence of a spring or springs. Now springs in granite or hard slate do not wear away the substance of the rock in the same way as they do when they come through limestone. And moreover, the natures of the two rocks are quite different. There are fissures and cavities in the limestone which are wanting, or which are at any rate not so common or perpetually recurrent in the other rock. Now if it should be, as I surmise, that the reservoir was ever fed by a spring passing through a streak or bed of limestone, we shall probably find that in the progress of time the rock became worn and that the spring found a way in some other direction—either some natural passage through a gap or fissure already formed, or by a channel made for itself."

"And then?"

"And then the process is easily understandable. The spring naturally sent its waters where there was the least resistance, and they found their way out on some level lower than the top of the hill. You perhaps noticed the peculiar formation of the hill, specially on its went side—great sloping tables of rock suddenly ended by a wall of a different stratum—a sort of serrated edge all the way down the inclined plane; you could not miss seeing it, for it cuts the view like the teeth of a saw! Now if the water, instead of rising to the top and then trickling down the old channel, which is still noticeable, had once found a vent on one of those shelving planes it would gradually fill up the whole cavity formed by the two planes, unless in the meantime it found some natural escape. As we know, the mountain is covered in a number of places with a growth or formation of bog, and this water, once accumulating under the bog, would not only saturate it, but would raise it—being of less specific gravity than itself—till it actually floated. Given such a state of things as this, it would only require sufficient time for the bog to become soft and less cohesive than when it was more dry and compact, and you have a dangerous bog, something like the Carpet of Death that we spoke of this morning."

"So far I can quite understand," said I. "But if this be so, how can the bog shift as this one has undoubtedly done? It seems, so far, to be hedged with walls of rock. Surely these cannot move."

Sutherland smiled. "I see you do apprehend! Now we are at the second stage. Did you notice as we went across the hill side that there were distinct beds or banks of clay?"

"Certainly! do they come in?"

"Of course! If my theory is correct, the shifting is due to them."

"Explain!"

"So far as I can. But here I am only on surmise, or theory pure and simple. I may be all wrong, or I may be right—I shall know more before

I am done with Shleenanaher. My theory is that the shifting is due to the change in the beds of clay, as for instance by rains washing them by degrees to lower levels—this is notably the case in that high clay bank just opposite the Snake's Pass. The rocks are fixed, and so the clay becomes massed in banks between them, perhaps aided in the first instance by trees falling across the chasm or opening. But then the perpetually accumulating water from the spring has to find a way of escape; and as it cannot cut through the rock it rises to the earth bed, till it either tops the bed of clay which confines it or finds a gap or fissure through which it can escape. In either case it makes a perpetually deepening channel for itself, for the soft clay yields little by little to the stream passing over it, and so the surface of the outer level falls, and the water escapes, to perhaps find new reservoirs ready made to receive it, and a similar process as before takes place."

"Then the bog extends and the extended part takes the place of the old bog which gradually drains."

"Just so! but such would of course depend on the level; there might be two or more reservoirs, each with a deep bottom of its own and united only near the surface; or if the bank or bed of clay lay on the surface of one shelving rock, the water would naturally drain to the lowest point and the upper land would be shallow in proportion."

"But," I ventured to remark, "if this be so, one of two things must happen; either the water would wear away the clay so quickly, that the accumulation would not be dangerous, or else the process would be a very gradual one, and would not be attended with such results as we are told of. There would be a change in the position of the bog, but there would not be the upheaval and complete displacement and chaos that I have heard of, for instance, with regard to this very bog of Knockcalltecrore.

"Your 'if' is a great peacemaker! If what I have supposed were all, then the result would be as you have said; but there are lots of other supposes; as yet we have only considered one method of change. Suppose, for instance, that the water found a natural means of escape—as, for instance, where this very bog sends a stream over the rocks into the Cliff Fields—it would not attack the clay bed at all, unless under some unusual pressure. Then suppose that when such pressure had come the water did not rise and top the clay bed, but that it found a small fissure part of the way down. Suppose there were several such reservoirs as I have mentioned—and from the formation of the ground I think it very likely, for in several places jutting rocks from either side come close together, and suggest a sort of gap or canon in the rock formation, easily forming it into a reservoir. Then if the barrier between the two upper ones were to be weakened, and a sudden weight of water were to be thrown on the lower wall; suppose such wall were to partially collapse, and bring down, say, a clay bank, which would make a temporary barrier loftier than any yet existing, but only temporary; suppose that the quick accumulation of waters behind this barrier lifted the whole mass of water and slime and bog to its utmost height. Then, when such obstruction had been reached, the whole lower barrier, weakened by infiltration and attacked with sudden and new force, would give way at once, and the stream, kept down from above by the floating bog, would force its way along the bed rock and lift the whole spongy mass resting on it. Then with this new extent of bog suddenly saturated and weakened—demoralized as it were—and devoid of resisting power, the whole floating mass of the upper bog might descend on it, mingle with it, become incorporated with its semi-fluid substance, and form a new and dangerous quagmire incapable of sustaining solid weight, but leaving behind on the higher level only the refuse and sediment of its former existence—all the rubble and grit too heavy to float, and which would gradually settle down on the upper bed rock."

"Really, Dick, you put it most graphically. What a terrible thing it would be to live on the line of such a change."

"Terrible, indeed! At such a moment a house in the track of the movement—unless it were built on the rock—would go down like a ship in a storm. Go down solid and in a moment, without warning and without hope!"

"Then with such a neighbour as a shifting bog, the only safe place for a house would be on a rock."—Before my eyes, as I spoke, rose the vision of Murdock's house, resting on its knoll of rock, and I was glad for one reason that there, at least, would be safety for Joyce—and his daughter.

"Exactly! Now Murdock's house is as safe as a church. I must look at his new house when I go up tomorrow."

As I really did not care about Murdock's future, I asked no further questions; so we sat in silence and smoked in the gathering twilight.

There was a knock at the door. I called "Come in." The door opened slowly, and through a narrow opening Andy's shock head presented itself.

"Come in, Andy!" said Dick. "Come here and try if you can manage a glass of punch!"

"Begor!" was Andy's sole expression of acquiescence. The punch was brewed and handed to him.

"Is that as good as Widow Kelligan's?" I asked him. Andy grinned:—

"All punch is good, yer 'an'rs. Here's both yer good healths, an' here's 'The Girls' an'"—turning to me, "'the Bog.'" He winked, threw up his hand—and put down the empty glass. "Glory be to God" was his grace after—drink.

"Well, Andy! what is it?" said Dick.

"I've heerd," said he, "that yer 'an'rs isn't goin' in the mornin' to Shleenanaher, and I thought that yez couldn't do betther nor dhrive over to Knocknacar to-morra an' spind the day there."

"And why Knocknacar?" said I.

Andy twirled his cap between his hands in a sheepish way. I felt that he was acting a part, but could not see any want of reality. With a little hesitation he said:—

"I've gother from what yer 'an'rs wor sayin' on the car this mornin', that yez is both intherested in bogs—an' there's the beautifulest bit iv bog in all the counthry there beyant. An', moreover, it's a lovely shpot intirely. If you gintlemin have nothin' betther to do, ye'd dhrive over there—if ye'd take me advice."

"What kind of bog is it, Andy?" said Dick. "Is there anythin' peculiar about it. Does it shift?"

Andy grinned a most unaccountable grin:—

"Begor, it does, surr!" he answered quickly. "Sure all bogs does shift!" And he grinned again.

"Andy," said Dick, laughing, "you have some joke in your mind. What is it?"

"Oh, sorra wan, surr—ask the masther there."

As it did not need a surgical operation to get the joke intended into the head of a man—of whatever nationality—who understood Andy's allusion, and as I did not want to explain it, I replied:—

"Oh, don't ask me, Andy; I'm no authority on the subject," and I looked rather angrily at him, when Dick was not looking.

Andy hastened to put matters right—he evidently did not want to lose his day's hire on the morrow:—

"Yer 'an'rs! ye may take me wurrd for it—there's a bog beyant at Knocknacar which'll intherest yez intirely—I remimber it meself a lot higher up the mountain whin I was a spalpeen—an' it's been crawlin' down iver since. It's a mighty quare shpot intirely!"

This settled the matter, and we arranged forthwith to start early on the following morning for Knocknacar, Andy, before he left, having a nightcap—out of a tumbler.

We were astir fairly early in the morning, and having finished a breakfast sufficiently substantial to tide us over till dinner time, we started on our journey. The mare was in good condition for work, the road was level and the prospect fine, and altogether we enjoyed our drive immensely. As we looked back we could see Knockcalltecrore rising on the edge of the coast away to our right, and seemingly surrounded by a network of foam-girt islands, for a breeze was blowing freshly from the south-west.

At the foot of the mountain—or rather, hill—there was a small, clean-looking sheebeen. Here Andy stopped and put up the mare; then he brought us up a narrow lane bounded by thick hedges of wild briar to where we could see the bog which was the object of our visit. Dick's foot was still painful, so I had to give him an arm, as on yesterday. We crossed over two fields, from which the stones had been collected and placed in heaps. The land was evidently very rocky, for here and there— more especially in the lower part—the grey rock cropped up in places. At the top of the farthest field, Andy pointed out an isolated rock rising sharply from the grass.

"Look there, yer 'an'rs; whin I remimber first, that rock was as far aff from the bog as we are now from the boreen—an' luk at it now! why, the bog is close to it, so it is." He then turned and looked at a small heap of stones. "Murther! but there is a quare thing. Why that heap, not a year ago, was as high as the top iv that rock. Begor, it's bein' buried, it is!"

Dick looked quite excited as he turned to me and said:—

"Why, Art, old fellow! here is the very thing we were talking about. This bog is an instance of the gradual changing of the locality of a bog by the filtration of its water through the clay beds resting on the bed-rock. I wonder if the people here will let me make some investigations! Andy, who owns this land?"

"Oh, I can tell yer 'an'r that well enough; it's Misther Moriarty from Knockaltecrore. Him, surr," turning to me, "that ye seen at Widda Kelligan's that night in the shtorm."

"Does he farm it himself?"

"No, surr—me father rints it. The ould mare was riz on this very shpot."

"Do you think your father will let me make some investigations here, if I get Mr. Moriarty's permission also?"

"Throth, an' he will, surr—wid all the plisure in life—iv coorse," he added, with native shrewdness, "if there's no harrum done to his land—or, if there's harrum done, it's ped for."

"All right, Andy," said I; "I'll be answerable for that part of it."

We went straight away with Andy to see the elder Sullivan. We found him in his cabin at the foot of the hill—a hale old man of nearly eighty, with all his senses untouched, and he was all that could be agreeable. I told him who I was, and that I could afford to reimburse him if any damage should be done. Dick explained to him that, so far from doing harm, what he would do would probably prevent the spreading of the bog, and would in such case much enhance the value of his holding, and in addition give him the use of a spring on his land. Accordingly we went back to make further investigations. Dick had out his note-book in an instant, and took accurate note of everything; he measured and probed the earth, tapped the rocks with the little geological hammer which he always carried, and finally set himself down to make an accurate map of the locality, I acting as his assistant in the measurements. Andy left us for a while, but presently appeared, hot and flushed. As he approached, Dick observed:—

"Andy has been drinking the health of all his relatives. We must keep him employed here, or we may get a spill going home."

The object of his solicitude came and sat on a rock beside us, and looked on. Presently he came over, and said to Dick:—

"Yer 'an'r, can I help ye in yer wurrk? Sure, if ye only want wan hand to help ye, mayhap mine id do. An' thin his 'an'r here might hop up to the top iv the mountain; there's a mighty purty view there intirely, an' he could enjoy it, though ye can't get up wid yer lame fut."

"Good idea!" said Dick. "You go up on top, Art. This is very dull work, and Andy can hold the tape for me as well as you or anyone else. You can tell me all about it when you come down."

"Do, yer 'an'r. Tell him all ye see!" said Andy, as I prepared to ascend. "If ye go up soft be the shady parts, mayhap ye'd shtrike another bit of bog be the way."

I had grown so suspicious of Andy's *double entente*, that I looked at him keenly, to see if there was any fresh joke on; but his face was immovably grave, and he was seemingly intent on the steel tape which he was holding.

I proceeded up the mountain. It was a very pleasant one to climb, or rather to ascend, for it was nearly all covered with grass. Here and there, on the lower half, were clumps of stunted trees, all warped eastwards by the prevailing westerly wind—alders, mountain-ash, and thorn. Higher up these disappeared, but there was still a pleasant sprinkling of hedgerows. As the verdure grew on the south side higher than on the north or west, I followed it and drew near the top. As I got closer, I heard some one singing. "By Jove," said I to myself, "the women of this country have sweet voices!"—indeed, this was by no means the first time I had noticed the fact. I listened, and as I drew nearer to the top of the hill, I took care not to make any noise which might disturb the singer. It was an odd sensation to stand in the shadow of the hill-top, on that September day, and listen to *Ave Maria* sung by the unknown voice of an unseen singer. I made a feeble joke all to myself:—

"My experience of the girls of the West is that of *vox et prætereus nihil.*"

There was an infinity of pathos in the voice—some sweet, sad yearning, as though the earthly spirit was singing with an unearthly voice—and the idea came on me with a sense of conviction that some deep unhappiness underlay that appeal to the Mother of Sorrows. I listened, and somehow felt guilty. It almost seemed that I was profaning some shrine of womanhood, and I took myself to task severely in something of the following strain:—

"That poor girl has come to this hill top for solitude. She thinks she is alone with Nature and Nature's God, and pours forth her soul freely; and you, wretched, tainted man, break in on the sanctity of her solitude—of her prayer. For shame! for shame!"

Then—men are all hypocrites!—I stole guiltily forward to gain a peep at the singer who thus communed with Nature and Nature's God, and the sanctity of whose solitude and prayer I was violating.

A tuft of heath grew just at the top; behind this I crouched, and parting its luxuriance looked through.

For my pains I only saw a back, and that back presented in the most ungainly way of which graceful woman is capable. She was seated on the ground, not even raised upon a stone. Her knees were raised to the level of her shoulders, and her outstretched arms confined her legs below the knees—she was, in fact, in much the same attitude as boys are at games of cockfighting. And yet there was something very touching in the attitude—something of self-oblivion so complete that I felt a renewed feeling of guiltiness as an intruder.—Whether her reasons be aesthetic, moral, educational, or disciplinary, no self-respecting woman ever sits in such a manner when a man is by.

The song died away, and then there was a gulp and a low suppressed moan. Her head drooped between her knees, her shoulders shook, and I could see that she was weeping. I wished to get away, but for a few moments I was afraid to stir lest she should hear me. The solitude, now that the vibration of her song had died out of the air, seemed oppressive. In those few seconds a new mood seemed to come over her. She suddenly abandoned her dejected position, and, with the grace and agility of a young fawn, leaped to her feet. I could see that she was tall and exquisitely built, on the slim side—what the French call *svelte*. With a grace and pathos which were beyond expression she stretched forth her arms towards the sea, as to something that she loved, and then, letting them fall by her side, remained in a kind of waking dream.

I slipped away, and when I was well out of sight, ran down the hill about a hundred yards, and then commenced the re-ascent, making a fair proportion of noise as I came—now striking at the weeds with my heavy stick, now whistling, and again humming a popular air.

When I gained the top of the hill I started as though surprised at seeing any one, much less a girl, in such a place. I think I acted the part well—again I say that at times the hypocrite in us can be depended upon! She was looking straight towards me, and certainly, so far as I could tell, took me in good faith. I doffed my hat and made some kind of stammering salutation as one would to a stranger—the stammering not being, of course, in the routine of such occasions, but incidental to the special circumstances. She made me a graceful curtsey, and a blush overspread her cheeks. I was afraid to look too hard at her, especially at first, lest I should frighten her away, but I stole a glance towards her at every moment when I could.

How lovely she was! I had heard that along the West coast of Ireland there are traces of Spanish blood and Spanish beauty; and here was a living evidence of the truth of the hearsay. Not even at sunset in the parades of Madrid or Seville, could one see more perfect beauty of the Spanish type—beauty perhaps all the more perfect for being tempered with northern calm. As I said, she was tall and beautifully proportioned. Her neck was long and slender, gracefully set in her rounded shoulders, and supporting a beautiful head borne with the free grace of the lily on its stem. There is nothing in woman more capable of complete beauty than the head, and, crowned as this head was with a rich mass of hair as black and as glossy as the raven's wing, it was a thing to remember. She wore no bonnet, but a grey homespun shawl was thrown loosely over her shoulders; her hair was coiled in one rich mass at the top and back of her head, and fastened with an old-fashioned tortoiseshell comb. Her face was a delicate oval, showing what Rossetti calls "the pure wide curve from ear to chin." Luxuriant black eyebrows were arched over large black-blue eyes swept by curling lashes of extraordinary length, and showed off the beauty of a rounded, ample forehead—somewhat sunburnt, be it said. The nose was straight and wide between the eyes, with delicate sensitive nostrils; the chin wide and firm, and the mouth full and not small, with lips of scarlet, forming a perfect Cupid's bow, and just sufficiently open to show two rows of small teeth, regular and white as pearls. Her dress was that of a well-to-do peasant—a sort of body or jacket of printed chintz over a dress or petticoat of homespun of the shade of crimson given by a madder dye. The dress was short, and showed trim ankles in grey homespun with pretty feet in thick country-made wide-toed shoes. Her hands were shapely, with long fingers, and were very sunburnt and manifestly used to work.

As she stood there, with the western breeze playing with her dress and tossing about the stray ends of her raven tresses, I thought that I had never in my life seen anything so lovely. And yet she was only a peasant girl, manifestly and unmistakably, and had no pretence of being anything else.

She was evidently as shy as I was, and for a little while we were both silent. As is usual, the woman was the first to recover her self-possession, and whilst I was torturing my brain in vain for proper words to commence a conversation, she remarked:—

"What a lovely view there is from here. I suppose, sir, you have never been on the top of this hill before?"

"Never," said I, feeling that I was equivocating if not lying. "I had no idea that there was anything so lovely here." I meant this to have a double meaning, although I was afraid to make it apparent to her. "Do you often come up here?" I continued.

"Not very often. It is quite a long time since I was here last; but the view seems fairer and dearer to me every time I come." As she spoke the words, my memory leaped back to that eloquent gesture as she raised her arms.

I thought I might as well improve the occasion and lay the foundation for another meeting without giving offence or fright, so I said:—

"This hill is quite a discovery; and as I am likely to be here in this neighbourhood for some time, I dare say I shall often find myself enjoying this lovely view."

She made no reply or comment whatever to this statement. I looked over the scene, and it was certainly a fit setting for so lovely a figure; but it was the general beauty of the scene, and not, as had hitherto been the case, one part of it only that struck my fancy. Away on the edge of the coast-line rose Knockcalltecrore; but it somehow looked lower than before, and less important. The comparative insignificance was of course due to the fact that I was regarding it from a superior altitude, but it seemed to me that it was because it did not now seem to interest me so much. That sweet voice through the darkness seemed very far away now—here was a voice as sweet, and in such a habitation! The invisible charm with which Shleenanaher had latterly seemed to hold me—or the spell which it had laid upon me, seemed to pass away, and I found myself smiling that I should ever have entertained such an absurd idea.

Youth is not naturally stand off, and before many minutes the two visitors to the hill-top had laid aside reserve and were chatting freely. I had many questions to ask of local matters, for I wanted to find out what I could of my fair companion without seeming to be too inquisitive; but she seemed to fight shy of all such topics, and when we parted my ignorance of her name and surroundings remained as profound as it had been at first. She, however, wanted to know all about London. She knew it only by hearsay; for some of the questions which she asked me were amazingly simple—manifestly she had something of the true peasant belief that London is the only home of luxury, power, and learning. She was so frank, however, and made her queries with such a gentle modesty, that something within my heart seemed to grow, and grow; and the conviction was borne upon me that I stood before my fate. Sir Geraint's exclamation rose to my lips:—

"Here, by God's rood, is the one maid for me!"

One thing gave me much delight. The sadness seemed to have passed quite away—for the time at all events. Her eyes, which had at the first been glassy with recent tears, were now lit with keenest interest, and she seemed to have entirely forgotten the cause of her sorrow.

"Good!" thought I to myself complacently. "At least I have helped to brighten her life, though it be but for one hour."

Even whilst I was thinking she rose up suddenly—we had been sitting on a boulder—"Goodness! how the time passes!" she said; "I must run home at once."

"Let me see you home," I said eagerly. Her great eyes opened, and she said with a grave simplicity that took me "way down" to use American slang:—

"Why?"

"Just to see that you get home safely," I stammered. She laughed merrily:—

"No fear for me. I'm safer on this mountain than anywhere in the world—almost," she added, and the grave, sad look stole again over her face.

"Well, but I would like to," I urged. Again she answered with grave, sweet seriousness:—

"Oh, no, sir: that would not do. What would folk say to see me walking with a gentleman like you?" The answer was conclusive. I shrugged my shoulders because I was a man, and had a man's petulance under disappointment; and then I took off my hat and bowed—not ironically, but cheerfully, so as to set her at ease—for I had the good fortune to have been bred a gentleman. My reward came when she held out her hand frankly and said:—

"Good-bye, sir," gave a little graceful curtsey, and tripped away over the edge of the hill.

I stood bareheaded looking at her until she disappeared. Then I went to the edge of the little plateau and looked over the distant prospect of land and sea, with a heart so full that the tears rushed to my eyes. There are those who hold that any good emotion is an act of prayer! If this be so, then on that wild mountain-top as fervent a prayer as the heart of man is capable of went up to the Giver of all good things!

When I reached the foot of the mountain I found Dick and Andy waiting for me at the sheebeen. As I came close Dick called out:—

"What a time you were, old chap. I thought you had taken root on the hill-top! What on earth kept you?"

"The view from the top is lovely beyond compare," I said, as an evasive reply.

"Is what ye see there more lovelier nor what ye see at Shleenanaher?" said Andy with seeming gravity.

"Far more so!" I replied instantly and with decision.

"I tould yer 'an'r there was somethin' worth lukin' at," said he. "An' may I ask if yer 'an'r seen any bog on the mountain?"

I looked at him with a smile. I seemed to rather like his chaff now. "Begor I did, yer 'an'r," I answered, mimicking his accent.

We had proceeded on our way for a long distance, Andy apparently quite occupied with his driving—Dick studying his note-book, and I quite content with my thoughts—when Andy said, apropos of nothing and looking at nobody:—

"I seen a young girrul comin' down the hill beyant, a wee while before yer 'an'r. I hope she didn't disturb any iv yez?"

The question passed unnoticed, for Dick apparently did not hear and I did not feel called upon to answer it.

I could not have truthfully replied with a simple negative or positive.

VI

CONFIDENCES

The next day Sutherland would have to resume his work with Murdock—but on his newly-acquired land. I could think of his visit to Knockcalltecrore without a twinge of jealousy; and for my own part I contemplated a walk in a different direction. Dick was full of his experiment regarding the bog at Knocknacar, and could talk of nothing else—a disposition of things which suited me all to nothing, for I had only to acquiesce in all he said, and let my own thoughts have free and pleasant range.

"I have everything cut and dry in my head, and I'll have it all on paper before I sleep tonight," said the enthusiast. "Unfortunately, I am tied for a while longer to the amiable Mr. Murdock; but since you're good enough, old fellow, to offer to stay to look after the cutting, I can see my way to getting along. We can't begin until the day after tomorrow, for I can't by any possibility get old Moriarty's permission before that. But then we'll start in earnest. You must get some men up there and set them to work at once. By tomorrow evening I'll have an exact map ready for you to work by, and all you will have to do will be to see that the men are kept up to the mark, look at the work now and then and take a note of results. I expect it will take quite a week or two to make the preliminary drainage, for we must have a decided fall for the water. We can't depend on less than twenty or thirty feet, and I should not be surprised if we want twice as much. I suppose I shan't see you till tomorrow night; for I'm going up to my room now, and shall work late, and I must be off early in the morning. As you're going to have a walk I suppose I may take Andy, for my foot is not right yet?"

"By all means," I replied, and we bade each other good night.

When I went to my own room I locked the door and looked out of the open window at the fair prospect bathed in soft moonlight. For a long time I stood there. What my thoughts were I need tell no young man or young woman, for without shame I admitted to myself that I was over head and ears in love. If any young person of either sex requires any further enlightenment, well! then, all I can say is that their education in life has been shamefully neglected, or their opportunities have been scant; or, worse still, some very grave omisssion has been made in their equipment for the understanding of life.—If any one, not young, wants such enlightenment I simply say—'sir or madam, either you are a fool or your memory is gone!'

One thing I will say, that I never felt so much at one with my kind; and before going to bed I sat down and wrote a letter of instructions to my agent, directing him to make accurate personal inquiries all over the estate, and at the forthcoming rent-day make such remissions of rent as would relieve any trouble or aid in any plan of improvements such as his kinder nature could guess at or suggest.

I need not say that for a long time I did not sleep, and although my thoughts were full of such hope and happiness that the darkness seemed ever changing into sunshine, there were, at times, such harrowing thoughts of difficulties to come, in the shape of previous attachments—of my being late in my endeavours to win her as my wife—of my never been able to find her again—that, now and again, I had to jump from my bed and pace the floor. Towards daylight I slept, and went through a series of dreams of alternating joy and pain. At first hope held full sway, and my sweet experience of the day became renewed and multiplied. Again I climbed the hill and saw her and heard her voice—again the tearful look faded from her eyes— again I held her hand in mine and bade good-bye, and a thousand happy fancies filled me with exquisite joy. Then doubts began to come. I saw her once more on the hill-top—but she was looking out for some other than myself, and a shadow of disappointment passed over her sweet face when she recognized me. Again, I saw myself kneeling at her feet and imploring her love, while only cold, hard looks were my lot; or I found myself climbing the hill, but never able to reach the top—or on reaching it finding it empty. Then I would find myself hurrying through all sorts of difficult places— high, bleak mountains, and lonely wind-swept strands—dark paths through gloomy forests, and over sun-smitten plains, looking for her whom I had lost, and in vain trying to call her—for I could not remember her name. This last nightmare was quite a possibility, for I had never heard it.

I awoke many times from such dreams in an agony of fear; but after a time both pleasure and pain seemed to have had their share of my sleep, and I slept the dreamless sleep that Plato eulogizes in the "Apologia Socratis."

I was awakened to a sense that my hour of rising had not yet come by a knocking at my door. I opened it, and on the landing without saw Andy standing, cap in hand.

"Hullo, Andy!" I said. "What on earth do you want?"

"Yer 'an'r 'll parden me, but I'm jist off wid Misther Sutherland; an' as I undherstand ye was goin' for a walk, I made bould t' ask yer 'an'r if ye'll give a missage to me father?"

"Certainly, Andy! With pleasure."

"Maybe ye'd tell him that I'd like the white mare tuk off the grash an' gave some hard 'atin' for a few days, as I'll want her brung into Wistport before long."

"All right, Andy! Is that all?"

"That's all, yer 'an'r." Then he added, with a sly look at me:—

"May be ye'll keep yer eye out for a nice bit o' bog as ye go along."

"Get on, Andy," said I. "Shut up! you ould corncrake." I felt I could afford to chaff with him as we were alone.

He grinned, and went away. But he had hardly gone a few steps when he returned and said, with an air of extreme seriousness:—

"As I'm goin' to Knockcalltecrore, is there any message I kin take for ye to Miss Norah?"

"Oh, go on!" said I. "What message should I have to send, when I never saw the girl in my life?"

For reply he winked at me with a wink big enough to cover a perch of land, and, looking back over his shoulder so that I could see his grin to the last, he went along the corridor—and I went back to bed.

It did not strike me till a long time afterwards—when I was quite close to Knocknacar—how odd it was that Andy had asked me to give the message to his father. I had not told him I was even coming in the direction—I had not told anyone—indeed, I had rather tried to mislead when I spoke of taking a walk that day, by saying some commonplace about 'the advisability of breaking new ground' and so forth. Andy had evidently taken it for granted; and it annoyed me somewhat that he could find me so transparent. However, I gave the message to the old man, to which he promised to attend, and had a drink of milk, which is the hospitality of the west of Ireland farmhouse. Then, in the most nonchalant way I could, I began to saunter up the hill.

I loitered awhile here and there on the way up. I diverted my steps now and then as if to make inquiry into some interesting object. I tapped rocks and turned stones over, to the discomfiture of various swollen pale-coloured worms and nests of creeping things. With the end of my stick I dug up plants, and made here and there unmeaning holes in the ground as though I were actuated by some direct purpose known to myself and not understood of others. In fact I acted as a hypocrite in many harmless and unmeaning ways, and rendered myself generally obnoxious to the fauna and flora of Knocknacar.

As I approached the hill-top my heart beat loudly and fast, and a general supineness took possession of my limbs, and a dimness came over my sight and senses. I had experienced something of the same feeling at other times in my life—as, for instance, just before my first fight when a school boy, and when I stood up to make my maiden speech at the village debating society. Such feelings—or lack of feelings—however, do not kill; and it is the privilege and strength of advancing years to know this fact.

I proceeded up the hill. I did not whistle this time, or hum, or make any noise—matters were far too serious with me for any such levity. I reached the top—and found myself alone! A sense of blank disappointment came over me—which was only relieved when, on looking at my watch, I found that it was as yet still early in the forenoon. It was three o'clock yesterday when I had met—when I had made the ascent.

As I had evidently to while away a considerable time, I determined to make an accurate investigation of the hill of Knocknacar—much, very much fuller than I had made as yet. As my unknown had descended the hill by the east, and would probably make the ascent—if she ascended at all—by the same side; and as it was my object not to alarm her, I determined to confine my investigations to the west side. Accordingly I descended about half way down the slope, and then commenced my prying into the secrets of Nature under a sense of the just execration of me and my efforts on the part of the whole of the animate and inanimate occupants of the mountain side.

Hours to me had never seemed of the same inexhaustible proportions as the hours thus spent. At first I was strong with a dogged patience; but this in time gave way to an impatient eagerness, that merged into a despairing irritability. More than once I felt an almost irresistible inclination to rush to the top of the hill and shout, or conceived an equally foolish idea to make a call at every house, cottage and cabin, in the neighbourhood. In this latter desire my impatience was somewhat held in check by a sense of the ludicrous; for as I thought of the detail of the doing it, I seemed to see myself when trying to reduce my abstract longing to a concrete effort, meeting only jeers and laughter from both men and women—in my seemingly asinine effort to make inquiries regarding a person whose name even I did not know, and for what purpose I could assign no sensible reason.

I verily believe I must have counted the leaves of grass on portions of that mountain. Unfortunately, hunger or thirst did not assail me, for they would have afforded some diversion to my thoughts. I sturdily stuck to my resolution not to ascend to the top until after three o'clock, and I gave myself much *kudos* for the stern manner in which I adhered to my resolve.

My satisfaction at so bravely adhering to my resolution, in spite of so much mental torment and temptation, may be imagined when, at the expiration of the appointed time, on ascending to the hill-top, I saw my beautiful friend sitting on the edge of the plateau and heard her first remark after our mutual salutations:—

"I have been here nearly two hours, and am just going home! I have been wondering and wondering what on earth you were working at all over the hillside! May I ask, are you a botanist?"

"No!"

"Or a geologist?"

"No!"

"Or a naturalist?"

"No!"

There she stopped; this simple interrogation as to the pursuits of a stranger evidently struck her as unmaidenly, for she blushed and turned away.

I did not know what to to say; but youth has its own wisdom—which is sincerity—and I blurted out:—

"In reality I was doing nothing; I was only trying to pass the time."

There was a query in the glance of the glorious blue-black eyes and in the lifting of the ebon lashes; and I went on, conscious as I proceeded that the ground before me was marked "Dangerous":—

"The fact is, I did not want to come up here till after three, and the time seemed precious long, I can tell you."

"Indeed, But you have missed the best part of the view. Between one and two o'clock, when the sun strikes in between the islands—Cusheen there to the right, and Mishear—the view is the finest of the whole day."

"Oh, yes," I answered, "I know now what I have missed."

Perhaps my voice betrayed me. I certainly felt full of bitter regret; but there was no possibility of mistaking the smile which rose to her eyes and faded into the blush that followed the reception of the thought.

There are some things which a woman *cannot* misunderstand or fail to understand; and surely my regret and its cause were within the category.

It thrilled through me, with a sweet intoxication, to realize that she was not displeased. Man is predatory even in his affections, and there is some conscious power to him which follows the conviction that the danger of him—which is his intention—is recognized.

However, I thought it best to be prudent, and to rest on success—for a while, at least. I therefore commenced to talk of London, whose wonders were but fresh to myself, and was rewarded by the bright smile that had now become incorporated with my dreams by day and by night.

And so we talked—talked in simple companionship; and the time fled by on golden wings. No word of love was spoken or even hinted at, but with joy and gratitude unspeakable I began to realize that we were *en rapport*. And more than this, I realized that the beautiful peasant girl had great gifts—a heart of gold, a sweet, pure nature, and a rare intelligence. I gathered that she had had some education, though not an extensive one, and that she had followed up at home such subjects as she had learned in school. But this was all I gathered. I was still as ignorant as ever of her name, and all else beside, as when I had first heard her sweet voice on the hill-top.

Perhaps I might have learned more, had there been time; but the limit of my knowledge had been fixed. The time had fled so quickly, because so happily, that neither of us had taken account of it; and suddenly, as a long red ray struck over the hill-top from the sun now preparing for his plunge into the western wave, she jumped to her feet with a startled cry:—

"The sunset! What am I thinking of! Good-night! good-night! No, you must not come—it would never do! Good night!" And before I could say a word, she was speeding down the eastern slope of the mountain.

The revulsion from such a dream of happiness made me for the moment ungrateful; and I felt that it was with an angry sneer on my lip that I muttered as I looked at her retreating form:—

"Why are the happy hours so short—whilst misery and anxiety spread out endlessly?"

But as the red light of the sunset smote my face, a better and a holier feeling came to me; and there on the top of the hill I knelt and prayed, with the directness and fervour that are the spiritual gifts of youth, that every blessing might light on her—the *arrière pensée* being—her, my wife. Slowly I went down the mountain after the sun had set; and when I got to the foot, I stood bareheaded for a long time, looking at the summit which had given me so much happiness.

Do not sneer or make light of such moments, ye whose lives are grey. Would to God that the grey-haired and grey-souled watchers of life, could feel such moments once again!

I walked home with rare briskness, but did not feel tired at all by it—I seemed to tread on air. As I drew near the hotel, I had some vague idea of hurrying at once to my own room, and avoiding dinner altogether as something too gross and carnal for my present exalted condition; but a moment's reflection was sufficient to reject any such folly. I therefore achieved the other extreme, and made Mrs. Keating's kindly face beam by the vehemence with which I demanded food. I found that Dick had not yet returned—a fact which did not displease me, as it insured me a temporary exemption from Andy's ill-timed banter, which I did not feel in a humour to enjoy at present.

I was just sitting down to my dinner when Dick arrived. He too had a keen appetite; and it was not until we had finished our fish, and were well into our roast duck, that conversation began. Once he was started, Dick was full of matters to tell me. He had seen Moriarty—that was what had kept him so late—and had got his permission to investigate and experiment on the bog. He had thought out the whole method of work to be pursued, and had, during Murdock's dinner-time, made to scale a rough diagram for me to work by. We had our cigars lit before he had exhausted himself on this subject. He had asked me a few casual questions about my walk, and, so as not to arouse any suspicions, I had answered him vaguely that I had had a lovely day, had enjoyed myself immensely, and had seen some very pretty things—all of which was literally and exactly true. I had then asked him as to how he had got on with his operations in connection with the bog. It amused me to think how small and secondary a place Shleenanaher, and all belonging to it, now had in my thoughts. He told me that they had covered a large portion of the new section of the bog—that there was very little left to do now, in so far as the bog was concerned; and he descanted on the richness and the fine position of Murdock's new farm.

"It makes me angry," said he, "to think that that human-shaped wolf should get hold of such a lovely spot, and oust such a good fellow as the man whom he has robbed—yes! it is robbery, and nothing short of it. I feel something like a criminal myself for working for such a wretch at all."

"Never mind, old chap," said I; "you can't help it. Whatever he may have done wrong, you have had neither act nor part in it. It will all come right in time!" In my present state of mind I could not imagine that there was, or could be, anything in the world that would not come all right in time.

We strolled into the street, and met Andy, who immediately hurried up to me:—

"Good evenin', yer 'an'r! An' did ye give me insthructions to me father?"

"I did, Andy; and he asked me to tell you that all shall be done exactly as you wish."

"Thank yer 'an'r." He turned away, and my heart rejoiced, for I thought I would be free from his badinage; but he turned and came back, and asked with a servility which I felt to be hypocritical and assumed:—

"Any luck, yer 'an'r, wid bogs today?" I know I got red as I answered him:—

"Oh, I don't know! Yes! a little—not much."

"Shure an' I'm glad to hear it, surr! but I might have known be the luk iv ye and be yer shtep. Faix! it's aisy known whin a man has been lucky wid bogs!" The latter sentence was spoken in a pronounced "aside."

Dick laughed, for although he was not in the secret he could see that there was some fun intended. I did not like his laugh, and said hotly:—

"I don't understand you, Andy!"

"Is it undershtand me ye don't do? Well, surr, if I've said anythin' that I shouldn't, I ax yer pardon. Bogs isn't to be lightly shpoke iv at all, at all!" then, after a pause:—"Poor Miss Norah!"

"What do you mean?" said I.

"Shure yer 'an'r, I was only pityin' the poor crathur. Poor thing, but this'll be a bitther blow to her intirely!" The villain was so manifestly acting a part, and he grinned at me in such a provoking way, that I got quite annoyed.

"Andy, what do you mean? out with it!" I said hotly.

"Mane, yer 'an'r? Sure nawthin'. All I mane is, poor Miss Norah! Musha, but it'll be the sore thrial to her. Bad cess to Knocknacar anyhow!"

"This is infernal impertinence! Here——" I was stopped by Dick's hand on my breast:—

"Easy, easy, old chap! What is this all about? Don't get angry, old man. Andy is only joking, whatever it is. I'm not in the secret myself, and so can give no opinion; but there is a joke somewhere. Don't let it go beyond a joke."

"All right, Dick," said I, having had time to recover my temper. "The fact is that Andy has started some chaff on me about bogs—meaning girls thereby—every time he mentions the word to me; and now he seems to accuse me in some way about a girl that came to meet her father that night I left him home at Knockcalltecrore. You know, Joyce, that Murdock has ousted from his farm. Now, look here, Andy! You're a very good fellow, and don't mean any harm; but I entirely object to the way you're going on. I don't mind a button about a joke. I hope I'm not such an ass as to be thin-skinned about a trifle, but it is another matter when you mention a young lady's name alongside mine. You don't think of the harm you may do. People are very talkative, and generally get a story the wrong end up. If you mention this girl—whatever her name is——"

"Poor Miss Norah!" struck in Andy, and then ostentatiously corrected himself—"I big yer 'an'r's pardon, Miss Norah, I mane."

"This Miss Norah along with me," I went on, "and especially in that objectionable form, people may begin to think she is wronged in some way, and you may do her an evil that you couldn't undo in all your lifetime. As for me, I never even saw the girl. I heard her speak in the dark for about half a minute, but I never set eyes on her in my life. Now, let this be the last of all this nonsense! Don't worry me any more; but run in and tell Mrs. Keating to give you a skinful of punch, and to chalk it up to me."

Andy grinned, ducked his head, and made his exit into the house as though propelled or drawn by some unseen agency. When I remarked this to Dick he replied, "Some spirit draws him, I dare say."

Dick had not said a word beyond advising me not to lose my temper. He did not appear to take any notice of my lecture to Andy, and puffed unconcernedly at his cigar till the driver had disappeared. He then took me by the arm and said:—

"Let us stroll a bit up the road." Arm in arm we passed out of the town and into the silence of the common. The moon was rising, and there was a soft, tender light over everything. Presently, without looking at me, Dick said:—

"Art, I don't want to be inquistive or to press for any confidences, but you and I are too old friends not to be interested in what concerns each other. What did Andy mean? Is there any girl in question?"

I was glad to have a friend to whom to open my mind, and without further thought I answered:—

"There is, Dick!"

Dick grasped my arm and looked keenly into my face, and then said:

"Art! Answer me one question—answer me truly, old fellow, by all you hold dear—answer me on your honour!"

"I shall, Dick! What is it?"

"Is it Norah Joyce?" I had felt some vague alarm from the seriousness of his manner, but his question put me at ease again, and, with a high heart, I answered:—

"No! Dick. It is not." We strolled on, and after a pause, that seemed a little oppressive to me, he spoke again:—

"Andy mentioned a poor 'Miss Norah'—don't get riled, old man— and you both agreed that a certain young lady was the only one alluded to. Are you sure there is no mistake? Is not your young lady called Norah?" This was a difficult question to answer, and made me feel rather awkward. Being awkward, I got a little hot:—

"Andy's an infernal fool. What I said to him—you heard me——"

"Yes! I heard you."

"——was literally and exactly true. I never set eyes on Norah Joyce in my life. The girl I mean, the one you mean also, was one I saw by chance yesterday—and today—on the top of Knocknacar."

"Who is she?"—there was a more joyous sound in Dick's voice.

"Eh! eh!" I stammered. "The fact is, Dick, I don't know."

"What is her name?"

"I don't know."

"You don't know her name?"

"No."

"Where does she come from?"

"I don't know. I don't know anything about her, except this, Dick, that I love her with all my heart and soul!" I could not help it—I could not account for it—but the tears rushed to my eyes, and I had to keep my head turned away from Dick lest he should notice me. He said nothing, and when I had surreptitiously wiped away what I thought were unmanly tears of emotion, I looked round at him. He, too, had his head turned away and, and if my eyes did not deceive me, he too had some unmanly signs of emotion.

"Dick!" said I. He turned on the instant. We looked in one another's faces, and the story was all told. We grasped hands warmly.

"We're both in the same boat, old boy," said he.

"Who is it, Dick?"

"Norah Joyce!"——I gave a low whistle.

"But," he went on, "you are well ahead of me. I have never even exchanged a word with her yet. I have only seen her a couple of times; but the whole world is nothing to me beside her. There! I've nothing to tell. *Veni, Vidi, Victus sum!*—I came, I saw, I was conquered. She has beauty enough, and if I'm not an idiot, worth enough to conquer a nation!—Now, tell me all about yours."

"There's nothing to tell, Dick; as yet I have only exchanged a few words. I shall hope to know more soon." We walked along in silence, turning our steps back to the hotel.

"I must hurry and finish up my plans tonight so as to be ready for you tomorrow. You won't look on it as a labour to go to Knocknacar, old chap!" said he, slapping me on the back.

"Nor you to go to Shleenanaher," said I, as we shook hands and parted for the night.

It was quite two hours after this when I began to undress for bed. I suppose the whole truth, however foolish, must be told, but those two hours were mainly spent in trying to compose some suitable verses to my unknown. I had consumed a vast amount of paper—consumed literally, for what lover was ever yet content to trust his unsuccessful poetic efforts to the waste basket?—and my grate was thickly strewn with filmy ashes. Hitherto the Muse had persistently and successfully evaded me. She did not even grant me a feather from her wing, and my 'woeful ballad made to my mistress' eyebrow' was amongst the things that were not. There was a gentle tap at the door. I opened it, and saw Dick with his coat off. He came in.

"I thought I would look in, Art, as I saw the light under your door, and knew that you had not gone to bed. I only wanted to tell you this. You don't know what a relief it is to me to be able to speak of it to any living soul—how maddening it is to me to work for that scoundrel

Murdock. You can understand now why I flared up at him so suddenly ere yesterday. I have a strong conviction on me that his service is devil's service as far as my happiness is concerned—and that I shall pay some terrible penalty for it."

"Nonsense, old fellow," said I, "Norah only wants to see you to know what a fine fellow you are. You won't mind my saying it, but you are the class of man that any woman would be proud of!"

"Ah! old chap," he answered sadly, "I'm afraid it will never get that far. There isn't, so to speak, a fair start for me. She has seen me already—worse luck!—has seen me doing work which must seem to her to aid in ruining her father. I could not mistake the scornful glance she has thrown on me each time we have met. However, *che sara sara!* It's no use fretting beforehand. Good night!"

VII

VANISHED

W e were all astir shortly after daylight on Monday morning. Dick's foot was well enough for his walk to Knockcalltecrore, and Andy came with me to Knocknacar, as had been arranged, for I wanted his help in engaging labourers and beginning the work. We got to the shebeen about nine o'clock, and Andy having put up the mare went out to get labourers. As I was morally certain that at that hour in the morning there would be no chance of seeing my unknown on the hilltop, I went at once to the bog, taking my map with me and studying the ground where we were to commence operations.

Andy joined me in about half-an-hour with five men—all he had been able to get in the time. They were fine strapping young fellows and seemed interested in the work, so I thought the contingent would be strong enough. By this time I had the ground marked out according to the plan, and so without more ado we commenced work.

We had attacked the hill some two hundred feet lower down than the bog, where the land suddenly rose steeply from a wide sloping extent of wilderness of invincible barrenness. It was over this spot that Sutherland hoped ultimately to send the waters of the bog. We began at the foot and made a trench some four feet wide at the bottom, and with sloping walls, so that when we got in so far the drain would be twenty feet deep, the external aperture would measure about twice as much.

The soil was heavy and full of moderate-sized boulders, but was not unworkable, and amongst us we came to the conclusion that a week of solid work would, bar accidents and our coming across unforeseen difficulties, at any rate break the back of the job. The men worked in sections—one marking out the trench by cutting the surface to some foot-and-a-half deep, and the others following in succession. Andy sat on a stone hard by, filled his pipe, and endeavoured in his own cheery way to relieve the monotony of the labour of the others. After about an hour he grew tired and went away—perhaps it was that he became interested in a country car, loaded with persons, that came down the road and stopped a few minutes at the shebeen on its way to join the main road to Carnaclif.

Things went steadily on for some time. The men worked well, and I possessed my soul in such patience as I could, and studied the map and the ground most carefully. When dinner-time came the men went off each to his own home, and as soon as the place was free from them I hurried to the top of the mountain. The prospect was the same as yesterday. There was the same stretch of wild moor and rugged coast, of clustering islands and foam-girt rocks—of blue sky laden with such masses of luminous clouds as are only found in Ireland. But all was to me dreary and desolate, for the place was empty and *she* was not there. I sat down to wait with what patience I could. It was dreary work at best; but at any rate there was hope—and its more immediate kinsman, expectation—and I waited. Somehow the view seemed to tranquillize me in some degree. It may have been that there was some unconscious working of the mind which told me in some imperfect way that in a region quite within my range of vision, nothing could long remain hidden or unknown. Perhaps it was the stilly silence of the place. There was hardly a sound—the country people were all within doors at dinner, and even the sounds of their toil were lacking. From the west came a very faint breeze, just enough to bring the far-off, eternal roar of the surf. There was scarcely a sign of life. The cattle far below were sheltering under trees, or in the shadows of hedges, or standing still knee-deep in the pools of the shallow streams. The only moving thing which I could see was the car which had left so long before, and was now far off, and was each moment becoming smaller and smaller as it went into the distance.

So I sat for quite an hour with my heart half sick with longing, but she never came. Then I thought I heard a step coming up the path at the far side. My heart beat strangely. I sat silent, and did not pretend to hear. She was walking more slowly than usual, and with a firmer tread. She was coming. I heard the steps on the plateau, and a voice came:—

"Och! an' isn't it a purty view, yer 'an'r?" I leaped to my feet with a feeling that was positively murderous. The revulsion was too great, and I broke into a burst of semi-hysterical laughter. There stood Andy—with ragged red head and sun-scorched face—in his garb of eternal patches, bleached and discoloured by sun and rain into a veritable coat of many colours—gazing at the view with a rapt expression, and yet with one eye half-closed in a fixed but unmistakable wink, as though taking the whole majesty of nature into his confidence.

When he heard my burst of laughter he turned to me quizzically:—

BRAM STOKER

"Musha! but it's the merry gentleman yer 'an'r is this day. Shure the view here is the laughablest thing I ever see!" and he affected to laugh, but in such a soulless, unspontaneous way that it became a real burlesque. I waited for him to go on. I was naturally very vexed, but I was afraid to say anything lest I might cause him to interfere in *this* affair—the last thing on earth that I wished for.

He did go on; no one ever found Andy abashed or ill at ease:—

"Begor! but yer 'an'r lepped like a deer when ye heerd me shpake. Did ye think I was goin' to shoot ye? Faix! an' I thought that ye wor about to jump from aff iv the mountain into the say, like a shtag."

"Why, what do you know about stags, Andy? There are none in this part of the country, are there?" I thought I would drag a new subject across his path. The ruse of the red herring drawn across the scent succeeded!

"Phwhat do I know iv shtags? Faix, I know this, that there does be plinty in me Lard's demesne beyant at Wistport. Sure wan iv thim got out last autumn an' nigh ruined me garden. He kem in at night an' ate up all me cabbages an' all the vigitables I'd got. I frightened him away a lot iv times, but he kem back all the same. At last I could shtand him no longer, and I wint meself an' complained to the Lard. He tould me he was very sorry fur the damage he done, 'an',' sez he, 'Andy, I think he's a bankrup,' sez he, 'an' we must take his body.' 'How is that, Me Lard?' sez I. Sez he, 'I give him to ye, Andy. Do what ye like wid him!' An' wid that I wint home an' I med a thrap iv a clothes line wid a loop in it, an' I put it betune two threes; and shure enough in the night I got him."

"And what did you do with him, Andy?" said I.

"Faith, surr, I shkinned him and ate him!" He said this just in the same tone in which he would speak of the most ordinary occurrence, leaving the impression on one's mind that the skinning and eating were matters done at the moment and quite offhand.

I fondly hoped that Andy's mind was now in quite another state from his usual mental condition; but I hardly knew the man yet. He had the true humorist's persistence, and before I was ready with another intellectual herring he was off on the original track.

"I thrust I didn't dishturb yer 'an'r. I know some gintlemin likes to luk at views and say nothin'. I'm tould that a young gintleman like yer 'an'r might be up on top iv a mountain like this, an' he'd luk at the view so hard day afther day that he wouldn't even shpake to a purty girrul—if there was wan forninst him all the time!"

"Then they lied to you, Andy!" I said this quite decisively.

"Faix, yer 'an'r, an' it's glad I am to hear that same, for I wouldn't like to think that a young gintleman was afraid of a girrul, however purty she might be."

"But, tell me, Andy," I said, "what idiot could have started such an idea? And even if it was told to you, how could you be such a fool as to believe it?"

"Me belave it! Surr, I did't belave a wurrd iv it—not until I met yer 'an'r." His face was quite grave, and I was not sorry to find him in a sober mood, for I wanted to have a serious chat with him. It struck me that he, having relatives at Knocknacar, might be able to give me some information about my unknown.

"Until you met me, Andy! Surely I never gave you any ground for holding such a ridiculous idea?"

"Begor, yer 'an'r, but ye did. But p'raps I had betther not say any more—yer 'an'r mightn't like it."

This both surprised and nettled me, and I was determined now to have it out, so I said, "You quite surprise me, Andy. What have I ever done? Do not be afraid! Out with it," for he kept looking at me in a timorous kind of way.

"Well, then, yer 'an'r, about poor Miss Norah?"

This was a surprise, but I wanted to know more.

"Well, Andy, what about her?"

"Shure, an' didn't you refuse to shpake iv her intirely an' sot on me fur only mintionin' her—an' she wan iv the purtiest girruls in the place."

"My dear Andy," said I, "I thought I had explained to you, last night, all about that. I don't suppose you quite understand; but it might do a girl in her position harm to be spoken about with a—a man like me."

"Wid a man like you—an' for why? Isn't she as good a girrul as iver broke bread?"

"Oh, it's not that, Andy; people might think harm."

"Think harrum!—phwhat harrum—an' who'd think it?"

"Oh, you don't understand—a man in your position can hardly know."

"But, yer 'an'r, I don't git comprehindin'! What harrum could there be, an' who'd think it? The people here is all somethin' iv me own position—workin' people—an' whin they knows a girrul is a good, dacent girrul, why should they think harrum because a nice young gintleman goes out iv his way to shpake to her?—Doesn't he shpake to the quality like himself, an' no wan thinks any harrum iv ayther iv them?"

Andy's simple, honest argument made me feel ashamed of the finer sophistries belonging to the more artificial existence of those of my own station.

"Sure, yer 'an'r, there isn't a bhoy in Connaught that wouldn't like to be shpoke of wid Miss Norah. She's that good, that even the nuns in Galway, where she was at school, loves her and thrates her like wan iv themselves, for all she's a Protestan'."

"My dear Andy," said I, "don't you think you're a little hard on me? You're putting me in the dock, and trying me for a series of offences that I never even thought of committing with regard to her or any one else. Miss Norah may be an angel in petticoats, and I'm quite prepared to take it for granted that she is so—your word on the subject is quite enough for me. But just please to remember that I never set eyes on her in my life. The only time I was ever in her presence was when you were by yourself, and it was so dark that I could not see her, to help her when she fainted. Why, in the name of common sense, you should keep holding her up to me, I do not understand."

"But yer 'an'r said that it might do her harrum even to mintion her wid you."

"Oh, well, Andy, I give it up—it's no use trying to explain. Either you *won't* understand, or I am unable to express myself properly."

"Surr, there can be only one harrum to a girrul from a gintleman," he laid his hand on my arm, and said this impressively—whatever else he may have ever said in jest, he was in grim earnest now—"an' that's whin he's a villain. Ye wouldn't do the black thrick, and desave a girrul that thrusted ye?"

"No, Andy, no! God forbid! I would rather go to the highest rock on some island there beyond, where the surf is loudest, and throw myself into the sea, than do such a thing. No! Andy, there are lots of men that hold such matters lightly, but I don't think I'm one of them. Whatever sins I have, or may ever have upon my soul, I hope such a one as *that* will never be there."

All the comment Andy made was, "I thought so!" Then the habitual quizzical look stole over his face again, and he said:—

"There does be some that does fear Braches iv Promise. Mind ye, a man has to be mighty careful on the subject, for some weemin is that 'cute, there's no bein' up to them."

Andy's sudden change to this new theme was a little embarrassing, since the idea leading to it—or rather preceding it—had been one purely personal to myself; but he was off, and I thought it better that he should go on.

"Indeed!" said I.

"Yes, surr. Oh, my! but they're 'cute. The first thing that a girrul does when a man looks twice at her, is t' ask him to write her a letther, an' thin she has him—tight."

"How so, Andy?"

"Well, ye see, surr, when you're writin' a letther to a girrul, ye can't begin widout a 'My dear' or a 'My darlin' '—an' thin she has the grip iv the law onto ye! An' ye do be badgered be the councillors, an' ye do be frowned at be the judge, an' ye do be laughed at be the people, an' ye do have to pay yer money—an' there ye are!"

"I say, Andy," said I, "I think you must have been in trouble yourself in that way—you seem to have it all off pat!"

"Oh, throth, not me, yer 'an'r. Glory be to God! but I niver was a defindant in me life—an' more betoken, I don't want to be—but I was wance a witness in a case iv the kind."

"And what did you witness?"

"Faix, I was called to prove that I seen the gintleman's arrum around the girrul's waist. The councillors made a deal out iv that—just as if it warn't only manners to hould up a girrul on a car!"

"What was the case, Andy? Tell me all about it."

I did not mind his waiting, as it gave me an excuse for staying on the top of the hill. I knew I could easily get rid of him when she came—if she came—by sending him on a message.

"Well, this was a young woman what had an action agin Shquire Murphy iv Ballynashoughlin himself—a woman as was no more nor a mere simple governess!"

It would be impossible to convey the depth of social unimportance conveyed by his tone and manner; and coming from a man of "shreds and patches," it was more than comic. Andy had his good suit of frieze and homespun; but whilst he was on mountain duty, he spared these and appeared almost in the guise of a scarecrow.

"Well! what happened?"

"Faix, whin she tould her shtory the shquire's councillor luked up at the jury, an' he whispered a wurrd to the shquire and his 'an'r wrote out a shlip iv paper an' handed it to him, an' the councillor ups an' says he: 'Me Lard and Gintlemin iv the Jury, me client is prepared to have the honour iv the lady's hand if she will so, for let bygones be bygones.'

An' sure enough they was married on the Sunday next four weeks; an' there she is now dhrivin' him about the counthry in her pony-shay, an' all the quality comin' to tay in the garden, an' she as affable as iver to all the farmers round. Aye, an' be the hokey, the shquire himself sez that it was a good day for him whin he sot eyes on her first, an' that he don't know why he was such a dam fool as iver to thry to say 'no' to her, or to wish it."

"Quite a tale with a moral, Andy! Bravo! Mrs. Murphy."

"A morial is it? Now may I make bould to ask yer 'an'r what morial ye take out iv it?

"The moral, Andy, that I see is, When you see the right woman go for her for all you're worth, and thank God for giving you the chance." Andy jumped up and gave me a great slap on the back.

"Hurro! more power to yer elbow! but it's a bhoy afther me own h'arrt y' are. I big yer pardon, surr, for the liberty; but it's mighty glad I am."

"Granted, Andy; I like a man to be hearty, and you certainly are. But why are you so glad about me?"

"Because I like yer 'an'r. Shure in all me life I niver see so much iv a young gintleman as I've done iv yer 'an'r. Surr, I'm an ould man compared wid ye—I'm the beginnin' iv wan, at any rate, an' I'd like to give ye a wurrd iv advice—git marrid while ye can! I tell ye this, surr, it's not whin the hair is beginnin' to git thin on to the top iv yer head that a nice young girrul 'ill love ye for yerself. It's the people that goes all their lives makin' money and lukin' after all kinds iv things that's iv no kind iv use to thim, that makes the mishtake. Suppose ye do git marrid when ye're ould and bald, an' yer legs is shaky, an' ye want to be let sit close to the fire in the warrum corner, an' ye've lashins iv money that ye don't know what to do wid! Do you think that it's thin that yer wives does be dhramin' iv ye all the time and worshippin' the ground ye thrid? Not a bit iv it! They do be wantin'—aye and thryin' too—to help God away wid ye!"

"Andy," said I, "you preach, on a practical text, a sermon that any and every young man ought to hear!" I thought I saw an opening here for gaining some information and jumped in.

"By Jove! you set me off wishing to marry! Tell me, is there any pretty girl in this neighbourhood that would suit a young man like me?"

"Oho! begor, there's girruls enough to shute any man."

"Aye, Andy—but pretty girls!"

"Well surr, that depinds. Now what might be yer 'anr's idea iv a purty girrul?"

"My dear Andy, there are so many different kinds of prettiness that it is hard to say."

"Faix, an' I'll tell ye if there's a girrul to shute in the counthry, for bedad I think I've seen thim all. But you must let me know what would shute ye best?"

"How can I well tell that, Andy, when I don't know myself? Show me the girl, and I'll very soon tell you."

"Unless I was to ax yer 'an'r questions!" this was said very slily.

"Go on, Andy! there is nothing like the Socratic method."

"Very well thin! I'll ax two kinds iv things, an' yer 'an'r will tell me which ye'd like like the best!"

"All right, go on."

"Long or short?"

"Tall; not short, certainly."

"Fat or lane?"

"Fie! fie! Andy, for shame; you talk as if they were cattle or pigs."

"Begor, there's only wan kind iv fat an' lane that I knows of; but av ye like I'll call it thick or thin; which is it?"

"Not too fat, but certainly not skinny." Andy held up his hands in mock horror:—

"Yer 'an'r shpakes as if ye was talkin' iv powlthry."

"I mean Andy," said I with a certain sense of shame, "she is not to be either too fat or too lean, as you put it."

"Ye mane 'shtreaky'!"

"Streaky!" said I, "what do you mean?" He answered promptly:—

"Shtreaky,—thick an' thin—like belly bacon." I said nothing. I felt certain it would be useless and out of place. He went on:—

"Nixt, fair or dark?"

"Dark, by all means."

"Dark be it, surr. What kind iv eyes might she have?"

"Ah! eyes like darkness on the bosom of the azure deep!"

"Musha! but that's a quare kind iv eye fur a girrul to have intirely! Is she to be all dark, surr, or only the hair of her?"

"I don't mean a nigger, Andy!" I thought I would be even with him for once in a way. He laughed heartily.

"Oh! my but that's a good wan. Be the hokey, a girrul can be dark enough fur any man widout bein' a nagur. Glory be to God, but I niver seen a faymale naygur meself, but I suppose there's such things; God's very good to all his craythurs! But, barrin' naygurs, must she be all dark?"

"Well not of necessity, but I certainly prefer what we call a brunette."

"A bru-net. What's that now; I've heerd a wheen o' quare things in me time, but I niver heerd a woman called that before."

I tried to explain the term; he seemed to understand, but his only comment was:—

"Well, God is very good," and then went on with his queries.

"How might she be dressed?" he looked very sly as he asked the question.

"Simply! The dress is not particular—that can easily be altered. For myself, just at present, I should like her in the dress they all wear here, some pretty kind of body and a red petticoat."

"Thrue for ye!" said Andy. Then he went over the list ticking off the items on his fingers as he went along:—

"A long, dark girrul, like belly bakin, but not a naygur, some kind iv a net, an' wid a rid petticoat, an' a quare kind iv an eye! Is that the kind iv a girrul that yer 'an'r wants to set yer eyes on?"

"Well," said I, "item by item, as you explaim them, Andy, the description is correct; but I must say, that never in my life did I know a man to so knock the bottom out of romance as you have done in summing-up the lady's charms."

"Her charrums, is it? Be the powers! I only tuk what yer 'an'r tould me. An' so that's the girrul that id shute yer?"

"Yes! Andy. I think she would." I waited in expectation, but he said nothing. So I jogged his memory:—

"Well!" He looked at me in a most peculiar manner, and said slowly and impressively:—

"Thin I can sahtisfy yer 'an'r. There's no such girrul in all Knocknacar!" I smiled a smile of triumph:—

"You're wrong for once, Andy. I saw such a girl only yesterday, here on the top of this mountain, just where we're sitting now."

Andy jumped up as if he had been sitting on an anthill, and had suddenly been made aware of it. He looked all round in a frightened way, but I could see that he was only acting, and said:—

"Glory be to God! but maybe it's the fairies, it was, or the pixies! Shure they do say that there's lots an' lots an' lashins iv them on this hill. Don't ye have nothin' to say to thim, surr! There's only sorra follys thim. Take an ould man's advice, an' don't come up here any more. The shpot is dangerous to ye. If ye want to see a fine girrul go to Shleenanaher, an' have a good luk at Miss Norah in the daylight."

"Oh, bother Miss Norah!" said I. "Get along with you—do! I think you've got Miss Norah on the brain; or perhaps you're in love with her yourself." Andy murmured *sotto voce,* but manifestly for me to hear:—

"Begor, I am, like the rist iv the bhoys—av course!"

Here I looked at my watch, and found it was three o'clock, so thought it was time to get rid of him.

"Here," said I "run down to the men at the cutting and tell them that I'm coming down presently to measure up their work, as Mr. Sutherland will want to know how they've got on."

Andy moved off. Before going, however, he had something to say, as usual:—

"Tell me, Misther Art"—this new name startled me, Andy had evidently taken me into his public family—"do ye think Misther Dick"—this was another surprise—"has an eye on Miss Norah?" There was a real shock this time.

"I see him lukin' at her wance or twice as if he'd like to ate her; but, bedad, it's no use if he has, for she wouldn't luk at him. No wondher! an' him helpin' to be takin' her father's houldin' away from him."

I could not answer Andy's question as to poor old Dick's feelings, for such was his secret, and not mine; but I determined not to let there be any misapprehension regarding his having a hand in Murdock's dirty work, so I spoke hotly:—

"You tell anyone that dares to say that Dick Sutherland has any act or part, good or bad—large or small—in that dirty ruffian's dishonourable conduct, that he is either a knave or a fool—at any rate he is a liar! Dick is simply a man of science engaged by Murdock, as any other man of science might be, to look after some operations in regard to his bog."

Andy's comment was made *sotto voce,* so I thought it better not to notice it.

"Musha! but the bogs iv all kinds is gettin' mixed up quarely. Here's another iv them. Misther Dick is engaged to luk afther the bogs. An' so he does, but his eyes goes wandherin' among thim. There does be bogs iv all kinds now all over these parts. It's quare times we're in, or I'm gettin' ould!"

With this Parthian shaft Andy took himself down the hill, and presently I saw the good effects of his presence in stimulating the workmen to more ardent endeavours, for they all leaned on their spades whilst he told them a long story, which ended in a tumult of laughter.

I might have enjoyed the man's fun, but I was in no laughing humour. I had got anxious long ago because *she* had not visited the hill-top. I looked all round, but could see no sign of her anywhere. I waited and waited, and the time truly went on leaden wings. The afternoon sun smote the hill-top with its glare, more oppressive always than even the noontide heat.

I lingered on and lingered still, and hope died within me.

When six o'clock had come I felt that there was no more chance for me that day; so I went sadly down the hill, and, after a glance for Dick's sake at the cutting, sought the sheebeen where Andy had the horse ready harnessed in the car. I assumed as cheerful an aspect as I could, and flattered myself that I carried off the occasion very well. It was not at all flattering, however, to my histrionic powers to hear Andy, as we were driving off, whisper in answer to a remark deploring how sad I looked, made by the old lady who kept the sheebeen:—

"Whisht! Don't appear to notice him, or ye'll dhrive him mad. Me opinion is that he's been wandherin' on the mountain too long, an' tamperin' wid the rings on the grass—you know—an' that he has seen the fairies!" Then he said aloud and ostentatiously:—

"Gee up! ye ould corncrake—ye ought to be fresh enough—ye've niver left the fut iv the hill all the day,"—then turning to me, "An' sure, surr, it's goin' to the top that takes it out iv wan—ayther a horse or a man."

I made no answer, and in silence we drove to Carnaclif, where I found Dick impatiently waiting dinner for me.

I was glad to find that he was full of queries concerning the cutting, for it saved me from the consideration of subjects more difficult to answer satisfactorily. Fortunately I was able to give a good account of the time spent, for the work done had far exceeded my expectations. I thought that Dick was in much better spirits than he had been; but it was not until the subject of the bog at Knocknacar was completely exhausted that I got any clue on the subject. I then asked Dick if he had had a good time at Shleenanaher?

"Yes!" he answered. "Thank God! the work is nearly done. We went over the whole place today and there was only one indication of iron. This was in the bog just beside an elbow where Joyce's land—his present land—touches ours; no! I mean on Murdock's, the scoundrel!" He was quite angry with himself for using the word "ours" even accidentally.

"And has anything come of it?" I asked him.

"Nothing! Now that he knows it is there, he would not let me go near it on any account. I'm in hopes he'll quarrel with me soon in order to get rid of me, so that he may try by himself to fish it—whatever it may be—out of the bog. If he does quarrel with me! Well! I only hope he will; I have been longing for weeks past to get a chance at him. Then she'll believe, perhaps——" He stopped.

"You saw her today, Dick!"

"How did you know that?"

"Because you look so happy, old man!"

"Yes! I did see her; but only for a moment. She drove up in the middle of the day, and I saw her go up to the new house. But she didn't even see me," and his face fell. Presently he asked:—

"You didn't see your girl?"

"No, Dick, I did not! But how did you know?"

"I saw it in your face when you came in!"

We sat and smoked in silence. The interruption came in the shape of Andy:—

"I suppose, Masther Art, the same agin to-morra—unless ye'd like me to bring ye wid Masther Dick to see Shleenanaher—ye know the shpot, surr—where Miss Norah is!"

He grinned, and as we said nothing, made his exit.

VIII

A Visit to Joyce

With renewed hope I set out in the morning for Knocknacar.
It is one of the many privileges of youth that a few hours' sleep will change the darkest aspect of the entire universe to one of the rosiest tint. Since the previous evening, sleeping and waking, my mind had been framing reasons and excuses for the absence of. . . !—it was a perpetual grief to me that I did not even know her name. The journey to the mountain seemed longer than usual; but, even at the time, this seemed to me only natural under the circumstances.

Andy was today seemingly saturated or overwhelmed with a superstitious gravity. Without laying any personal basis for his remarks, but accepting as a standpoint his own remark of the previous evening concerning my having seen a fairy, he proceeded to develop his fears on the subject. I will do him the justice to say that his knowledge of folklore was immense, and that nothing but a gigantic memory for detail, cultivated to the full, or else an equally stupendous imaginitaon working on the facts that momentarily came before his view, could have enabled him to keep up such a flow of narrative and legend. The general result to me was, that if I had been inclined to believe such matters I would have remained under the impression that, although the whole seaboard, with adjacent mountains, from Westport to Galway, was in a state of plethora as regards uncanny existences, Knocknacar, as a habitat for such, easily bore off the palm. Indeed, that remarkable mountain must have been a solid mass of gnomes, fairies, pixies, leprachauns, and all genii, species and varieties of the same. No Chicago grain-elevator in the early days of a wheat corner could have been more solidly packed. It would seem that so many inhabitants had been allured by fairies, and consequently had mysteriously disappeared, that this method of minimisation of the census must have formed a distinct drain on the local population, which, by the way, did not seem to be excessive.

I reserved to myself the right of interrogating Andy on this subject later in the day, if, unhappily, there should be any opportunity. Now that we had drawn near the hill, my fears began to return.

Whilst Andy stabled the mare I went to the cutting and found the men already at work. During the night there had evidently been a considerable drainage from the cutting, not from the bog but entirely local. This was now Friday morning, and I thought that if equal progress were made in the two days, it would be quite necessary that Dick should see the working on Sunday, and advise before proceeding further.

As I knew that gossip and the requirements of his horse would keep Andy away for a little while, I determined to take advantage of his absence to run up to the top of the hill, just to make sure that no one was there. It did not take long to get up, but when I arrived there was no reward, except in the shape of a very magnificent view. The weather was evidently changing, for great clouds seemed to gather from the west and south, and far away over the distant rim of the horizon the sky was as dark as night. Still the clouds were not hurrying as before a storm, and the gloom did not seem to have come shoreward as yet; it was rather a presage of prolonged bad weather than bad itself. I did not remain long, as I wished to escape Andy's scrutiny. Indeed, as I descended the hill I began to think that Andy had become like the "Old Man of the Sea," and that my own experience seemed likely to rival that of Sinbad.

When I arrived at the cutting I found Andy already seated, enjoying his pipe. When he saw me he looked up with a grin, and said audibly:—

"The Good People don't seem to be workin' so 'arly in the mornin'! Here he is safe an' sound amongst us."

That was a very long day. Whenever I thought I could do so, without attracting too much attention, I strolled to the top of the hill, but only to suffer a new disappointment.

At dinner-time I went up and sat all the time. I was bitterly disappointed, and also began to be seriously alarmed. I seemed to have lost my unknown.

When the men got back to their work, and I saw Andy beginning to climb the hill in an artless, purposeless manner, I thought I would kill two birds with one stone, and, whilst avoiding my incubus, make some inquiries. As I could easily see from the top of the hill, there were only a few houses all told in the little hamlet; and including those most isolated, there were not twenty in all. Of these I had been in the sheebeen and in old Sullivan's, so that a stroll of an hour or two, properly organized, would cover the whole ground; and so I set out on my task to try and get some sight or report of my unknown. I knew I could always get an opportunity of opening conversation by asking for a light for my cigar.

It was a profitless task. Two hours after I had started I returned to the top of the hill as ignorant as I had gone, and the richer only by some dozen or more drinks of milk, for I found that the acceptance of some form of hospitality was an easy opening to general conversation. The top was still empty, but I had not been there a quarter of an hour when I was joined by Andy. His first remark was evidently calculated to set me at ease:—

"Begor, yer 'an'r comes to the top iv this hill nigh as often as I do meself."

I felt that my answer was inconsequential as well as ill-tempered:—

"Well, why on earth, Andy, do you come so often? Surely there is no need to come, unless you like it."

"Faix! I came this time lest yer 'an'r might feel lonely. I niver see a man yit be himself on top iv a hill that he didn't want a companion—iv some kind or another."

"Andy," I remarked, as I thought, rather cuttingly, "you judge life and men too much by your own experience. There are people and emotions which are quite out of your scope—far too high, or perhaps too low, for your psychic or intellectual grasp."

Andy was quite unabashed. He looked at me admiringly.

"It's a pity yer 'an'r isn't a mimber iv Parlyment. Shure, wid a flow iv language like that, ye could do anythin'!"

As satire was no use I thought I would draw him out on the subject of the fairies and pixies.

"I suppose you were looking for more fairies; the supply you had this morning was hardly enough to suit you, was it?"

"Begor, it's meself is not the only wan that does be lukin' for the fairies!" and he grinned.

"Well, I must say, Andy, you seem to have a good supply on hand. Indeed, it seems to me that if there were any more fairies to be located on this hill it would have to be enlarged, for it's pretty solid with them already, so far as I can gather."

"Augh! there's room for wan more! I'm tould there's wan missin' since ere yistherday."

It was no good trying to beat Andy at this game, so I gave it up and sat silent. After a while he asked me:—

"Will I be dhrivin' yer 'an'r over to Knockcalltecrore?"

"Why do you ask me?"

"I'm thinking it's glad yer 'an'r will be to see Miss Norah."

"Upon my soul, Andy, you are too bad. A joke is a joke, but there are limits to it; and I don't let any man joke with me when I prefer not. If you want to talk of your Miss Norah, go and talk to Mr. Sutherland about her. He's there every day and can make use of your aid! Why on earth do you single me out as your father confessor? You're unfair to the girl, after all, for if I ever do see her I'm prepared to hate her."

"Ah! yer 'an'r would'nt be that hard! What harrum has the poor crathur done that ye'd hate her—a thing no mortial man iver done yit?"

"Oh, go on! don't bother me any more; I think it's about time we were getting home. You go down to the sheebeen and rattle up that old corncrake of yours; I'll come down presently and see how the work goes on."

He went off, but came back as usual; I could have thrown something at him.

"Take me advice, surr—pay a visit to Shleenanaher, an' see Miss Norah!" and he hurried down the hill.

His going did me no good; no one came, and after a lingering glance around, and noting the gathering of the rain clouds, I descended the hill.

When I got up on the car I was not at all in a talkative humour, and said but little to the group surrounding me. I heard Andy account for it to them:—

"Whisht! don't notice his 'an'r's silence! It's stupid wid shmokin' he is. He lit no less nor siventeen cigars this blissed day. Ax the neighbours av ye doubt me. Gee up!"

The evening was spent with Dick as the last had been. I knew that he had seen his girl; he knew that I had not seen mine, but neither had anything to tell. Before parting he told me that he expected to shortly finish his work at Knockcalltecrore, and asked me if I would come over.

"Do come," he said, when I expressed a doubt. "Do come, I may want a witness," so I promised to go.

Andy had on his best suit, and a clean wash, when he met us smiling in the early morning, "Look at him," I said, "wouldn't you know he was going to meet his best girl?"

"Begor," he answered, "mayhap we'll all do that same!"

It was only ten o'clock when we arrived at Knockcalltecrore, and went up the boreen to Murdock's new farm. The Gombeen Man was standing at the gate with his watch in his hand. When we came up, he said:—

"I feared you would be late. It's just conthract time now. Hadn't ye bethter say good-bye to your frind an' git to work?" He was so transparently inclined to be rude, and possibly to pick a quarrel, that I whispered a warning to Dick. To my great satisfaction he whispered back:—

"I see he wants to quarrel; nothing in the world will make me lose temper today." Then he took out his pocket-book, searched for and found a folded paper; opening this he read: "'and the said Richard Sutherland shall be at liberty to make use of such assistant as he may choose or appoint whensoever he may wish during the said engagement at his own expense.' You see, Mr. Murdock, I am quite within the four walls of the agreement, and exercise my right. I now tell you formally tbat Mr. Arthur Severn has kindly undertaken to assist me for today." Murdock glared at him for a minute, and then opened the gate and said:—

"Come in, gintlemin." We entered.

"Now, Mr. Murdoch!" said Dick, briskly, "what do you wish done today? Shall we make further examination of the bog where the iron indication is, or shall we finish the survey of the rest of the land?"

"Finish the rough survey!"

The operation was much less complicated than when we had examined the bog. We simply "quartered" the land, as the Constabulary say when they make search for hidden arms; and taking it bit by bit, passed the magnet over its surface. We had the usual finds of nails, horseshoes, and scrap iron, but no result of importance. The last place we examined was the house. It was a much better built and more roomy structure than the one he had left. It was not, however, like the other, built on a rock, but in a sheltered hollow. Dick pointed out this to me, and remarked:—

"I don't know but that Joyce is better off, all told, in the exchange. I wouldn't care myself to live in a house built in a place like this, and directly in the track of the bog."

"Not even," said I, "if Norah was living in it too?"

"Ah, that's another thing! With Norah I'd take my chance and live in the bog itself, if I could get no other place."

When this happened, our day's work was nearly done, and very soon we took our leave for the evening, Murdock saying, as I thought rather offensively:—

"Now, you, sir, be sure to be here in time on Monday morning."

"All right!" said Dick, nonchalantly; and we passed out. In the boreen, he said to me:—

"Let us stroll up this way, Art," and we walked up the hill towards Joyce's house, Murdock coming down to his gate and looking at us. When we came to Joyce's gate, we stopped. There was no sign of Norah; but Joyce himself stood at his door. I was opening the gate when he came forward.

"Good evening, Mr. Joyce," said I. "How is your arm? I hope quite well by this time. Perhaps you don't remember me—I had the pleasure of giving you a seat up here in my car, from Mrs. Kelligan's, the night of the storm."

"I remember well," he said; "and I was thankful to you, for I was in trouble that night—it's all done now." And he looked round the land with a sneer, and then he looked yearningly towards his old farm.

"Let me introduce my friend, Mr. Sutherland," said I.

"I ask yer pardon, sir. An' I don't wish to be rude—but I don't want to know him. He's no frind to me and mine!"

Dick's honest, manly face grew red with shame. I thought he was going to say something angrily, so cut in as quickly as I could:—

"You are sadly mistaken, Mr. Joyce; Dick Sutherland is too good a gentleman to do wrong to you or any man. How can you think such a thing?"

"A man what consorts wid me enemy can be no frind of mine!"

"But he doesn't consort with him; he hates him. He was simply engaged to make certain investigations for him as a scientific man. Why, I don't suppose you yourself hate Murdock more than Dick does."

"Thin I ax yer pardon, sir," said Joyce. "I like to wrong no man, an' I'm glad to be set right."

Things were going admirably, and we were all beginning to feel at ease, when we saw Andy approach. I groaned in spirit—Andy was gradually taking shape to me as an evil genius. He approached, and making his best bow, said:—

"Fine evenin', Misther Joyce. I hope yer arrum is betther—an' how is Miss Norah?"

"Thank ye kindly, Andy; both me arm and the girl's well."

"Is she widin?"

"No! she wint this mornin' to stay over Monday in the convent. Poor girl! she's broken-hearted, lavin' her home and gettin' settled here. I med the changin' as light for her as I could—but weemin takes things to heart more nor min does, an' that's bad enough, God knows!"

"Thrue for ye," said Andy. "This gintleman here, Masther Art, says he hasn't seen her since the night she met us below in the dark."

"I hope," said Joyce, "you'll look in and see us, if you're in these parts, sir, whin she comes back. I know she thought a dale of your kindness to me that night."

"I'll be here for some days, and I'll certainly come, if I may."

"And I hope I may come, too, Mr. Joyce," said Dick, "now that you know me."

"Ye'll be welkim, sir."

We all shook hands, coming away; but as we turned to go home, at the gate we had a surprise. There, in the boreen, stood Murdock—livid with fury. He attacked Dick with a tirade of the utmost virulence: He called him every name he could lay his tongue to—traitor, liar, thief, and indeed exhausted the whole terminology of abuse, and accused him of stealing his secrets and of betraying his trust. Dick bore the ordeal splendidly; he never turned a hair, but calmly went on smoking his cigar. When Murdock had somewhat exhausted himself and stopped, he said calmly:—

"My good fellow, now that your ill-manners are exhausted, perhaps you will tell me what it is all about?"

Whereupon Murdock opened again the vials of his wrath. This time he dragged us all into it—I had been brought in as a spy, to help in betraying him, and Joyce had suborned him to the act of treachery. For myself I fired up at once, and would have struck him, only that Dick laid his hand on me, and in a whisper cautioned me to desist.

"Easy, old man—easy! Don't spoil a good position. What does it matter what a man like that can say? Give him rope enough! we'll have our turn in time, don't fear!"

I held back, but unfortunately Joyce pressed forwards. He had his say pretty plainly.

"What do ye mane, ye ill-tongued scoundhrel, comin' here to make a quarrel? Why don't ye shtay on the land you have robbed from me, and have us alone? I am not like these gintlemen here, that can afford to hould their tongues and despise ye—I'm a man like yerself, though I hope I'm not the wolf that ye are—fattenin' on the blood of the poor! How dare you say I suborned any one—me that never told a lie, or done a dirty thing in me life? I tell you, Murtagh Murdock, I put my mark upon ye once—I see it now comin' up white through the red of yer passion! Don't provoke me further, or I'll put another mark on ye that ye'll carry to yer grave!"

No one said a word more. Murdock moved off and entered his own house; Dick and I said "good night" to Joyce again, and went down the boreen.

IX

My New Property

The following week was a time to me of absolute bitterness. I went each day to Knocknacar, where the cutting was proceeding at a rapid rate. I haunted the hill-top, but without the slightest result. Dick had walked over with me on Sunday, and had been rejoiced at the progress made; he said that if all went well we could about Friday next actually cut into the bog. Already there was a distinct infiltration through the cutting, and we discussed the best means to achieve the last few feet of the work so as not in any way to endanger the safety of the men working.

All this time Dick was in good spirits. His meeting with Norah's father had taken a great and harrowing weight off his mind, and to him all things were now possible in the future. He tried his best to console me for my disappointment. He was full of hope—indeed he refused to see anything but a delay, and I could see that in his secret heart he was not altogether sorry that my love affair had received a temporary check. This belief was emphasized by the tendency of certain of his remarks to the effect that marriages between persons of unequal social status were inadvisable—he, dear old fellow, seemingly in his transparent honesty unaware that he was laying himself out with all his power to violate his own principles.

But all the time I was simply heartbroken. To say that I was consumed with a burning anxiety would be to to understate the matter; I was simply in a fever. I could neither eat nor sleep satisfactorily, and—sleeping or waking—my brain was in a whirl of doubts, conjectures, fears and hopes. The most difficult part to bear was my utter inability to do anything. I could not proclaim my love or my loss on the hill-top; I did not know where to make inquiries, and I had no idea who to inquire for. I did not even like to tell Dick the full extent of my woes.

Love has a modesty of its own, whose lines are boldly drawn, and whose rules are stern.

On more than one occasion I left the hotel secretly—after having ostensibly retired for the night—and wended my way to Knocknacar. As I passed through the sleeping country I heard the dogs bark in the cottages as I went by, but little other sound I ever heard except the booming of the distant sea. On more than one of these occasions I was drenched with rain—for the weather had now become thoroughly unsettled. But I heeded it not; indeed the physical discomfort—when I felt it—was in some measure an anodyne to the torture of my restless soul.

I always managed to get back before daylight, so as to avoid any questioning. After three or four days, however, the "boots" of the hotel began evidently to notice the state of my clothes and boots, and ventured to speak to me. He cautioned me against going out too much alone at night, as there were two dangers—one from the moonlighters who now and again raided the district, and who, being composed of the scum of the countryside—"corner-boys" and loafers of all kinds—would be only too glad to find an unexpected victim to rob; and the other, lest in wandering about I should get into trouble with the police under suspicion of being one of these very ruffians.

The latter difficulty seemed to me to be even more obnoxious than the former; and to avoid any suspicion I thought it best to make my night wanderings known to all. Accordingly, I asked Mrs. Keating to have some milk and bread and butter left in my room each night, as I would probably require something after my late walk. When she expressed surprise as to my movements, I told her that I was making a study of the beauty of the country by night, and was much interested in moonlight effects. This last was an unhappy setting forth of my desires, for it went round in a whisper amongst the servants and others outside the hotel, until at last it reached the ears of an astute Ulster-born policeman, from whom I was much surprised to receive a visit one morning. I asked him to what the honour was due. His answer spoke for itself:—

"From information received A come to talk till ye regardin' the interest ye profess to take in moonlichtin'."

"What on earth do you mean?" I asked.

"A hear ye're a stranger in these parts—an' as ye might take away a wrong impression weth ye—A thenk it ma duty to tell ye that the people round here are nothin' more nor less than leears—an' that ye mustn't believe a sengle word they say."

"Really," said I, "I am quite in the dark. Do try and explain. Tell me what it is all about."

"Why, A larn that ye're always out at nicht all over the country, and that ye've openly told people here that ye're interested in moon-lichtin'."

"My dear sir, some one is quite mad! I never said such a thing—indeed, I don't know anything about moon-lighting."

"Then why do ye go out at nicht?"

"Simply to see the country at night—to look at the views—to enjoy effects of moonlight."

"There ye are, ye see—ye enjoy the moonlicht effect."

"Good lord! I mean the view—the purely æsthetic effect—the chiaroscuro—the pretty pictures!"

"Oh, aye! A see now—A ken weel! Then A needn't trouble ye further. But let ma tell ye that it's a dangerous practice to walk out be nicht. There's many a man in these parts watched and laid for. Why in Knockcalltecrore there's one man that's in danger all the time. An' as for ye—why ye'd better be careful that yer nicht wanderins doesn't bring ye ento trouble," and he went away.

At last I got so miserable about my own love affair that I thought I might do a good turn to Dick; and so I determined to try to buy from Murdock his holding on Knockcalltecrore, and then to give it to my friend, as I felt that the possession of the place, with power to re-exchange with Joyce, would in no way militate against his interests with Norah.

With this object in view I went out one afternoon to Knockcalltecrore, when I knew that Dick had arranged to visit the cutting at Knocknacar. I did not tell anyone where I was going, and took good care that Andy went with Dick. I had acquired a dread of that astute gentleman's inferences.

It was well in the afternoon when I got to Knockcalltecrore. Murdock was out at the edge of the bog making some investigations on his own account with the aid of the magnets. He flew into a great rage when he saw me, and roundly accused me of coming to spy upon him. I disclaimed any such meanness, and told him that he should be ashamed of such a suspicion. It was not my cue to quarrel with him, so I restrained myself as well as I could, and quietly told him that I had come on a matter of business.

He was anxious to get me away from the bog, and took me into the house; here I broached my subject to him, for I knew he was too astute a man for my going round the question to be of any use.

At first my offer was a confirmation of his suspicion of me as a spy; and, indeed, he did not burke this aspect of the question in expressing his opinion.

"Oh, aye!" he sneered. "Isn't it likely I'm goin' to give up me land to ye, so that ye may hand it over to Mr. Sutherland—an' him havin' saycrets from me all the time—maybe knowin' where what I want to find is hid. Didn't I know it's a thraitor he is, an' ye a shpy."

"Dick Sutherland is no traitor and I am no spy. I wouldn't hear such words from anyone else; but, unfortunately, I know already that your ideas regarding us both are so hopelessly wrong that it's no use trying to alter them. I simply came here to make you an offer to buy this piece of land. The place is a pretty one, and I, or some friend of mine, may like some day to put up a house here. Of course if you don't want to sell there's an end to the matter; but do try to keep a decent tongue in your head—if you can."

My speech had evidently some effect on him, for he said:—

"I didn't mane any offinse—an' as for sellin', I'd sell anything in the wurrld av I got me price fur it!"

"Well! why not enter on this matter? You're a man of the world, and so am I. I want to buy; I have money and can afford to give a good price, as it is a fancy with me. What objection have you to sell?"

"Ye know well enough I'll not sell—not yit, at all evints. I wouldn't part wid a perch iv this land fur all ye cud offer—not till I'm done wid me sarch. I mane to get what I'm lukin' fur—if it's there!"

"I quite understand! Well! I am prepared to meet you in the matter. I am willing to purchase the land—it to be given over to me at whatever time you may choose to name. Would a year suit you to make your investigations?"

He thought for a moment—then took out an old letter, and on the back of it made some calculations. Then he said:—

"I suppose ye'd pay the money down at wanst?"

"Certainly," said I, "the very day I get possession." I had intended paying the money down, and waiting for possession as a sort of inducement to him to close with me; but there was so much greed in his manner that I saw I would do better by holding off payment until I got possession. My judgment was correct, for his answer surprised me:—

"A month'll do what I wanted; or, to be certain, say five weeks from today. But the money would have to be payed to the minit."

"Certainly!" said I. "Suit yourself as to time, and let me know the terms, so that I can see if we agree. I suppose you will want to see your attorney, so name any day to suit you."

"I'm me own attorney! Do ye think I'd thrust any iv them wid me affairs? Whin I have a law suit I'll have thim, but not before. If ye want to know me price I'll tell it to ye now."

"Go on," said I, concealing my delight as well as I could.

He accordingly named a sum which, to me, accustomed only as I had hitherto been to the price of land in a good English county, seemed very small indeed.

"He evidently thought he was driving a hard bargain, for he said with a cunning look:—

"I suppose ye'll want to see lawyers and the like. So you may; but only to see that ye get ye bargin hard and fast. I'll not discuss the terrums wid anyone else; an' if y' accept, ye must sign me a writin' now, that ye buy me land right here, an' that ye'll pay the money widin a month before ye take possession on the day we fix."

"All right," said I. "That will suit me quite well. Make out your paper in duplicate, and we will both sign. Of course, you must put in a clause guaranteeing title, and allowing the deed to be made with the approval of my solicitor, not as to value, but as to form and completeness.

"That's fair!" he said, and sat down to draw up his papers. He was evidently a bit of a lawyer—a gombeen man must be—and he knew the practical matters of law affecting things in which he was himself interested. His Memorandum of Agreement was, so far as I could judge, quite complete and as concise as possible. He designated the land sold, and named the price which was to be paid into the account in his name in the Galway Bank before twelve o'clock noon on the 27th September, or which might be paid in at an earlier date, with the deduction of two per cent. per annum as discount—in which case the receipt was to be given in full and an undertaking to give possession at the appointed time, namely Wednesday, 27 Oct., at 12 noon.

We both signed the memorandum, he having sent the old woman who came up from the village to cook for him for the old schoolmaster to witness the signatures. I arranged that when I should have seen my solicitor and have had the deed proper drafted, I would see him again. I then came away, and got back at the hotel a little while before Dick arrived.

Dick was in great spirits; his experiment with the bog had been quite successful. The cutting had advanced so far that the clay wall hemming in the bog was actually weakened, and with a mining cartridge, prepared for the purpose, he had blown up the last bit of bank remaining. The bog had straightway begun to pour into the opening, not merely from the top, but simultaneously to the whole depth of the cutting.

"The experience of that first half-hour of the rush," went on Dick, "was simply invaluable.' I do wish you had been there, old fellow. It was in itself a lesson on bogs and their reclamation."

It just suited my purpose that he should do all the talking at present, so I asked him to explain all that happened. He went on:—

"The moment the cartridge exploded the whole of the small clay bank remaining was knocked to bits and was carried away by the first rush. There had evidently been a considerable accumulation of water just behind the bank; and at the first rush this swept through the cutting and washed it clean. Then the bog at the top, and the water in the middle, and the ooze below all struggled for the opening. I could see that the soft part of the bog actually floated. Naturally the water got away first. The bog proper, which was floating, jammed in the opening, and the ooze began to drain out below it. Of course, this was only the first rush; it will be running for days before things begin to settle; and then we shall be able to make some openings in the bog and see if my theories are tenable, in so far as the solidification is concerned. I am only disappointed in one thing."

"What is that?"

"That it will not enlighten us much regarding the bog at Shleenanaher, for I cannot find any indication here of a shelf of rock such as I imagine to be at the basis of the shifting bog. If I had had time I would like to have made a cutting into some of the waste where the bog had originally been. I daresay that Joyce would let me try now if I asked him."

I had my own fun out of my answer:—

"Oh! I'm sure he will; but even if he won't let you now, he may be inclined to in a month or two when things have settled down a bit."

His answer startled me.

"Do you know, Art, I fear it's quite on the cards that in a month or two there may be some settling down up there that may be serious for some one."

"How do you mean?"

"Simply this—that I am not at all satisfied about Murdock's house. There is every indication of it being right in the track of the bog in case it should shift again; and I would not be surprised if that hollow where it stands was right over the deepest part of the natural reservoir, where the rock slopes into the ascending stratum. This wet weather looks bad;

and already the bog has risen somewhat. If the rain lasts I wouldn't like to live in that house after five or six weeks."

A thought struck me:—

"Did you tell this to Murdock?"

"Certainly! the moment the conviction was in my mind."

"When was that now? just for curiosity!"

"Last night, before I came away." A light began to dawn on me, as to Murdock's readiness to sell the land. I did not want to have to explain anything, so I did not mention the subject of my purchase, but simply asked Dick:—

"And what did our upright friend say?"

"He said, in his own sweet manner, that it would last as long as he wanted it, and that after that it might go to hell—and me too, he added, with a thoughtfulness that was all his own."

When I went to my room that night I thought over the matter. For good or ill I had bought the property, and there was no going back now; indeed I did not wish to go back, for I thought that it would be a fine opportunity for Dick to investigate the subject. If we could succeed in draining the bog and reclaiming it, it would be a valuable addition to the property.

That night I arranged to go over on the following day to Galway, my private purpose being to consult a solicitor; and I wrote to my bankers in London, directing that an amount something over the sum required to effect my purchase should be lodged forthwith to an account to be opened for me at the Galway Bank.

Next day I drove to Galway, and there, after a little inquiry, found a solicitor, Mr. Caicy, of whom every one spoke well. I consulted him regarding the purchase. He arranged to do all that was requisite, and to have the deed of purchase drawn. I told him that I wished the matter kept a profound secret. He agreed to meet my wishes in this respect, even to the extent that when he should come to Carnaclif to make the final completion with Murdock, he would not pretend to know me. We parted on the best of terms, after I had dined with him, and had consumed my share of a couple of bottles of as fine old port as is to be had in all the world.

Next day I returned to Carnaclif in the evening and met Dick.

Everything had gone right during the two days. Dick was in great spirits; he had seen his Norah during the day, and had exchanged salutations with her. Then he had gone to Knocknacar, and had seen a great change in the bog, which was already settling down into a more solid form. I simply told him I had been to Galway to do some banking and other business. It was some consolation to me in the midst of my own unhappiness to know that I was furthering the happiness of my friend.

On the third day from this Mr. Caicy was to be over with the deed, and the following day the sale was to be completed, I having arranged with the bank to transfer on that day the purchase money for the sale to the account of Mr. Murdock. The two first days I spent mainly on Knocknacar, going over each day ostensibly to look at the progress made in draining the bog, but in reality in the vain hope of seeing my unknown. Each time I went, my feet turned naturally to the hill-top; but on each visit I felt only a renewal of my sorrow and disappointment. I walked on each occasion to and from the hill, and on the second day—which was Sunday—went in the morning and sat on the top many hours, in the hope that some time during the day, it being a holiday, she might be able to find her way there once again!

When I got to the top, the chapel bells were ringing in all the parishes below me to the west, and very sweetly and peacefully the sounds came through the bright crisp September air. And in some degree the sound brought peace to my soul, for there is so large a power in even the aspirations and the efforts of men towards good, that it radiates to unmeasurable distance. The wave theory that rules our knowledge of the distribution of light and sound, may well be taken to typify, if it does not not control the light of divine love, and the beating in unison of human hearts.

I think that during these days I must have looked, as well as felt, miserable; for even Andy did not make any effort to either irritate or draw me. On the Sunday evening, when I was on the strand behind the hotel, he lounged along, in his own mysterious fashion, and after looking at me keenly for a few moments, came up close, and said to me in a grave, pitying halfwhisper:—

"Don't be afther breakin' yer harrt, yer 'an'r. Divil mend the fairy girrul. Sure isn't she vanished intirely? Mark me now! there's no sahtisfaction at all, at all, in them fairy girruls. Faix! but I would'nt like to see a fine young gintleman like yer 'an'r, become like Yeoha, the Sigher, as they called him in the ould times."

"And who might that gentleman be, Andy?" I asked, with what appearance of cheerful interest I could muster up.

"Begor! it's a prince he was that married onto a fairy girrul, what wint an' was tuk off be a fairy man what lived in the same mountain as she done herself. Sure thim fairy girruls has mostly a fairy man iv their own somewheres, that they love betther nor they does mortials. Jist you take me advice, Master Art, fur ye might do worser! Go an take a luk at Miss Norah, an ye'll soon forget the fairies. There's a rale girrul av ye like!"

I was too sad to make any angry reply, and before I could think of any other kind, Andy lounged away whistling softly—for he had, like many of his class, a very sweet whistle—the air of *Savourneen Deelish*.

The following day Mr. Caicy turned up at the hote according to his promise. He openly told Mrs. Keating, of whom he had often before been a customer, that he had business with Mr. Murdock. He was, as usual with him, affable to all, "passing the time of day" with the various inhabitants of all degrees, and, as if a stranger, entering into conversation with me as we sat at lunch in the coffee-room. When we were alone he whispered to me that all was ready; that he had made an examination of the title, for which Murdock had sent him all the necessary papers, and that the deed was complete and ready to be signed. He told me he was going over that day to Knockcalltecrore, and would arrange that he would be there the next day, and that he would take care to have some one to witness the signatures.

On the following morning, when Dick went off with Andy to Knocknacar, and Mr. Caicy drove over to Knockcalltecrore, where I also shortly took my way on another car.

We met at Murdock's house. The deed was duly completed, and Mr. Caicy handed over to Murdock the letter from the bank that the lodgment had been made.

The land was now mine; and I was to have possession on the 27th of October. Mr. Caicy took the deed with him; and with it took also instructions to draw out a deed making the property over to Richard Sutherland. He went straight away to Galway; whilst I, in listless despair, wandered out on the hill-side to look at the view.

X

In the Cliff Fields

I went along the mountain-side until I came to the great ridge of rocks which, as Dick had explained to me, protected the lower end of Murdock's farm from the westerly wind. I climbed to the top to get a view, and then found that the ridge was continuous, running as far as the Snake's Pass where I had first mounted it. Here, however, I was not as then above the sea, for I was opposite what they had called the Cliff Fields, and a very strange and beautiful sight it was.

Some hundred and fifty feet below me was a plateau of seven or eight acres in extent, and some two hundred and fifty feet above the sea. It was sheltered on the north by a high wall of rock like that I stood on, serrated in the same way, as the strata ran in similar layers. In the centre there rose a great rock with a flat top some quarter of an acre in extent. The whole plateau, save this one bare rock, was a mass of verdure. It was watered by a small stream which fell through a deep narrow cleft in the rocks, where the bog drained itself from Murdock's present land. The after-grass was deep, and there were many clumps of trees and shrubs— none of them of considerable height except a few great stone-pines which towered aloft and dared the fury of the western breeze. But not all the beauty of the scene could hold my eyes—for seated on the rocky table in the centre, just as I had seen her on the hill-top at Knocknacar, sat a girl to all intents the ditto of my unknown.

My heart gave a great bound, and in the tumult of hope that awoke within my breast the whole world seemed filled with sunshine. For an instant I almost lost my senses; my knees shook, and my eyes grew dim. Then came a horrible suspense and doubt. It was impossible to believe that I should see my unknown here when I least expected to see her. And then came the man's desire of action.

I do not know how I began. To this day I cannot make out whether I took a bee-line for that isolated table of rock, and from where I was, slid or crawled down the face of the rock, or whether I made a detour to the same end. All I can recollect is that I found myself scrambling over some large boulders, and then passing through the deep heavy grass at the foot of the rock.

Here I halted to collect my thoughts—a moment sufficed. I was too much in earnest to need any deliberation, and there was no choice of ways. I only waited to be sure that I would not create any alarm by unnecessary violence.

Then I ascended the rock. I did not make more noise than I could help; but I did not try to come silently. She had evidently heard steps, for she spoke without turning round:—

"Am I wanted?" Then, as I was passing across the plateau, my step seemed to arouse her attention; for at a bound she leaped to her feet, and turned with a glad look that went through the shadow on my soul, as the sunshine strikes through the mist.

"Arthur!" She almost rushed to meet me; but stopped suddenly—for an instant grew pale—and then a red flush crimsoned her face and neck. She put up her hands before her face, and I could see the tears drop through her fingers.

As for myself, I was half-dazed. When I saw that it was indeed my unknown, a wild joy leaped to my heart; and then came the revulsion from my long pent-up sorrow and anxiety; and as I faltered out—"At last! at last!"—the tears sprang unbidden to my eyes. There is, indeed, a dry-eyed grief, but its corresponding joy is as often smit with sudden tears.

In an instant I was by her side, and had her hand in mine. It was only for a moment, for she withdrew it with a low cry of maidenly fear—but in that moment of gentle, mutual pressure, a whole world had passed, and we knew that we loved.

We were silent for a time, and then we sat together on a boulder— she edging away from me shyly.

What matters it of what we talked? There was not much to say— nothing that was new—the old, old story that has been told since the days when Adam, waking, found that a new joy had entered into his life. For those whose feet have wandered in Eden, there is no need to speak; for those who are yet to tread the hallowed ground, there is no need either—for in the fulness of time their knowledge will come.

It was not till we had sat some time that we exchanged any sweet words—they were sweet, although to any one but ourselves they would have seemed the most absurd and soulless commonplaces.

We spoke, and that was all. It is of the nature of love that it can from airy nothings win its own celestial food!

Presently I said—and I pledge my word that this was the first speech that either of us had made, beyond the weather and the view, and such lighter topics:—

"Won't you tell me your name? I have so longed to know it, all these weary days."

"Norah—Norah Joyce! I thought you knew."

This was said with a shy lifting of the eyelashes, which were as suddenly and as shyly dropped again.

"Norah!" As I spoke the word—and my whole soul was in its speaking—the happy blush overspread her face again. "Norah! What a sweet name! Norah! No, I did not know it; if I had known it, when I missed you from the hill-top at Knocknacar, I should have sought you here."

Somehow her next remark seemed to chill me:—

"I thought you remembered me, from that night when father came home with you?"

There seemed some disappointment that I had so forgotten.

"That night," I said, "I did not see you at all. It was so dark, that I felt like a blind man—I only heard your voice."

"I thought you remembered my voice."

The disappointment was still manifest. Fool that I was!—that voice, once heard, should have sunk into my memory for ever.

"I thought your voice was familiar when I heard you on the hill-top; but when I saw you, I loved you from that moment—and then every other woman's voice in the world went, for me, out of existence!" She half arose, but sat down again, and the happy blush once more mantled her cheek—I felt that my peace was made. "My name is Arthur." Here a thought struck me—struck me for the first time, and sent through me a thrill of unutterable delight. The moment she had seen me she had mentioned my name—all unconsciously, it is true—but she had mentioned it. I feared, however, to alarm her by attracting her attention to it as yet, and went on:—"Arthur Severn—but I think you know it."

"Yes; I heard it mentioned up at Knocknacar."

"Who by?"

"Andy the driver. He spoke to my aunt and me when we were driving down, the day after we—after we met on the hill-top the last time."

Andy! And so my jocose friend knew all along! Well, wait! I must be even with him!

"Your aunt?"

"Yes; my aunt Kate. Father sent me up to her, for he knew it would distress me to see all our things moved from our dear old home—all my mother's things. And father would have been distressed to see me grieved, and I to see him. It was kind of him; he is always so good to me."

"He is a good man, Norah—I know that; I only hope he won't hate me."

"Why?"—This was said very faintly.

"For wanting to carry off his daughter. Don't go, Norah. For God's sake, don't go! I shall not say anything you do not wish; but if you only knew the agony I have been in since I saw you last—when I thought I had lost you—you would pity me—indeed you would! Norah, I love you! No! you must listen to me—you must! I want you to be my wife—I shall love and honour you all my life! Don't refuse me, dear; don't draw back—for I love you!—I love you!"

There, it was all out. The pent-up waters find their own course.

For a minute, at least, Norah sat still. Then she turned to me very gravely, and there were tears in her eyes:—

"Oh, why did you speak like that, sir?—why did you speak like that? Let me go!—let me go! You must not try to detain me!"—I stood back, for we had both risen—"I am conscious of your good intention—of the honour you do me—but I must have time to think. Good-bye!"

She held out her hand. I pressed it gently—I dared not do more—true love is very timid at times!—She bowed to me, and moved off.

A sudden flood of despair rushed over me—the pain of the days when I thought I had lost her could not be soon forgotten, and I feared that I might lose her again.

"Stay, Norah!—stay one moment!" She stopped and turned round. "I may see you again, may I not? Do not be cruel!—may I not see you again?"

A sweet smile lit up the perplexed sadness of her face:—

"You may meet me here tomorrow evening, if you will," and she was gone.

Tomorrow evening! Then there was hope; and with gladdened heart I watched her pass across the pasture and ascend a path over the rocks. Her movements were incarnate grace; her beauty and her sweet presence filled the earth and air. When she passed from my sight, the sunlight seemed to pale and the warm air to grow chill.

For a long while I sat on that table-rock, and my thoughts were of heavenly sweetness—all, save one which was of earth—one brooding fear that all might not be well—some danger I did not understand.

And then I too arose, and took my way across the plateau, and climbed the rock, and walked down the boreen on my way for Carnaclif.

And then, and for the first time, did a thought strike me—one which for a moment made my blood run cold—Dick!

Aye—Dick! What about him? It came to me with a shudder, that my happiness—if it should be my happiness—must be based on the pain of my friend. Here, then, there was perhaps a clue to Norah's strange gravity! Could Dick have made a proposal to her? He admitted having spoken to her—why should he, too, not have been impulsive? Why should it not be that he, being the first to declare himself, had got a favourable answer, and that now Norah was not free to choose?

How I cursed the delay in finding her—how I cursed and found fault with everyone and everything! Andy especially came in for my ill-will. He, at any rate, knew that my unknown of the hill-top at Knocknacar was none other than Norah!

And yet, stay! who but Andy persisted in turning my thoughts to Norah, and more than once suggested my paying a visit to Shleenanaher to see her? No! Andy must be acquitted at all points: common justice demanded that. Who, then, was I to blame? Not Andy—not Dick, who was too noble and too loyal a friend to give any cause for such a thought. Had he not asked me at the first if the woman of my fancy was not this very woman; and had he not confessed his own love only when I answered him that it was not? No! Dick must be acquitted from blame!

Acquitted from blame! Was that justice? At present he was in the position of a wronged man, and it was I who had wronged him—in ignorance certainly, but still the wrong was mine. And now what could I do? Should I tell Dick? I shrank from such a thing; and as yet there was little to tell. Not till tomorrow evening should I know my fate; and might not that fate be such that it would be wiser not to tell Dick of it? Norah had asked for time to consider my offer. If it should be that she had already promised Dick, and yet should have taken time to consider another offer, would it be fair to tell Dick of such hesitation, even though the result was a loyal adherance to her promise to him? Would such be fair either to him or to her? No! he must not be told—as yet, at all events.

How, then, should I avoid telling him, in case the subject should crop up in the course of conversation? I had not told him of any of my late visits to Knockcalltecrore, although, God knows! they were taken not in my own interest, but entirely in his; and now an explanation seemed impossible.

Thus revolving the situation in my mind as I walked along, I came to the conclusion that the wisest thing I could do was to walk to some other place and stay there for the night. Thus I might avoid questioning altogether. On the morrow I could return to Carnaclif, and go over to Shleenanaher at such a time that I might cross Dick on the way, so that I might see Norah and get her answer without anyone knowing of my visit. Having so made up my mind, I turned my steps towards Roundwood, and when I arrived there in the evening sent a wire to Dick:—

"Walked here, very tired; sleep here tonight; probably return tomorrow."

The long walk did me good, for it made me thoroughly tired, and that night, despite my anxiety of mind, I slept well—I went to sleep with Norah's name on my lips.

The next day I arrived at Carnaclif about mid-day. I found that Dick had taken Andy to Knockcalltecrore. I waited until it was time to leave, and then started off. About half a mile from the foot of the boreen I went and sat in a clump of trees, where I could not be seen, but from which I could watch the road; and presently saw Dick passing along on Andy's car. When they had quite gone out of sight, I went on my way to the Cliff Fields.

I went with mingled feelings. There was hope, there was joy at the remembrance of yesterday, there was expectation that I would see her again—even though the result might be unhappiness, there was doubt, and there was a horrible, haunting dread. My knees shook, and I felt weak as I climbed the rocks. I passed across the field and sat on the table-rock.

Presently she came to join me. With a queenly bearing she passed over the ground, seeming to glide rather than to walk. She was very pale, but as she drew near I could see in her eyes a sweet calm.

I went forward to meet her, and in silence we shook hands. She motioned to the boulder, and we sat down. She was less shy than yesterday, and seemed in many subtle ways to be, though not less girlish, more of a woman.

When we sat down I laid my hand on hers and said—and I felt that my voice was hoarse:—

"Well!"

She looked at me tenderly, and said in a sweet, grave voice:—

"My father has a claim on me that I must not overlook. He is all alone; he has lost my mother, and my brother is away, and is going into a different sphere of life from us. He has lost his land that he prized and valued, and that has been ours for a long, long time; and now that he is sad and lonely, and feels that he is growing old, how could I leave him? He that has always been so good and kind to me all my life!" Here the sweet eyes filled with tears. I had not taken away my hand, and she had not removed hers; this negative of action gave me hope and courage.

"Norah! answer me one thing. Is there any other man between your heart and me?"

"Oh no! no!" Her speech was impulsive; she stopped as suddenly as she began. A great weight seemed lifted from my heart; and yet there came a qualm of pity for my friend. Poor Dick! poor Dick!

Again we were silent for a minute. I was gathering courage for another question.

"Norah!"—I stopped; she looked at me.

"Norah! if your father had other objects in life, which would leave you free, what would be your answer to me?"

"Oh, do not ask me! Do not ask me!" Her tone was imploring; but there are times when manhood must assert itself, even though the heart be torn with pity for woman's weakness. I went on:—

"I must, Norah! I must! I am in torture till you tell me. Be pitiful to me! Be merciful to me! Tell me, do you love me? You know I love you, Norah. Oh God! how I love you! The world has but one being in it for me; and you are that one! With every fibre of my being—with all my heart and soul, I love you! Won't you tell me, then, if you love me?"

A flush as rosy as dawn came over her face, and timidly she asked me, "Must I answer? Must I?"

"You must, Norah!"

"Then, I do love you! God help us both! but I love you! I love you!" and tearing away her hand from mine, she put both hands before her face and burst into a passionate flood of tears.

There could be but one ending to such a scene. In an instant she was in my arms. Her will and mine went down before the sudden flood of passion that burst upon us both. She hid her face upon my breast, but I raised it tenderly, and our lips met in one long, loving, passionate kiss.

We sat on the boulder, hand in hand, and whispering confessed to each other, in the triumph of our love, all those little secrets of the growth of our affection that lovers hold dear. That final separation, which had been spoken of but a while ago, was kept out of sight by mutual consent; the dead would claim its dead soon enough. Love lives in the present and in the sunshine finds its joy.

Well, the men of old knew the human heart, when they fixed upon the butterfly as the symbol of the soul; for the rainbow is but sunshine through a cloud, and love, like the butterfly, takes the colours of the rainbow on its aery wings!

Long we sat in that beauteous spot. High above us towered the everlasting rocks; the green of nature's planting lay beneath our feet; and far off the reflection of the sunset lightened the dimness of the soft twilight over the wrinkled sea.

We said little, as we sat hand in hand; but the silence was a poem, and the sound of the sea, and the beating of our hearts were hymns of praise to nature and to nature's God.

We spoke no more of the future; for now that we knew that we were each beloved, the future had but little terror for us. We were content!

When we had taken our last kiss, and parted beneath the shadow of the rock, I watched her depart through the gloaming to her own home; and then I too took my way. At the foot of the Boreen I met Murdock, who looked at me in a strange manner, and merely growled some reply to my salutation.

I felt that I could never meet Dick tonight. Indeed, I wished to see no human being, and so I sat for long on the crags above the sounding sea; and then wandered down to the distant beach. To and fro I went all the night long, but ever in sight of the hill, and ever and anon coming near to watch the cottage where Norah slept.

In the early morning, I took my way to Roundwood, and going to bed, slept until late in the day.

When I woke, I began to think of how I could break my news to Dick. I felt that the sooner it was done the better. At first I had a vague idea of writing to him from where I was, and explaining all to him; but this, I concluded, would not do—it seemed too cowardly a way to deal with so true and loyal a friend—I would go now and await his arrival at Carnaclif, and tell him all, at the earliest moment when I could find an opportunity.

I drove to Carnaclif, and waited his coming impatiently, for I intended, if it were not too late, to afterwards drive over to Shleenanaher, and see Norah—or at least the house she was in.

Dick arrived a little earlier than usual, and I could see from the window that he was grave and troubled. When he got down from the car, he asked if I were in, and being answered in the affirmative, ordered dinner to be put on the table as soon as possible, and went up to his room.

I did not come down until the waiter came to tell me that dinner was ready. Dick had evidently waited also, and followed me down. When he came into the room, he said heartily:—

"Hallo! Art, old fellow, welcome back, I thought you were lost," and shook hands with me warmly.

Neither of us seemed to have much appetite, but we pretended to eat, and sent away platesfull of food, cut up into the smallest proportions. When the apology for dinner was over, Dick offered me a cigar, lit his own, and said:—

"Come out for a stroll on the sand, Art; I want to have a chat with you." I could feel that he was making a great effort to appear hearty, but there was a hollowness about his voice, which was not usual. As we went through the hall, Mrs. Keating handed me my letters, which had just arrived.

We walked out on the wide stretch of fine hard sand, which lies westwards from Carnaclif when the tide is out, and were a considerable distance from the town before a word was spoken. Dick turned to me, and said:—

"Art! what does it all mean?"

I hesitated for a moment, for I hardly knew where to begin—the question, so comprehensive and so sudden, took me aback. Dick went on:—

"Art! two things I have always believed; and I won't give them up without a struggle. One is that there are very few things that, no matter how strange or wrong they look, won't bear explanation of some kind; and the other is that an honourable man does not grow crooked in a moment. Is there anything, Art, that you would like to tell me?"

"There is, Dick! I have a lot to tell; but won't you tell me what you wish me to speak about?" I was just going to tell him all, but it suddenly occurred to me that it would be wise to know something of what was amiss with him first.

"Then I shall ask you a few questions! Did you not tell me that the girl you were in love with was not Norah Joyce?"

"I did; but I was wrong. I did not know it at the time—I only found it out, Dick, since I saw you last!"

"Since you saw me last! Did you not then know that I loved Norah Joyce, and that I was only waiting a chance to ask her to marry me?"

"I did!" I had nothing to add here; it came back to me that I had spoken and acted all along without a thought of my friend.

"Have you not of late payed many visits to Shleenanaher; and have you not kept such visits quite dark from me?"

"I have, Dick."

"Did you keep me ignorant on purpose?"

"I did! But those visits were made entirely on your account."—I stopped, for a look of wonder and disgust spread over my companion's face.

"On my account! on my account! And was it, Arthur Severn, on my account that you asked, as I presume you did, Norah Joyce to marry you—I take it for granted that your conduct was honourable, to her at any rate—the woman whom I had told you I loved, and that I wished to marry, and that you assured me that you did not love, your heart being fixed on another woman? I hate to speak so, Art! but I have had black thoughts, and am not quite myself—was this all on my account?" It was a terrible question to answer, and I paused; Dick went on:—

"Was it on my account that you, a rich man, purchased the home that she loved; whilst I, a poor one, had to stand by and see her father despoiled day by day, and, because of my poverty, had to go on with a hateful engagement, which placed me in a false position in her eyes?"

Here I saw daylight. I could answer this scathing question:—

"It was, Dick—entirely on your account!" He drew away from me, and stood still, facing me in the twilight as he spoke:—

"I should like you to explain, Mr. Severn—for your own sake—a statement like that."

Then I told him, with simple earnestness, all the truth. How I had hoped to further his love, since my own seemed so hopeless—how I had bought the land intending to make it over to him, so that his hands might be strong to woo the woman he loved—how this and nothing else had taken me to Shleenanaher; and that whilst there I had learned that my own unknown love and Norah were one and the same—of my proposal to her; and here I told him humbly how in the tumult of my own passion I had forgotten his—whereat he shrugged his shoulders—and of my long anxiety till her answer was given. I told him that I had stayed away the first night at Roundwood, lest I should be betrayed into any speech which would lack in loyalty to him as well as to her. And then I told him of her decision not to leave her father—touching but lightly on the confession of her love, lest I should give him needless pain; I did not dare to avoid it lest I should mislead him to his further harm. When I had finished he said softly:—

"Art, I have been in much doubt!"

I thought a moment, and then remembered that I had in my pocket the letters which had been handed to me at the hotel, and that amongst them there was one from Mr. Caicy at Galway. This letter I took out and handed to Dick.

"There is a letter unopened. Open it and it may tell you something. I know my word will suffice you; but this is in justice to us both."

Dick took the letter and broke the seal. He read the letter from Caicy, and then holding up the deed so that the dying light of the west should fall on it, read it. The deed was not very long. When he finished it he stood for a moment with his hands down by his sides; then he came over to me, and laying his hands, one of which grasped the deed, on my shoulders, said:—

"Thank God, Art, there need be no bitterness between me and thee—all is as you say, but oh! old fellow!"—and here he laid his head on my shoulder and sobbed—"my heart is broken! All the light has gone out of my life!"

His despair was only for a moment. Recovering himself as quickly as he had been overcome, he said:—

"Never mind, old fellow, only one of us must suffer; and, thank God! my secret is with you alone—no one else in the wide world even suspects. She must never know! Now tell me all about it; don't fear that it will hurt me. It will be something to know that you are both happy. By the way, this had better be torn up; there is no need for it now!" Having torn the paper across, he put his arm over my shoulder as he used to do when we were boys; and so we passed into the gathering darkness.

Thank God for loyal and royal manhood! Thank God for the heart of a friend that can suffer and remain true! And thanks, above all, that the lessons of tolerance and forgiveness, taught of old by the Son of God, are now and then remembered by the sons of men.

XI

Un Mauvais Quart d'Heure

When we were strolling back to the hotel Dick said to me:—

"Cheer up, old fellow! You need'nt be the least bit downhearted. Go soon and see Joyce. He will not stand in the girl's way, you may be sure. He is a good fellow, and loves Norah dearly—who could help it!" He stopped for a moment here, and choked a great sob, but went on bravely:—

"It is only like her to be willing to sacrifice her own happiness; but she must not be let do that. Settle the matter soon! Go tomorrow to see Joyce. I shall go up to Knocknacar instead of working with Murdock; it will leave the coast clear for you." Then we went into the hotel; and I felt as if a great weight had been removed.

When I was undressing I heard a knock. "Come in," I called, and Dick entered. Dear old fellow! I could see that he had been wrestling with himself, and had won. His eyes were red, but there was a noble manliness about him which was beyond description.

"Art," said he, "I wanted to tell you something, and I thought it ought to be told now. I would'nt like the night to close on any wrong impression between you and me. I hope you feel that my suspicion about fair play and the rest of it is all gone."

"I do! old fellow! quite."

"Well, you are not to get thinking of me as in any way wronged in the matter, either by accident or design. I have been going over the whole matter to try and get the heart of the mystery; and I think it only fair to say that no wrong could be done to me. I never spoke a single word to Norah in my life. Nor did she to me. Indeed, I have seen her but seldom, though the first time was enough to finish me. Thank God! we have found out the true state of affairs before it was too late. It might have been worse, old lad! it might have been worse! I don't think there's any record—even in the novels—of a man's life being wrecked over a girl he did'nt know. We don't get hit to death at sight, old boy! It's only skin deep this time, and though skin deep hurts the most, it doesn't kill! I thought I would tell you what I had worked out, for I knew we were such old friends that it would worry you and mar your happiness to think I was wretched. I hope—and I honestly expect—that by tomorrow I shall be all right, and able to enjoy the sight of both your happiness—as, please God! I hope such is to be."

We wrung each other's hands; and I believe that from that moment we were closer friends than ever. As he was going out Dick turned to me, and said:—

"It is odd about the legend, isn't it! The Snake is in the Hill still, if I am not mistaken. He told me all about your visits and the sale of the land to you, in order to make mischief. But his time is coming; St. Patrick will lift that crozier of his before long!"

"But the Hill holds us all!" said I; and as I spoke there was an ominous feeling over me. "We're not through yet; but it will be all right now."

The last thing I saw was a smile on his face as he closed the door.

The next morning Dick started for Knocknacar. It had been arranged the night before that he should go on Andy's car, as I preferred walking to Shleenanaher. I had more than one reason for so doing, but that which I kept in the foreground of my own mind—and which I almost persuaded myself was the chief—if not the only reason—was that I did not wish to be troubled with Andy's curiosity and impertinent badinage. My real and secret reason, however, was that I wished to be alone so that I might collect my thoughts, and acquire courage for what the French call *un mauvais quart d'heure*.

In all classes of life, and under all conditions, this is an ordeal eminently to be dreaded by young men. No amount of reason is of the least avail to them—there is some horrible, lurking, unknown possibility which may defeat all their hopes, and may, in addition, add the flaming aggravation of making them appear ridiculous! I summed up my own merits, and, not being a fool, found considerable ground for hope. I was young, not bad looking—Norah loved me; I had no great bogey of a past secret or misdeed to make me feel sufficiently guilty to fear a just punishment falling upon me; and, considering all things, I was in a social position and of wealth beyond the dreams of a peasant—howsoever ambitious for his daughter he might be.

And yet I walked along those miles of road that day with my heart perpetually sinking into my boots, and harassed with a vague dread which made me feel at times an almost irresistible inclination to run away. I can only compare my feelings, when I drew in sight of the hilltop, with those which animate the mind of a young child when coming in sight of the sea in order to be dipped for the first time.

There is, however, in man some wholesome fear of running away, which at times either takes the place of resolution, or else initiates the mechanical action of guiding his feet in the right direction—of prompting his speech and regulating his movement. Otherwise no young man, or very few at least, would ever face the ordeal of asking the consent of the parents of his *inamorata*. Such a fear stood to me now; and with a seeming boldness I approached Joyce's house. When I came to the gate I saw him in the field not far off, and went up to speak to him.

Even at that moment, when the dread of my soul was greatest, I could not but recall an interview which I had had with Andy that morning, and which was not of my seeking, but of his.

After breakfast I had been in my room, making myself as smart as I could, for of course I hoped to see Norah—when I heard a knock at the door, timid but hurried. When I called to "come in," Andy's head appeared; and then his whole body was by some mysterious wriggle conveyed through the partial opening of the door. When within, he closed it, and, putting a finger to his lip, said in a mysterious whisper:—

"Masther Art!"

"Well Andy! what is it?"

"Whisper me now! Shure I don't want to see yer 'an'r so onasy in yer mind."

I guessed what was coming, so interrupted him, for I was determined to get even with him.

"Now, Andy! if you have any nonsense about your 'Miss Norah,' I don't want to hear it."

"Whisht! surr; let me shpake. I mustn't kape Misther Dick waitin'. Now take me advice! an' take a luk out to Shleenanaher. Ye may see some wan there what ye don't ixpect!"—this was said with a sly mysteriousness, impossible to describe.

"No! no! Andy," said I, looking as sad as I could, "I can see no one there that I don't expect."

"They do say, surr, that the fairies does take quare shapes; and your fairy girrul may have gone to Shleenanaher. Fairies may want to take the wather like mortials."

"Take the water, Andy! what do ye mean?"

"What do I mane! why what the quality does call say-bathin'. An' maybe, the fairy girrul has gone too!"

"Ah! no, Andy," said I, in as melancholy a way as I could, "my fairy girl is gone. I shall never see her again!"

Andy looked at me very keenly; and then a twinkle came in his eye and he said, slapping his thigh:—

"Begor! but I believe yer 'an'r is cured! Ye used to be that melancholy that bedad it's meself what was gettin' sarious about ye; an' now it's only narvous ye are! Well! if the fairy is gone, why not see Miss Norah? Sure wan sight iv her 'd cure all the fairy spells what iver was cast. Go now, yer 'an'r, an' see her this day!"

I said with decision, "No, Andy, I will not go today to see Miss Norah. I have something else to do!"

"Oh, very well!" said he with simulated despondency. "If yer 'an'r won't, of course ye won't! but ye're wrong. At any rate, if ye're in the direction iv Shleenanaher, will ye go an' see th' ould man? Musha! but I'm thinkin' it's glad he'd be to see yer 'an'r."

Despite all I could do, I felt blushing up to the roots of my hair. Andy looked at me quizzically; and said oracularly, and with sudden seriousness:—

"Begor! if yer fairy girrul is turned into a fairy complately, an' has flew away from ye, maybe ould Joyce too 'd become a leprachaun! Hould him tight whin ye catch him! Remimber, wid leprachauns, if ye wance let thim go ye may niver git thim agin. But if ye hould thim tight, they must do whatsumiver ye wish! So they do say—but maybe I'm wrong— I'm itherfarin' wid a gintleman as was bit be a fairy, and knows more nor mortials does about thim! There's the masther callin'. Good bye, surr, an' good luck!" and with a grin at me over his shoulder, Andy hurried away. I muttered to myself:—

"If anyone is a fairy, my bold Andy, I think I can name him. You seem to know everything!"

This scene came back to me with renewed freshness. I could not but feel that Andy was giving me some advice. He evidently knew more than he pretended; indeed, he must have known all along of the identity of my unknown of Knocknacar with Norah. He now also evidently knew of my knowledge on the subject; and he either knew or guessed that I was off to see Joyce on the subject of his daughter.

In my present state of embarrassment, his advice was a distinct light. He knew the people, and Joyce especially; he also saw some danger to my hopes, and showed me a way to gain my object. I knew already that Joyce was a proud man, and I could quite conceive that he was an obstinate one; and I knew from general experience of life that there is no obstacle so difficult to surmount as the pride of an obstinate man. With all the fervour of my heart I prayed that, on this occasion, his pride might not in any way be touched, or arrayed against me.

When I saw him I went straight towards him, and held out my hand. He seemed a little surprised, but took it. Like Bob Acres, I felt my courage oozing out of the tips of my fingers, but with the remnant of it threw myself into the battle:—

"Mr. Joyce, I have come to speak to you on a very serious subject."

"A sarious subject! Is it concarnin' me?"

"It is."

"Go on! More throuble, I suppose?"

"I hope not, most sincerely. Mr. Joyce, I want to have your permission to marry your daughter!" If I had suddenly turned into a bird and flown away, I do not think I could have astonished him more. For a second or two he was speechless, and then said, in an unconscious sort of way:—

"Want to marry me daughter!"

"Yes, Mr. Joyce! I love her very dearly! She is a pearl amongst women; and if you will give your permission, I shall be the happiest man on earth. I can quite satisfy you as to my means. I am well to do; indeed, as men go, I am a rich man."

"Aye! sir, I don't doubt. I'm contint that you are what you say. But you never saw me daughter—except that dark night when you took me home."

"Oh yes, I have seen her several times, and spoken with her; but, indeed, I only wanted to see her once to love her!"

"Ye have seen her—and she never tould me! Come wid me!" He beckoned me to come with him, and strode at a rapid pace to his cottage, opened the door, and motioned me to go in. I entered the room—which was both kitchen and living room—to which he pointed. He followed.

As I entered, Norah, who was sewing, saw me and stood up. A rosy blush ran over her face; then she grew as white as snow as she saw the stern face of her father close behind me. I stepped forward, and took her hand; when I let it go, her arm fell by her side.

"Daughter!"—Joyce spoke very sternly, but not unkindly. "Do you know this gentleman?"

"Yes, father!"

"He tells me that you and he have met several times. Is it thrue?"

"Yes, father; but—"

"Ye never tould me! How was that?"

"It was by accident we met."

"Always be accident?" Here I spoke:—

"Always by accident—on her part." He interrupted me:—

"Yer pardon, young gentleman! I wish me daughter to answer me! Shpeak, Norah!"

"Always, father!—except once, and then I came to give a message—yes! it was a message, although from myself."

"What missage?"

"Oh father! don't make me speak! We are not alone! Let me tell you, alone! I am only a girl—and it is hard to speak."

His voice had a tear in it, for all its sternness, as he answered:—

"It is on a subject that this gentleman has spoke to me about—as mayhap he has spoke to you."

"Oh father!"—she took his hand, which he did not withdraw, and, bending over, kissed it and hugged it to her breast. "Oh father! what have I done that you should seem to mistrust me? You have always trusted me; trust me now, and don't make me speak till we are alone!"

I could not be silent any longer. My blood began to boil, that she I loved should be so distressed—whatsoever the cause, and at the hands of whomsoever, even her father.

"Mr. Joyce, you must let me speak! You would speak yourself to save pain to a woman you loved." He turned to tell me to be silent, but suddenly stopped; I went on:—"Norah," he winced as I spoke her name, "is entirely blameless. I met her quite by chance at the top of Knocknacar when I went to see the view. I did not know who she was—I had not the faintest suspicion; but from that moment I loved her. I went next day, and waited all day in the chance of seeing her; I did see her, but again came away in ignorance even of her name. I sought her again, day after day, day after day, but could get no word of her; for I did not know who she was, or where she came from. Then, by chance, and after many weary days, again I saw her in the Cliff Fields below, three days ago. I could no longer be silent, but told her that I loved her, and asked her to be my wife. She asked a while to think, and left me, promising to give me an answer on the next evening. I came again; and I got my answer." Here Norah, who was sobbing, with her face turned away, looked round, and said:—

"Hush! hush! You must not let father know. All the harm will be done!" Her father answered in a low voice:—

"All that could be done is done already, daughter. Ye never tould me!"

"Sir! Norah is worthy of all esteem. Her answer to me was that she could not leave her father, who was all alone in the world!" Norah turned away again, but her father's arm went round her shoulder. "She told me I must think no more of her; but, sir, you and I, who are men, must not let a woman, who is dear to us both make such a sacrifice." Joyce's face was somewhat bitter as he answered me:—

"Ye think pretty well of yerself, young sir, whin ye consider it a sacrifice for me daughter to shtay wid the father, who loves her, and who she loves. There was never a shadda on her life till ye came!" This was hard to hear, but harder to answer, and I stammered as I replied:—

"I hope I am man enough to do what is best for her, even if it were to break my heart. But she must marry some time; it is the lot of the young and beautiful!" Joyce paused a while, and his look grew very tender as he made answer softly:—

"Aye! thrue! thrue! the young birds lave the nist in due sayson—that's only natural." This seemed sufficient concession for the present; but Andy's warning rose before me, and I spoke:—

"Mr. Joyce, God knows! I don't want to add one drop of bitterness to either of your lives! only tell me that I may have hope, and I am content to wait and to try to win your esteem and Norah's love."

The father drew his daughter closer to him, and with his other hand stroked her hair, and said, whilst his eyes filled with tears:—

"Ye didn't wait for me esteem to win her love!" Norah threw herself into his arms and hid her face on his breast. He went on:—

"We can't undo what is done. If Norah loves ye—and it seems to me that she does—do I shpeak thrue, daughter?" The girl raised her face bravely, and looked in her father's eyes:—

"Yes! father." A thrill of wild delight rushed through me. As she dropped her head again, I could see that her neck had

"The colour of the budding rose's crest."

"Well! well!" Joyce went on, "Ye are both young yit. God knows what may happen in a year! Lave the girl free a bit to choose. She has not met many gentlemen in her time; and she may desave herself. Me darlin'! whativer is for your good shall be done, plase God!"

"And am I to have her in time?" The instant I had spoken I felt that I had made a mistake; the man's face grew hard as he turned to me:—

"I think for me daughter, sir, not for you! As it is, her happiness seems to be mixed up with yours—lucky for ye. I suppose ye must meet now and thin; but ye must both promise me that ye'll not meet widout me lave, or, at laste, me knowin' it. We 're not gentlefolk, sir, and we don't undherstand their ways. If ye were of Norah's and me own kind, I mightn't have to say the same; but ye're not."

Things were now so definite that I determined to make one more effort to fix a time when my happiness might be certain, so I asked:—

"Then if all be well, and you agree—as please God you shall when you know me better—when may I claim her?"

When he was face to face with a definite answer Joyce again grew stern. He looked down at his daughter and then up at me, and said, stroking her hair:—

"Whin the threasure of Knockcalltecrore is found, thin ye may claim her if ye will, an' I 'll freely let her go!" As he spoke, there came before my mind the strong idea that we were all in the power of the Hill—that it held us; however, as lightly as I could I spoke:—

"Then I would claim her now!"

"What do ye mane?"—this was said half anxiously, half fiercely.

"The treasure of Knockcalltecrore is here; you hold her in your arms!" He bent over her:—

"Aye! the threasure sure enough—the threasure ye would rob me of!" Then he turned to me, and said sternly, but not unkindly:—

"Go, now! I can't bear more at prisent; and even me daughter may wish to be for a while alone wid me!" I bowed my head and turned to leave the room; but as I was going out, he called me back:—

"Shtay! Afther all, the young is only young. Ye seem to have done but little harm—if any." He held out his hand; I grasped it closely, and from that instant it seemed that our hearts warmed to each other. Then I felt bolder, and stepping to Norah took her hand—she made no resistance—and pressed it to my lips, and went out silently. I had hardly left the door when Joyce came after me.

"Come agin in an hour," he said, and went in and shut the door.

Then I wandered to the rocks and climbed down the rugged path into the Cliff Fields. I strode through the tall grass and the weeds, rank with the continuous rain, and gained the table rock. I climbed it, and sat where I first had met my love, after I had lost her; and, bending, I kissed the ground where her feet had rested. And then I prayed as fervent a prayer as the heart of a lover can yield, for every blessing on the future of my beloved; and made high resolves that whatsoever might befall, I would so devote myself that, if a man's efforts could accomplish it, her feet should never fall on thorny places.

I sat there in a tumult of happiness. The air was full of hope, and love, and light; and I felt that in all the wild glory and fulness of nature the one unworthy object was myself.

When the hour was nearly up I went back to the cottage; the door was open, but I knocked on it with my hand. A tender voice called to me to come in, and I entered.

Norah was standing up in the centre of the room. Her face was radiant, although her sweet eyes were bright with recent tears; and I could see that in the hour which I had passed on the rock, the hearts of the father and the child had freely spoken. The old love between them had taken a newer and fuller and more conscious life—based, as God has willed it with the hearts of men, on the parent's sacrifice of self for the happiness of the child.

Without a word I took her in my arms. She came without bashfulness and without fear; only love and trust spoke in every look, and every moment. The cup of our happiness was full to the brim; and it seemed as though God saw, and, as of old with His completed plan of the world, was satisfied that all was good.

We sat, hand in hand, and told again and again the simple truths that lovers tell; and we built bright mansions of future hope. There was no shadow on us, except the shadow that slowly wrapped the earth in the wake of the sinking sun. The long, level rays of sunset spread through the diamond panes of the lattice, grew across the floor, and rose on the opposite wall; but we did not heed them until we heard Joyce's voice behind us:—

"I have been thinkin' all the day, and I have come to believe that it is a happy day for us all, sir. I say, though she is my daughter, that the man that won her heart should be a proud man, for it is a heart of gold. I must give her to ye. I was sorry at the first, but I do it freely now. Ye must guard and kape, and hould her as the apple of your eye. If ye should ever fail or falter, remimber that ye took a great thrust in takin' her from me that loved her much, and in whose heart she had a place— not merely for her own sake, but for the sake of the dead that loved her." He faltered a moment, but then coming over, put his hand in mine, and while he held it there, Norah put her arm around his neck, and laying her sweet head on his broad, manly breast, said softly:—

"Father, you are very good, and I am very, very happy!" Then she took my hand and her father's together, and said to me:—

"Remember, he is to be as your father, too; and that you owe him all the love and honour that I do!"

"Amen," I said, solemnly; and we three wrung each others' hands.

Before I went away, I said to Joyce:—

"You told me I might claim her when the treasure of the Hill was found. Well! give me a month, and perhaps, if I don't have the one you mean, I may have another." I wanted to keep, for the present, the secret of my purchase of the old farm, so as to make a happy surprise when I should have actual possession.

"What do ye mane?" he said.

"I shall tell you when the month is up," I answered; "or if the treasure is found sooner—but you must trust me till then."

Joyce's face looked happy as he strolled out, evidently leaving me a chance of saying good-bye alone to Norah; she saw it too, and followed him.

"Don't go father!" she said. At the door she turned her sweet face to me, and with a shy look at her father, kissed me, and blushed rosy red.

"That's right, me girl," said Joyce, "honest love is without shame! Ye need never fear to kiss your lover before me."

Again we stayed talking for a little while. I wanted to say good-bye again; but this last time I had to give the kiss myself. As I looked back from the gate, I saw father and daughter standing close together; he had his arm round her shoulder, and the dear head that I loved lay close on his breast, as they both waved me farewell.

I went back to Carnaclif, feeling as though I walked on air; and my thoughts were in the heaven that lay behind my footsteps as I went—though before me on the path of life.

XII

Bog-Fishing and Schooling

When I got near home, I met Dick, who had strolled out to meet me. He was looking much happier than when I had left him in the morning. I really believe that now that the shock of his own disappointment had passed, he was all the happier that my affair had progressed satisfactorily. I told him all that had passed, and he agreed with the advice given by Joyce, that for a little while, nothing should be said about the matter. We walked together to the hotel, I hurrying the pace somewhat, for it had begun to dawn upon me that I had eaten but little in the last twenty-four hours. It was prosaic, but true; I was exceedingly hungry. Joy seldom interferes with the appetite; it is sorrow or anxiety which puts it in deadly peril.

When we got to the hotel, we found Andy waiting outside the door. He immediately addressed me:—

"'Och musha! but it's the sad man I am this day! Here's Masther Art giv over intirely to the fairies. An' its leprachaun catchin', he has been onto this blissed day. Luk at him! isn't it full iv sorra he is. Give up the fairies, Masther Art!—Do thry an make him, Misther Dick!—an' take to fallin' head over ears in love wid some nice young girrul. Sure, Miss Norah herself, bad as she is, 'd be betther nor none at all, though she doesn't come up to Masther Art's rulin'!"

This latter remark was made to Dick, who immediately asked him:—

"What is that, Andy?"

"Begor! yer 'an'r, Masther Art has a quare kind iv a girrul in his eye intirely, wan he used to be lukin' for on the top iv Knocknacar—the fairy girrul yer 'an'r," he added to me in an explanatory manner.

"I suppose, yer 'an'r," turning to me, "ye haven't saw her this day?"

"I saw nobody to answer your description, Andy; and I fear I wouldn't know a fairy girl if I saw one," said I, as I passed into the house followed by Dick, whilst Andy, laughing loudly, went round to the back of the house, where the bar was.

That was, for me at any rate, a very happy evening. Dick and I sat up late and smoked, and went over the ground that we had passed, and the ground that we were, please God, to pass in time. I felt grateful to the dear old fellow, and spoke much of his undertakings both at Knocknacar and at Knokcalltecrore. He told me that he was watching carefully the experiment at the former place as a guide to the latter. After some explanations, he said:—

"There is one thing there which rather disturbs me. Even with the unusual amount of rain which we have had lately, the flow or drain of water from the bog is not constant; it does not follow the rains as I expected. There seems to be some process of silting, or choking, or damming up the walls of what I imagine to be the different sections or reservoirs of the bog. I cannot make it out, and it disturbs me; for if the same process goes on at Knockcalltecrore, there might be any kind of unforeseen disaster in case of the shifting of the bog. I am not at all easy about the way Murdock is going on there. Ever since we found the indication of iron in the bog itself, he has taken every occasion when I am not there to dig away at one of the clay banks that jut into it. I have warned him that he is doing a very dangerous thing, but he will not listen. Tomorrow, when I go up, I shall speak to him seriously. He went into Galway with a cart the night before last, and was to return by tomorrow morning. Perhaps he has some game on. I must see what it is."

Before we parted for the night we had arranged to go together in the morning to Knockcalltecrore, for of course I had made up my mind that each day should see me there.

In the morning, early, we drove over. We left Andy, as usual, in the boreen at the foot of the hill, and walked up together. I left Dick at Murdock's gate, and then hurried as fast as my legs could carry me to Joyce's.

Norah must have had wonderful ears. She heard my footsteps in the lane, and when I arrived at the gate she was there to meet me. She said, "Good morning," shyly, as we shook hands. For an instant she evidently feared that I was going to kiss her, there in the open where someone might see; but almost as quickly she realized that she was safe so far, and we went up to the cottage together. Then came my reward; for, when the door was closed, she put her arms round my neck as I took her in my arms, and our lips met in a sweet, long kiss. Our happiness was complete. Anyone who has met the girl he loved the day after his engagement to her, can explain why or how—if any explanation be required.

Joyce was away in the fields. We sat hand in hand, and talked for a good while; but I took no note of time.

Suddenly Norah looked up. "Hush!" she said. "There is a step in the boreen; it is your friend, Mr. Sutherland." We sat just a little further apart and let go hands. Then the gate clicked, and even I heard Dick's steps as he quickly approached. He knocked at the door; we both called out "Come in" simultaneously, and then looked at each other and blushed. The door opened and Dick entered. He was very pale, but in a couple of seconds his pallor passed away. He greeted Norah cordially, and she sweetly bade him welcome; then he turned to me:—

"I am very sorry to disturb you, old fellow, but would you mind coming down to Murdock's for a bit? There is some work which I wish you to give me a hand with."

I started up and took my hat, whispered good-bye to Norah, and went with him. She did not come to the door; but from the gate I looked back and saw her sweet face peeping through the diamond pane of the lattice.

"What is it, Dick?" I asked, as we went down the lane.

"A new start today. Murdock evidently thinks we have got on the track of something. He went into Galway for a big grapnel; and now we are making an effort to lift it—whatever 'it' is—out of the bog."

"By Jove!" said I, "things are getting close."

"Yes," said Dick. "And I am inclined to think he is right. There is most probably a considerable mass of iron in the bog. We have located the spot, and are only waiting for you, so as to be strong enough to make a cast."

When we got to the edge of the bog we found Murdock standing beside a temporary jetty, arranged out of a long plank, with one end pinned to the ground and the centre supported on a large stone, placed on the very edge of the solid ground, where a rock cropped up. Beside him was a very large grappling-iron, some four feet wide, attached to a coil of strong rope. When we came up, he saluted me in a half surly manner, and we set to work, Dick saying, as we began:—

"Mr. Severn, Mr. Murdock has asked us to help in raising something from the bog. He prefers to trust us, whom he knows to be gentlemen, than to let his secret be shared in with anyone else."

Dick got out on the end of the plank, holding the grapnel and a coil of the rope in his hand, whilst the end of the coil was held by Murdock.

I could see from the appearance of the bog that someone had been lately working at it, for it was all broken about as though to make a hole in it, and a long pole that lay beside where I stood was covered with wet and slime.

Dick poised the grapnel carefully, and then threw it out. It sank into the bog, slowly at first, but then more quickly; an amount of rope ran out which astonished me, for I knew that the bog must be at least so deep.

Suddenly the run of the rope ceased, and we knew that the grapnel had gone as far as it could. Murdock and I then held the rope, and Dick took the pole and poked and beat a passage for it through the bog up to the rock where we stood. Then he, too, joined us, and we all began to pull.

For a few feet we pulled in the slack of the rope. Then there was a little more resistance for some three or four feet, and we knew that the grapnel was dragging on the bottom. Suddenly there was a check, and Murdock gave a suppressed shout:—

"We have got it! I feel it! Pull away for your lives!"

We kept a steady pull on the rope. At first there was simply a dead weight, and in my own mind I was convinced that we had caught a piece of projecting rock. Murdock would have got unlimited assistance and torn out of the bog whatever it was that we had got hold of, even if he had to tear up the rocks by the roots; but Dick kept his head, and directed a long steady pull.

There was a sudden yielding, and then again resistance. We continued to pull, and then the rope began to come, but very slowly, and there was a heavy weight attached to it. Even Dick was excited now. Murdock shut his teeth, and scowled like a demon; it would have gone hard with anyone who came then between him and his prize. As for myself, I was in a tumult. In addition to the natural excitement of the time, there rose to my memory Joyce's words:—"When the treasure is found you may claim her if you will;"—and, although the need for such an occasion passed away with his more free consent, the effect that they had at the time produced on me remained in my mind.

Here, then, was the treasure at last; its hiding for a century in the bog had come to an end.

We pulled and pulled. Heavens! how we tugged at that rope. Foot after foot it came up through our hands, wet and slimy, and almost impossible to hold. Now and again it slipped from each of us in turns a few inches, and a muttered "steady! steady!" was all the sound heard. It took all three of us to hold the weight, and so no one could be spared to make an effort to further aid us by any mechanical appliance. The rope lay beside us in seemingly an endless coil. I began to wonder if it would ever end. Our breath began to come quickly, our hands were cramped. There came a new and more obstinate resistance. I could not account for it. Dick cried out:—

"It is under the roots of the bog; we must now take it up straight. Can you two hold on for a moment? and I shall get on the plank." We nodded, breath was too precious for unnecessary speech.

Dick slacked out after we had got our feet planted for a steady resistance. He then took a handful of earth, and went out on the plank a little beyond the centre and caught the rope. When he held it firmly with his clay-covered hands, he said:—

"Come now, Art. Murdock, you stay and pull." I ran to him, and, taking my hands full of earth, caught the rope also.

The next few minutes saw a terrible struggle. Our faces were almost black with the rush of blood in stooping and lifting so long and so hard, our hands and backs ached to torture, and we were almost in despair, when we saw the bog move just under us. This gave us new courage and new strength, and with redoubled effort we pulled at the rope.

Then up through the bog came a large mass. We could not see what it was, for the slime and the bog covered it solidly; but with a final effort we lifted it. Each instant it grew less weighty as the resistance of the bog was overcome, and the foul slimy surface fell back into its place and became tranquil. When we lifted and pulled the mass on the rock bank, Murdock rushed forward in a frenzied manner, and shouted to us:—

"Kape back! Hands off! It's mine, I say, all mine! Don't dar even to touch it, or I'll do ye a harrum! Here, clear off! this is my land! Go!" and he turned on us with the energy of a madman and the look of a murderer.

I was so overcome with my physical exertions that I had not a word to say, but simply in utter weariness threw myself upon the ground; but Dick, with what voice he could command, said:—

"You're a nice grateful fellow to men who have helped you! Keep your find to yourself, man alive; we don't want to share. You must know that as well as I do, unless your luck has driven you mad. Handle the thing yourself, by all means. Faugh! how filthy it is!" and he too sat down beside me.

It certainly was most filthy. It was a shapeless irregular mass, but made solid with rust and ooze and the bog surface through which it had been dragged. The slime ran from it in a stream; but its filth had no deterring power for Murdock, who threw himself down beside it and actually kissed the nauseous mass as he murmured:—

"At last! at last! me threasure! All me own!"

Dick stood up with a look of disgust on his handsome face:—

"Come away, Art; it's too terrible to see a man degraded to this pitch. Leave the wretch alone with his god!" Murdock turned to us, and said with savage glee:—

"No! shtay! Sthay an' see me threasure! It'll make ye happy to think of afther! An' ye can tell Phelim Joyce what I found in me own land—the land what I tuk from him." We stayed.

Murdock took his spade and began to remove the filth and rubbish from the mass. And in a very few moments his discovery proclaimed itself.

There lay before us a rusty iron gun-carriage! This was what we had dragged with so much effort from the bottom of the bog; and beside it Murdock sat down with a scowl of black disappointment.

"Come away!" said Dick. "Poor devil, I pity him! It is hard to find even a god of that kind worthless!" And so we turned and left Murdock sitting beside the gun-carriage and the slime, with a look of baffled greed which I hope never to see on any face again.

We went to a brook at the foot of the hill, Andy being by this time in the sheebeen about half a mile off. There we cleansed ourselves as well as we could from the hideous slime and filth of the bog, and then walked to the top of the hill to let the breeze freshen us up a bit if possible. After we had been there for a while, Dick said:—

"Now, Art, you had better run back to the cottage. Miss Joyce will be wondering what has become of you all this time, and may be frightened." It was so strange to hear her—Norah, my Norah—called "Miss Joyce," that I could not help smiling—and blushing whilst I smiled. Dick noticed and guessed the cause. He laid his hand on my shoulder, and said:—

"You will hear it often, old lad. I am the only one of all your friends privileged to hear of her by the name you knew her by at first. She goes now into your class and amongst your own circle; and, by George! she will grace it too—it or any circle—and they will naturally give to her folk the same measure of courtesy that they mete to each other. She is Miss Joyce—until she shall be Mrs. Arthur Severn!"

What a delicious thrill the very thought sent through me!

I went up to the cottage, and on entering found Norah still alone. She knew that I was under promise not to tell anything of Murdock's proceedings, but noticing that I was not so tidy as before—for my cleansing at the brook-side was a very imperfect one—went quietly and got a basin with hot water, soap, and a towel, and clothes brush, and said I must come and be made very tidy.

That toilet was to me a sweet experience, and is a sweet remembrance now. It was so wifely in its purpose and its method, that I went through it in a languorous manner—like one in a delicious dream. When, with a blush, she brought me her own brush and comb and began to smooth my hair, I was as happy as it is given to a man to be. There is a peculiar sensitiveness in their hair to some men, and to have it touched by hands that they love is a delicious sensation. When my toilet was complete Norah took me by the hand and made me sit down beside her. After a pause, she said to me with a gathering blush:—

"I want to ask you something."

"And I want to ask you something," said I. "Norah, dear! there is one thing I want much to ask you."

She seemed to suspect or guess what I was driving at, for she said:—

"You must let me ask mine first."

"No, no!" I replied. "You must answer me; and then, you know, you will have the right to ask what you like."

"But I do not want any right."

"Then it will be all the more pleasure to me to give a favour—if there can be any such from me to you."

Masculine persistence triumphed—men are always more selfish than women—and I asked my question:—

"Norah, darling—tell me when will you be mine—my very own? When shall we be married?"

The love-light was sweet in her eyes as she answered me with a blush that made perfect the smile on her lips:—

"Nay! You should have let me ask my question first."

"Why so, dearest?"

"Because, dear, I am thinking of the future. You know, Arthur, that I love you, and that whatever you wish, I would and shall gladly do; but you must think for me too. I am only a peasant girl—"

"Peasant!" I laughed. "Norah, you are the best lady I have ever seen! Why, you are like a queen—what a queen ought to be!"

"I am proud and happy, Arthur, that you think so; but still I am only a peasant! Look at me—at my dress. Yes! I know you like it, and I shall always prize it because it found favour in your eyes!" She smiled happily, but went on:—

"Dear, I am speaking very truly. My life and surroundings are not yours. You are lifting me to a higher grade in life, Arthur, and I want to be worthy of it and of you. I do not want any of your family or your friends to pity you and say, 'Poor fellow, he has made a sad mistake. Look at her manners—she is not of us.' I could not bear to hear or to know that such was said—that anyone should have to pity the man I love, and to have that pity because of me. Arthur, it would break my heart!"

As she spoke the tears welled up in the deep dark eyes and rolled unchecked down her cheeks. I caught her to my breast with the sudden instinct of protection, and cried out:—

"Norah! no one on earth could say such a thing of you—you who would lift a man, not lower him. You could not be ungraceful if you tried; and as for my family and friends, if there is one who will not hold out both hands to you and love you, he or she is no kin or friend of mine."

"But, Arthur, they might be right! I have learned enough to know that there is so much more to learn—that the great world you live in is so different from our quiet, narrow life here. Indeed, I do not mean to be nervous as to the future, or to make any difficulties; but, dear, I should like to be able to do all that is right and necessary as your wife. Remember, that when I leave here I shall not have one of my own kin or friends to tell me anything—from whom I could ask advice. They do not themselves even know what I might want—not one of them all! Your world and mine, dear, are so different—as yet."

"But, Norah, shall I not be always by your side to ask?"—I felt very superior and very strong as well as very loving as I spoke.

"Yes, yes; but oh! Arthur—can you not understand—I love you so that I would like to be, even in the eyes of others, all that you could wish. But, dear, you must understand and help me here. I cannot reason with you. Even now I feel my lack of knowledge, and it makes me fearful. Even now"—her voice died away in a sob, and she hid her beautiful eyes with her hand.

"My darling! my darling!" I said to her passionately—all the true lover in me awake—"Tell me what it is that you wish, so that I may try to judge with all my heart."

"Arthur! I want you to let me go to school—to a good school for a while—a year or two before we are married. Oh! I should work so hard! I should try so earnestly to improve—for I should feel that every hour of honest work brought me higher and nearer to your level!"

My heart was more touched than even my passion gave me words to tell—and I tried, and tried hard, to tell her what I felt—and in my secret heart a remorseful thought went up: "What have I done in my life to be worthy of so much love!"

Then, as we sat hand in hand, we discussed how it was to be done—for that it was to be done we were both agreed. I had told her that we should so arrange it that she should go for awhile to Paris, and then to Dresden, and finish up with an English school. That she could learn languages, and that amongst them would be Italian; but that she would not go to Italy until we went together—on our honeymoon. She bent her head and listened in silent happiness; and when I spoke of our journey together to Italy, and how we would revel in old-world beauty—in the softness and light and colour of that magic land—the delicate porcelain of her shell-like ear became tinged with pink, and I bent over and kissed it. And then she turned and threw herself on my breast, and hid her face.

As I looked I saw the pink spread downward and grow deeper and deeper, till her neck and all became flushed with crimson. And then she put me aside, rose up, and with big brave eyes looked me full in the face through all her deep embarrassment, and said to me:—

"Arthur, of course I don't know much of the great world, but I suppose it is not usual for a man to pay for the schooling of a lady before she is his wife—whatever might be arranged between them afterwards. You know that my dear father has no money for such a purpose as we have spoken of, and so if you think it is wiser, and would be less hardly spoken of in your family, I would marry you before I went—if—if you wished it. But we would wait till after I came from school to—to—to go to Italy," and whilst the flush deepened almost to a painful degree, she put her hands before her face and turned away.

Such a noble sacrifice of her own feelings and her own wishes—and although I felt it in my heart of hearts I am sure none but a woman could fully understand it—put me upon my mettle, and it was with truth I spoke:—

"Norah, if anything could have added to my love and esteem for you, your attitude to me in this matter has done it. My darling, I shall try hard all my life to be worthy of you, and that you may never, through any act of mine, decline for a moment from the standard you have fixed. God knows I could have no greater pride or joy than that this very moment I should call you my wife. My dear! my dear! I shall count the very hours until that happy time shall come. But all shall be as you wish. You will go to the schools we spoke of, and your father shall pay for them. He will not refuse, I know, and what is needed he shall have. If there be any way that he would prefer—that suits your wishes—it shall be done. More than this! if he thinks it right, we can be married before you go, and you can keep your own name until my time comes to claim you."

"No! no! Arthur. When once I shall bear your name I shall be too proud of it to be willing to have any other. But I want, when I do bear it, to bear it worthily—I want to come to you as I think your wife should come."

"My dear, dear Norah—my wife to be—all shall be as you wish."

Here we heard the footsteps of Joyce approaching.

"I had better tell him," she said.

When he came in she had his dinner ready. He greeted me warmly.

"Won't ye stay?" he said. "Don't go unless ye wish to!"

"I think, sir, Norah wants to have a chat with you when you have had your dinner."

Norah smiled a kiss at me as I went out. At the door I turned and said to to her:—

"I shall be in the Cliff Field in case I am wanted."

I went there straightway, and sat on the table rock in the centre of the fields, and thought and thought. In all my thought there was no cloud. Each day—each hour seemed to reveal new beauties in the girl I loved, and I felt as if all the world were full of sunshine, and all the future of hope; and I built new resolves to be worthy of the good fortune which had come upon me.

It was not long before Norah came to me, and said that she had told her father, and that he wished to speak with me. She said that he quite agreed about the school, and that there would be no difficulty made by him on account of any false pride about my helping in the task. We had but one sweet minute together on the rock, and one kiss; and then, hand in hand, we hurried back to the cottage, and found Joyce waiting for us, smoking his pipe.

Norah took me inside, and, after kissing her father, came shyly and kissed me also, and went out. Joyce began:—

"Me daughter has been tellin' me about the plan of her goin' to school, an' her an' me's agreed that it's the right thing to do. Of coorse, we're not of your class, an' if ye wish for her it is only right an' fair that she should be brought up to the level of the people that she's goin' into. It's not in me own power to do all this for her, an' although I did'nt give her the schoolin' that the quality has, I've done already more nor min like me mostly does. Norah knows more nor any girl about here—an' as ye're to have the benefit of yer wife's schoolin', I don't see no rayson why ye should'nt help in it. Mind ye this—if I could see me way to do it meself, I'd work me arms off before I'd let you or any one else come between her an' me in such a thing. But it'd be only a poor kind of pride that'd hurt the poor child's feelins, an' mar her future—an' so it'll be as ye both wish. Ye must find out the schools an' write me about them when ye go back to London." I jumped up and shook his hand.

"Mr. Joyce, I am more delighted than I can tell you; and I promise, on my honour, that you shall never in your life regret what you have done."

"I'm sure of that—Mr.—Mr.—"

"Call me Arthur!"

"Well! I must do it some day—Arthur—an' as to the matther that Norah told me ye shpoke of—that, if I'd wish it, ye'd be married first. Well! me own mind an' Norah's is the same—I'd rather that she come to you as a lady at wance—though God knows! it's a lady she is in all ways I iver see one in me life—barrin' the clothes!"

"That's true, Mr. Joyce! there is no better lady in all the land."

"Well, that's all settled. Ye'll let me know in good time about the schools, won't ye? an' now I must get back to me work," and he passed out of the house, and went up the hillside.

Then Norah came back, and with joy I told her that all had been settled; and somehow, we seemed to have taken another step up the ascent that leads from earth to heaven—and that all feet may tread, which are winged with hope.

Presently Norah sent me away for a while, saying that she had some work to do, as she expected both Dick and myself to come back to tea with them; and I went off to look for Dick.

I found him with Murdock. The latter had got over his disappointment, and had evidently made up his mind to trust to Dick's superior knowledge and intelligence. He was feverishly anxious to continue his search, and when I came up we held a long discussion as to the next measure to be taken. The afternoon faded away in this manner before Murdock summed up the matter thus:—

"The chist was carried on the gun-carriage, and where wan is th' other is not far off. The min couldn't have carried the chist far, from what ould Moynahan sez. His father saw the min carryin' the chist only a wee bit." Dick said:—

"There is one thing, Murdock, that I must warn you about. You have been digging in the clay bank by the edge of the bog. I told you before how dangerous this is; now, more than ever, I see the danger of it. It was only today that we got an idea of the depth of the bog, and it rather frightens me to think that with all this rain falling you should be tampering with what is more important to you than even the foundations of your house. The bog has risen far too much already, and you have only to dig perhaps one spadeful too much in the right place and you'll have a torrent that will sweep away all you have. I have told you that I don't like the locality of your house down in the hollow. If the bog ever moves again, God help you! You seem also to have been tampering with the stream that runs into the Cliff Fields. It is all very well for you to try to injure poor Joyce more than you have done—and that's quite enough, God knows!—but here you are actually imperilling your own safety. That stream is the safety valve of the bog, and if you continue to dam up that cleft in the rock you will have a terrible disaster. Mind now! I warn you seriously against what you are doing. And besides, you do not even know for certain that the treasure is here. Why, it may be anywhere on the mountain, from the brook below the boreen to the Cliff Fields; is the off chance worth the risk you run?" Murdock started when he mentioned the Cliff Fields, and then said suddenly:—

"If ye're afraid ye can go. I'm not."

"Man alive!" said Dick, "why not be afraid if you see cause for fear? I don't suppose I'm a coward any more than you are, but I can see a danger, and a very distinct one, from what you are doing. Your house is directly in the track in which the bog has shifted at any time this hundred years; and if there should be another movement, I would not like to be in the house when the time comes."

"All right!" he returned doggedly, "I'll take me chance; and I'll find the threasure, too, before many days is over!"

"Well; but be reasonable also, or you may find your death!"

"Well, if I do that's me own luk out. Ye may find yer death first!"

"Of course I may, but I see it my duty to warn you. The weather these last few weeks back has been unusually wet. The bog is rising as it is. As a matter of fact, it is nearly a foot higher now than it was when I came here first; and yet you are doing what must help to rise it higher still, and are weakening its walls at the same time." He scowled at me as he sullenly answered:—

"Well, all I say is I'll do as I like wid me own. I wouldn't give up me chance iv findin' the threasure now—no, not for God himself!"

"Hush! man; hush!" said Dick sternly, as we turned away. "Do not tempt Him, but be warned in time!"

"Let Him look out for Himself, an' I'll look out for meself," he answered with a sneer. "I'll find the threasure—an' if need be in spite iv God an' iv the Divil too!"

XIII

Murdock's Wooing

I think it was a real pleasure to Dick to get Norah's message that he was expected to tea that evening. Like the rest of his sex, he was not quite free from vanity; for when I told him, his first act was to look down at himself ruefully, and his first words were:—

"But I say, old lad! look at the mess I'm in; and these clothes are not much, anyhow."

"Never mind, Dick, you are as good as I am."

"Oh, well!" he laughed, "if you'll do, I suppose I needn't mind. We're both pretty untidy. No, begad," he added, looking me all over, "you're not out of the perpendicular with regard to cleanliness, anyhow. I say, Art! who's been tidying you up? Oh! I see! Forgive me, old lad; and quite natural, too! Miss Joyce should see you blush, Art! Why, you are as rosy as a girl!"

"Call her 'Norah,' Dick! it is more natural, and I am sure she will like it better. She is to look on you as a brother, you know!"

"All right, Art," he answered heartily, "but you must manage it for me, for I think I should be alarmed to do so unless I got a lead; but it will come easy enough after the first go off. Remember, we both always thought of her as 'Norah!'"

We went down towards the brook and met with Andy, who had the car all ready for us.

"Begor yer 'an'rs," said he, "I thought yez was lost intirely, or that the fairies had carried yez off; both iv yez this time."—This with a sly look at me, followed by a portentous wink to Dick. "An' I'm thinkin' it's about time fur somethin' to ate. Begor! but me stummick is cryin' out that me throat is cut!"

"You're quite right, Andy, as to the fact," said Dick, "but you are a little antecedent."

"An' now what's that, surr? Begor! I niver was called that name afore. Shure, an' I always thry to be dacent—divvle a man but can tell ye that! Antidacent indeed! Well now! what nixt?"

"It means, Andy, that we are going to be carried off by the fairies, and to have some supper with them too; and that you are to take this half-crown, and go over to Mother Kelligan's, and get her to try to dissipate that unnatural suspicion of capital offence wreaked on your thoracic region. Here, catch! and see how soon you can be off!"

"Hurroo! Begor, yer 'an'r, it's the larned gintleman y' are! Musha! but ye ought to be a councillor intirely! Gee-up! ye ould corncrake!" and Andy was off at full speed.

When we had got rid of him, Dick and I went down to the brook, and made ourselves look as tidy as we could. At least Dick did; for, as to myself, I purposely disarranged my hair—unknown to Dick—in the hope that Norah would take me in hand again, and that I might once more experience the delicious sensation of a toilet aided by her sweet fingers.

Young men's ideas, however, are very crude; no one who knew either the Sex or the World would have fallen into such an absurd hope. When I came in with Dick, Norah—in spite of some marked hints, privately and secretly given to her—did not make either the slightest remark on my appearance, or the faintest suggestion as to improving it.

She had not been idle in the afternoon. The room, which was always tidy, was as prettily arranged as the materials would allow. There were some flowers, and flag-leaves, and grasses tastefully placed about; and on the table, in a tumbler, was a bunch of scarlet poppies. The tablecloth, although of coarse material, was as white as snow, and the plates and cups, of common white and blue, were all that was required.

When Joyce came in from his bedroom, where he had been tidying himself, he looked so manly and handsome in his dark frieze coat with horn buttons, his wide unstarched shirt-collar, striped waistcoat, and cord breeches, with grey stockings, that I felt quite proud of him. There was a natural grace and dignity about him which suited him so well, that I had no wish to see him other than a peasant. He became the station, and there was no pretence. He made a rough kind of apology to us both:—

"I fear ye'll find things a bit rough, compared with what you're accustomed to, but I know ye'll not mind. We have hardly got settled down here yit; and me sisther, who always lives with us, is away with me other sisther that is sick, so Norah has to fare by herself; but gentlemen both—you, Mr. Sutherland; and you, Arthur—you're welcome!"

We sat down to table, and Norah insisted on doing all the attendance herself. I wanted to help her, and, when she was taking up a plate of cakes from the hearth, stooped beside her and said:—

"May not I help, Norah? Do let me!"

"No—no, dear," she whispered. "Don't ask me now—I'm a little strange yet—another time. You'll be very good, won't you, and help me not to feel awkward?"

Needless to say I sat at table for the rest of the meal, and feasted my eyes on my darling, whilst in common with the others I enjoyed the good things placed before us. But when she saw that I looked too long and too lovingly, she gave me such an imploring glance from her eloquent eyes, that for the remainder of the time I restrained both the ardour of my glance and its quantity within modest bounds.

Oh! but she was fair and sweet to look upon! Her dark hair was plainly combed back, and coiled modestly round her lovely head. She had on her red petticoat and chintz body, that she knew I admired so much; and on her breast she wore a great scarlet poppy, whose splendid colour suited well her dark and noble beauty. At the earliest opportunity, when tea was over, I whispered to her:—

"My darling, how well the poppy suits you. How beautiful you are. You are like the Goddess of Sleep!" She put her finger to her lips with a happy smile, as though to forbid me to pay compliments—before others. I suppose the woman has never yet been born—and never shall be—who would not like to hear her praises from the man she loves.

I had eaten potato-cakes before, but never such as Norah had made for us; possibly they seemed so good to me because I knew that her hands had made them. The honey, too, was the nicest I had tasted—for it was made by Norah's bees. The butter was perfect—for it was the work of her hands!

I do not think that a happier party ever assembled round a tea-table. Joyce was now quite reconciled to the loss of his daughter, and was beaming all over; and Dick's loyal nature had its own reward, for he too was happy in the happiness of those he loved—or else I was, and am, the most obtuse fool, and he the most consummate actor, that has been. As for Norah and myself, I know we were happy—as happy as it is given to mortals to be.

When tea was over, and Norah fetched her father's pipe and lighted it for him, she said to me with a sweet blush, as she called me by my name for the first time before a stranger:—

"I suppose, Arthur, you and Mr. Sutherland would like your own cigars best; but if you care for a pipe there are some new ones here," and she pointed them out. We lit our cigars, and sat round the fire; for in this damp weather the nights were getting a little chilly. Joyce sat on one side of the fire and Dick on the other. I sat next to Dick, and Norah took her place between her father and me, sitting on a little stool beside her father and leaning, her head against his knees, whilst she took the hand that was fondly laid over her shoulder and held it in her own. Presently, as the grey autumn twilight died away, and as the light from the turf fire rose and fell, throwing protecting shadows, her other hand stole towards my own—which was waiting to receive it; and we sat silent for a spell, Norah and I in an ecstasy of quiet happiness.

By-and-by we heard a click at the latch of the gate, and firm, heavy footsteps coming up the path. Norah jumped up, and peeped out of the window.

"Who is it, daughter?" said Joyce.

"Oh father! it is Murdock! What can he want?"

There was a knock at the door. Joyce rose up, motioning to us to sit still, laid aside his pipe, and went to the door and opened it. Every word that was spoken was perfectly plain to us all.

"Good evenin', Phelim Joyce!"

"Good evenin'! You want me?"

"I do." Murdock's voice was fixed and firm, as of one who has made up his mind.

"What is it?"

"May I come in? I want to shpake to ye particular."

"No, Murtagh Murdock! Whin a man comes undher me roof by me own consint, I'm not free wid him to spake me mind the same as whin he's outside. Ye haven't thrated me well, Murdock. Ye've been hard wid me; and there's much that I can't forgive!"

"Well! if I did, ye gev me what no other man has ever gave me yit widout repintin' it sore. Ye sthruck me a blow before all the people, an' I didn't strike ye back."

"I did, Murtagh; an' I'm sorry for it. That blow has been hangin' on me conscience iver since. I would take it back if I could; God knows that is thrue. Much as ye wronged me, I don't want such a thing as that to remimber when me eyes is closin'. Murtagh Murdock, I take it back, an' gladly. Will ye let me?"

"I will—on wan condition."

"What is it?"

"That's what I've kem here to shpake about; but I'd like to go in."

"No! ye can't do that—not yit, at any rate, till I know what ye want. Ye must remimber, Murtagh, that I've but small rayson to thrust ye!"

"Well, Phelim, I'll tell ye; tho' it's mortial hard to name it shtandin' widout the door like a thramp! I'm a warrum man; I've a power iv money put by, an' it brings me in much."

"I know! I know!" said the other bitterly. "God help me! but I know too well how it was gother up."

"Well! niver mind that now; we all know that. Anyhow, it *is* gother up. An' them as finds most fault wid the manes, mayhap 'd be the first to get hould iv it av they could. Well, anyhow, I'm warrum enough to ask any girrul in these parts to share it wid me. There's many min and weemin between this and Galway, that'd like to talk over the fortin iv their daughter wid Murtagh Murdock—for all he's a gombeen man."

As he spoke, the clasp of Norah's hand and mine grew closer. I could feel in her clasp both a clinging, as for protection, and a restraining power on myself. Murdock went on:—

"But there's none of thim girls what I've set me harrt on—except wan!" He paused. Joyce said quietly:—

"An' who, now, might that be?"

"Yer own daughther, Norah Joyce!" Norah's hand restrained me as I was instinctively rising.

"Go on!" said Joyce, and I could notice that there was a suppressed passion in his voice:—

"Well, I've set me harrt on her; and I'm willin' to settle a fortin on her, on wan condition."

"And what, now, might that be?"—the tone was of veiled sarcasm.

"She'll have all the money that I settle on her to dale wid as she likes—that is, the intherest iv it—as long as she lives; an' I'm to have the Cliff Fields that is her's, as me own to do what I like wid, an' that them an' all in them belongs to me." Joyce paused a moment before answering:—

"Is that all ye have to say?" Murdock seemed nonplussed, but after a slight pause he answered:—

"Yis!"

"An' ye want me answer?"

"Iv coorse!"

"Thin, Murtagh Murdock, I'd like to ask ye for why me daughter would marry you or the like of you? Is it because that yer beauty'd take a young girl's fancy—you that's known as the likest thing to a divil in these parts! Or is it because of yer kind nature? You that tried to ruin her own father, and that drove both her and him out of the home she was born in, and where her poor mother died! Is it because yer charácther is respicted in the counthry wheriver yer name is known?———" Here Murdock interrupted him:—

"I tould ye it's a warrum man I am"—he spoke decisively, as if his words were final—"an' I can, an' will, settle a fortin on her." Joyce answered slowly and with infinite scorn:—

"Thank ye, Mr. Murtagh Murdock, but me daughter is not for sale!"

There was a long pause. Then Murdock spoke again, and both suppressed hate and anger were in his voice:—

"Ye had betther have a care wid me. I've crushed ye wance, an' I'll crush ye agin! Ye can shpake scornful yerself, but mayhap the girrul would give a different answer."

"Then, ye had betther hear her answer from herself. Norah! Come here, daughter! Come here!"

Norah rose, making an imperative sign to me to keep my seat, and with the bearing of an empress passed across to the door and stood beside her father. She took no notice whatever of her wooer.

"What is it, father?"

"Now, Murdock, spake away! Say what ye have to say; an' take yer answer from her own lips." Murdock spoke with manifest embarrassment:—

"I've been tellin' yer father that I'd like ye for me wife!"

"I've heard all you said!"

"An' yer answer?"

"My father has answered for me!"

"But I want me answer from yer own lips. My! but it's the handsome girrul ye are this night!"

"My answer is 'No!'" and she turned to come back.

"Shtay!" Murdock's voice was nasty, so nasty that instinctively I stood up. No person should speak like that to the woman I loved. Norah stopped. "I suppose ye won't luk at me because ye have a young shpark on yer hands. I'm no fool! an' I know why ye've been down in the Fields. I seen yez both more nor wance; an' I'm makin' me offer knowin' what I know. I don't want to be too hard on ye, an' I'll say nothin' if ye dont dhrive me to. But remimber ye're in me power; an' ye've got to plase me in wan way or another. I knew what I was doin' whin I watched ye wid yer young shpark! Ye didn't want yer father to see him nigh the house!

Ye'd betther be careful, the both of ye. If ye don't intind to marry me, well, ye won't; but mind how ye thrate me or shpake to me, here or where there's others by; or be th' Almighty! I'll send the ugly whisper round the counthry about ye——"

Flesh and blood could not stand this. In an instant I was out in the porch, and ready to fly at his throat; but Norah put her arm between us.

"Mr. Severn!" she said in a voice which there was no gainsaying, "my father is here. It is for him to protect me here, if any protection is required from a thing like that!" The scorn of her voice made even Murdock wince, and seemed to cool both Joyce and myself, and also Dick, who now stood beside us.

Murdock looked from one to another of us for a moment in amazement, and then with a savage scowl, as though he were looking who and where to strike with venom, he fixed on Norah—God forgive him!

"An' so ye have him at home already, have ye! An' yer father prisent too, an' a witness. It's the sharp girrul ye are, Norah Joyce, but I suppose this wan is not the first!" I restrained myself simply because Norah's hand was laid on my mouth; Murdock went on:—

"An' so ye thought I wanted ye for yerself! Oh no! It's no bankrup's daughther for me; but I may as well tell ye why I wanted ye. It was because I've had in me hands, wan time or another, ivery inch iv this mountain, bit be bit, all except the Cliff Fields; and thim I wanted for purposes iv me own—thim as knows why, has swore not to tell"—this with a scowl at Dick and me—"But I'll have thim yit; an' have thim too widout thinkin' that me wife likes sthrollin' there wid sthrange min!"

Here I could restrain myself no longer; and to my joy on the instant—and since then whenever I have thought of it—Norah withdrew her hand as if to set me free. I stepped forward, and with one blow fair in the lips knocked the foul-mouthed ruffian head over heels. He rose in an instant, his face covered with blood, and rushed at me. This time I stepped out, and with an old football trick, taking him on the breast-bone with my open hand, again tumbled him over. He arose livid—but this time his passion was cold—and standing some yards off, said, whilst he wiped the blood from his face:—

"Wait! Ye'll be sorry yit ye shtruck that blow! Aye! ye'll both be sorry—sad an' sorry—an' for shame that ye don't reckon on! Wait!"—I spoke out:—

"Wait! yes, I shall wait, but only till the time comes to punish you. And let me warn you to be careful how you speak of this lady! I have shown you already how I can deal with you personally; next time—if there be a next time——" Here Murdock interrupted *sotto voce*—

"There'll be a next time; don't fear! Be God but there will!" I went on:—

"I shall not dirty my hands with you but I shall have you in gaol for slander."

"Gaol me, is it?" he sneered. "We'll see. An' so ye think ye're going to marry a lady, whin ye make an honest woman iv Norah Joyce, do ye? Luk at her! an' it's a lady ye're goin' to make iv her, is it? An' thim hands iv hers, wid the marks iv the milkin' an' the shpade on to them. My! but they'll luk well among the quality! won't they?" I was going to strike him again, but Norah laid her hand on my arm; so smothering my anger as well as I could, I said:—

"Don't dare to speak ill of people whose shoes you are not worthy to black; and be quick about your finishing your work at Shleenanaher, for you've got to go when the time is up. I won't have the place polluted by your presence a day longer than I can help."

Norah looked wonderingly at me and at him, for he had given a manifest start. I went on:—

"And as for these hands"—I took Norah's hands in mine—"perhaps the time may come when you will pray for the help of their honest strength—pray with all the energy of your dastard soul! But whether this may be or not, take you care how you cross her path or mine again, or you shall rue it to the last hour of your life. Come, Norah, it is not fit that you should contaminate your eyes or your ears with the presence of this wretch!" and I led her in. As we went I heard Joyce say:—

"An' listen to me! Niver you dare to put one foot across me mearin' again; or I'll take the law into me own hands!"

Then Dick spoke:—

"An' hark ye, Mr. Murdock! remember that you have to deal with me also in any evil that you attempt!" Murdock turned on him savagely:—

"As for you, I dismiss ye from me imploymint. Ye'll niver set foot on me land agin! Away wid ye!"

"Hurrah!" shouted Dick. "Mr. Joyce, you're my witness that he has discharged me, and I am free." Then he stepped down from the porch, and said to Murdock, in as exasperating a way as he could:—

"And, dear Mr. Murdock, wouldn't it be a pleasure to you to have it out with me here, now? Just a simple round or two—to see which is the best man? I am sure it would do you good—and me too! I can see you are simply spoiling for a fight. I promise you that there will be no legal consequences if you beat me, and if I beat you I shall take my chance. Do let me persuade you! Just one round;" and he began to take off his coat. Joyce, however, stopped him, speaking gravely:—

"No! Mr. Sutherland, not here! and let me warn ye, for ye're a younger man nor me, agin such anger. I sthruck that man wance, an' it's sorry I am for that same! No! not that I'm afeered of him"—answering the query in Dick's face—"but because, for a full-grown man to sthrike in anger is a sarious thing. Arthur there sthruck not for himself, but for an affront to his wife that's promised, an' he's not to be blamed." Norah here took my arm and held it tight; "but I say, wid that one blow that I've sthruck since I was a lad on me mind, 'Never sthrike a blow in anger all yer life long, unless it be to purtect one ye love!'" Dick turned to him, and said heartily:—

"You're quite right, Mr. Joyce, and I'm afraid I acted like a cad. Here! you clear off! Your very presence seems to infect better men than yourself, and brings them something nearer to your level. Mr. Joyce, forgive me! I promise I'll take your good lesson to heart."

They both came into the room; and Norah and I looking out of the window—my arm being around her—saw Murdock pass down the path and out at the gate.

We all took our places once again around the fire. When we sat down Norah instinctively put her hands behind her, as if to hide them—that ruffian's words had stung her a little; and as I looked, without, however, pretending to take any notice, I ground my teeth. But with Norah such an ignoble thought could be but a passing one; with a quick blush she laid her hand open on my knee, so that, as the fire-light fell on it, it was shown in all its sterling beauty. I thought the opportunity was a fair one, and I lifted it to my lips and said:—

"Norah! I think I may say a word before your father and my friend. This hand—this beautiful hand," and I kissed it again, "is dearer to me a thousand times, because it can do, and has done, honest work; and I only hope that in all my life I may be worthy of it." I was about to kiss it yet again, but Norah drew it gently away. Then she shifted her stool a little, and came closer to me. Her father saw the movement, and said simply:—

"Go to him, daughter. He is worth it!—he sthruck a good blow for ye this night." And so we changed places, and she leaned her head against my knee; her other hand—the one not held in mine—rested on her father's knee.

There we sat and smoked and talked for an hour or more. Then Dick looked at me and I at him, and we rose. Norah looked at me lovingly as we got our hats. Her father saw the look, and said:—

"Come, daughter! if you're not tired, suppose we see them down the boreen."

A bright smile and a blush came in her face; she threw a shawl over her head, and we went all together. She held her father's arm and mine; but by-and-by the lane narrowed, and her father went in front with Dick, and we two followed.

Was it to be wondered at, if we did lag a little behind them?—and if we spoke in whispers?—or, if now and again, when the lane curved and kindly bushes projecting threw dark shadows, our lips met?

When we came to the open space before the gate, we found Andy. He pretended to see only Dick and Joyce, and saluted them:—

"Begor! but it's the fine night, it is, Misther Dick, though more betoken the rain is comin' on agin soon. A fine night, Misther Joyce! and how's Miss Norah?—God bless her! Musha! but it's sorry I am that she didn't walk down wid ye this fine night! An' poor Masther Art—I suppose the fairies has got him agin?" Here he pretended to just catch sight of me. "Yer 'an'r, but it's the sorraful man I was—shure, an' I thought ye was tuk aff be the fairies—or, mayhap, it was houldin' a leprachaun that ye wor. An' my! but there's Miss Norah, too, comin' to take care iv her father! God bless ye, Miss Norah, Acushla!—but it's glad I am to see ye!"

"And I'm always glad to see you, Andy," she said, and shook hands with him.

Andy took her aside, and said, in a staccato whisper intended for us all:—

"Musha! Miss Norah, dear, may I ax ye somethin'?"

"Indeed you may, Andy. What is it?"

"Well, now, it's throubled in me mind I am about Masther Art—that young gintleman beyant ye, talkin' t' yer father!" the hypocritical villain pointed me out, as though she did not know me. I could see in the moonlight the happy smile on her face as she turned towards me.

"Yes, I see him!" she answered.

"Well, Miss Norah, the fairies got him on the top iv Knocknacar, and ivir since he's been wandherin' round lukin' fur wan iv thim. I thried to timpt him away be tellin' him iv nice girruls iv these parts—real girruls, not fairies. But he's that obstinate he wouldn't luk at wan iv thim—no, nor listen to me, ayther."

"Indeed!" she said, her eyes dancing with fun.

"An', Miss Norah, dear, what kind iv a girrul d'ye think he wanted to find?"

"I don't know, Andy—what kind?"

"Oh, begor! but it's meself can tell ye! Shure, it's a long, yalla, dark girrul, shtreaky—like—like he knows what—not quite a faymale nagur, wid a rid petticoat, an' a quare kind iv an eye!"

"Oh, Andy!" was all she said, as she turned to me smiling.

"Get along, you villain!" said I, and I shook my fist at him in fun; and then I took Norah aside, and told her what the "quare kind iv an eye" was that I had sought—and found.

Then we two said "Good-night" in peace, whilst the others in front went through the gate. We took—afterwards—a formal and perfectly decorous farewell, only shaking hands all round, before Dick and I mounted the car. Andy started off at a gallop, and his "Git up, ye ould corncrake!" was lost in our shouts of "Goodbye!" as we waved our hats. Looking back, we saw Norah's hands waving as she stood with her father's arm around her, and her head laid back against his shoulder, whilst the yellow moonlight bathed them from head to foot in a sea of celestial light.

And then we sped on through the moonlight and the darkness alike, for the clouds of the coming rain rolled thick and fast across the sky.

But for me the air was all aglow with rosy light, and the car was a chariot flying swiftly to the dawn!

XIV

A Trip to Paris

The next day was Sunday; and after church I came over early to Knockcalltecrore, and had a long talk with Norah about her school project. We decided that the sooner she began the better—she because, as she at first alleged, every month of delay made school a less suitable place for her—I because, as I took care not only to allege but to reiterate, as the period had to be put in, the sooner it was begun the sooner it would end, and so the sooner would my happiness come.

Norah was very sweet, and shyly told me that if such was my decided opinion, she must say that she too had something of the same view.

"I do not want you to be pained, dear, by any delay," she said, "made by your having been so good to me; and I love you too well to want myself to wait longer than is necessary,"—an admission that was an intoxicating pleasure to me.

We agreed that our engagement was, if not to be kept a secret, at least not to be spoken of unnecessarily. Her father was to tell her immediate relatives, so that there would not be any gossip at her absence, and I was to tell one or two of my own connexions—for I had no immediate relatives—and perhaps one or two friends who were rather more closely connected with me than those of my own blood. I asked to be allowed to tell also my solicitor, who was an old friend of my father's, and who had always had more than merely professional relations with me. I had reasons of my own for telling him of the purposed change in my life, for I had important matters to execute through him, so as to protect Norah's future in case my own death should occur before the marriage was to take place. But of this, of course, I did not tell her.

We had a happy morning together, and when Joyce came in we told him of the conclusion we had arrived at. He fully acquiesced; and then, when he and I were alone, I asked him if he would prefer to make the arrangements about the schools himself or by some solicitor he would name, or that should all be done by my solicitor? He told me that my London solicitor would probably know what to do better than anyone in his own part of the world; and we agreed that I was to arrange it with him.

Accordingly I settled with Norah that the next day but one I should leave for London, and that when I had put everything on a satisfactory footing I should return to Carnaclif, and so be for a little longer able to see my darling. Then I went back to the hotel to write my letters in time for post.

That afternoon I wrote to my solicitor, Mr. Chapman, and asked him to have inquiries made, without the least delay, as to what was the best school in Paris to which to send a young lady, almost grown up, but whose education had been neglected. I added that I should be myself in London within two days of my letter, and would hope to have the information.

That evening I had a long talk on affairs with Dick, and opened to him a project I had formed regarding Knockcalltecrore. This was that I should try to buy the whole of the mountain, right away from where the sandy peninsula united it to the mainland—for evidently it had ages ago been an isolated sea-girt rockbound island. Dick knew that already we held a large part of it—Norah the Cliff Fields, Joyce the upper land on the sea side, and myself the part that I had already bought from Murdock. He quite fell in with the idea, and as we talked it over he grew more and more enthusiastic.

"Why, my dear fellow," he said, as he stood up and walked about the room, "it will make the most lovely residence in the world, and will be a fine investment for you. Holding long leases, you will easily be able to buy the freehold, and then every penny spent will return many fold. Let us once be able to find the springs that feed the bog, and get them in hand, and we can make the place a paradise. The springs are evidently high up on the hill, so that we can not only get water for irrigating and ornamental purposes, but we can get power also! Why, you can have electric light, and everything else you like, at the smallest cost. And if it be, as I suspect, that there is a streak of limestone in the hill, the place might be a positive mine of wealth as well! We have not lime within fifty miles, and if once we can quarry the stone here we can do anything. We can build a harbour on the south side, which would be the loveliest place to keep a yacht in that ever was known—quite big enough for anything in these parts—as safe as Portsmouth, and of fathomless depth.

"Easy, old man!" I cried, for the idea made me excited too.

"But I assure you Art, I am within the truth!"

"I know it, Dick—and now I want to come to business!"

"Eh! how do you mean?" he said, looking puzzled.

Then I told him of the school project, and that I was going to London after another day to arrange it. He was delighted, and quite approved.

"It is the wisest thing I ever heard of!" was his comment. "But how do you mean about business?" he asked.

"Dick, this has all to be done; and it needs some one to do it. I am not a scientist nor an engineer, and this project wants the aid of both, or of one man who is the two. Will you do it for me—and for Norah?"

He seemed staggered for a moment, but said heartily:

"That I will—but it will take some time!"

"We can do it within two years," I answered, "and that is the time that Norah will be away. It will help to pass it!" and I sighed.

"A long time, indeed, but oh, what a time, Art! Just fancy what you are waiting for; there need be no unhappy moment, please God, in all those months."

Then I made him a proposition, to which he, saying that my offer was too good, at first demurred. I reasoned with him, and told him that the amount was little to me, as, thanks to my Great Aunt, I had more than I ever could use; and that I wanted to make Norah's country home a paradise on earth—so far as love and work and the means at command could do it; that it would take up all Dick's time, and keep him for the whole period from pursuing his studies; and that he would have to be manager as well as engineer, and would have to buy the land for me. I told him also my secret hope that in time he would take all my affairs in hand and manage everything for me.

"Buying the land will, I fancy, be easy enough," he said. "Two of the farms are in the market now, and all round here land is literally going abegging. However, I shall take the matter in hand at once, and write you to London, in case there should be anything before you get back." And thus we settled that night that I was, if possible, to buy the whole mountain. I wrote by the next post to Mr. Caicy, telling him that I had a project of purchase in hand, and that Mr. Sutherland would do everything for me during my absence, and that whatever he wished was to be done. I asked him to come over and see Dick before the week was out.

The next day I spoke to Joyce, and asked him if he would care to sell me the lease of the land he now held. He seemed rejoiced at the chance of being able to get away.

"I will go gladly, though, sure enough, I'll be sad for a while to lave the shpot where I was born, and where I've lived all me life. But whin

Norah is gone—an' sure she'll never be back, for I'm thinkin' that after her school ye'll want to get married at once—"

"That we shall!" I interrupted.

"An' right enough too! But widout her the place will be that lonesome that I don't think I could abear it! Me sister'll go over to Knocknacar to live wid me married sister there, that'll be only too happy to have her with her; and I'll go over to Glasgow where Eugene is at work. The boy wants me to come, and whin I wrote and tould him of Norah's engagement, he wrote at once askin' me to lave the Hill and come to him. He says that before the year is out he hopes to be able to keep himself—an' me, too, if we should want it—an' he wrote such a nice letter to Norah—but the girl will like to tell ye about that herself! I can't sell ye the Cliff Fields meself, for they belong to Norah; but if ye like to ask her I'm sure she'll make no objection."

"I should be glad to have them," I said, "but all shall be her's in two years!"

And then and there we arranged for the sale of the property. I made Joyce the offer; he accepted at once, but said it was more than it was worth.

"No," said I, "I shall take the chance! I intend to make improvements."

Norah did not make any objection to her father selling the Cliff Fields. She told me that as I wanted to have them, I might, of course; but she hoped I would never sell the spot, as it was very dear to her. I assured her that in this as in all other matters I would do as she wished, and we sealed the assurance with——. Never mind! we sealed it!

I spent the afternoon there, for it was to be my last afternoon with Norah until I came back from Paris. We went down for a while to the Cliff Fields and sat on the table rock and talked over all our plans. I told her I had a scheme regarding Knockcalltecrore, but that I did not wish to tell her about it as it was to be a surprise. It needed a pretty hard struggle to be able to keep her in the dark even to this extent—there is nothing more sweet to young lovers than to share a secret. She knew that my wishes were all for her, and was content.

When we got back to the cottage I said good-bye. This naturally took some time—a first good-bye always does!—and went home to get my traps packed ready for an early start in the morning—more especially as I wished, when in Galway, to give Mr. Caicy instructions as to transferring the two properties—Norah's and her father's.

When Dick came home, he and I had a long talk on affairs; and I saw that he thoroughly understood all about the purchase of the whole mountain. Then we said good-night, and I retired.

I did not sleep very well. I think I was too happy, and out of the completeness of my happiness there seemed to grow a fear—some dim haunting dread of a change—something which would reverse the existing order of things. And so in dreams the Drowsy God played at ball with me; now throwing me to a dizzy height of joy, and then, as I fell swiftly through darkness, arresting my flight into the nether gloom with some new sweet hope. It seemed to me that I was awake all the night—and yet I knew I must have slept for I had distinct recollections of dreams in which all the persons and circumstances lately present to my mind were strangely jumbled together. The jumble was kaleidoscopic; there was an endless succession of its phases, but the pieces all remained the same. There were moments when all seemed aglow with rosy light, and hard on them, others horrid with the gloom of despair or fear; but in all, the dominating idea was the mountain standing against the sunset, always as the embodiment of the ruling emotion of the scene—and always Norah's beautiful eyes shone upon me. I seemed to live over again in isolated moments all the past weeks; but in such a way that the legends and myths and stories of Knockcalltecrore which I had heard were embodied in each moment. Thus, Murdock had always a part in the gloomy scenes, and got inextricably mixed up with the King of the Snakes. They freely exchanged personalities, and at one time I could see the Gombeen Man defying St. Patrick, whilst at another the Serpent seemed to be struggling with Joyce, and, after twisting round the mountain, being only beaten off by a mighty blow from Norah's father, rushing to the sea through the Shleenanaher.

Towards morning, as I suppose the needs of the waking day became more present to my mind in the gradual process of awakening, the bent of my thoughts began to be more practical; the Saint and His Majesty of the Serpents began to disappear, and the two dim cuirassiers who, with the money chest, had through the earlier hours of the night been passing far athwart my dreams—appearing and disappearing equally mysteriously—took a more prominent, or, perhaps, a more real part. Then I seemed to see Murdock working in a grave, whose sides were ever crumbling in as he frantically sought the treasure chest, whilst the gun-carriage, rank with the slime of the bog, was high above him on the brink of the grave, projected blackly against the yellow moon. Every time this scene in its myriad variations came round, it changed to one where the sides of the grave began to tumble in, and Murdock in terror tried to scream out, but could make no sound, nor could he make any effort to approach Norah, whose strong hands were stretched out to aid him.

With such a preparation for waking is it any wonder that I suddenly started broad awake with a strong sense of something forgotten, and found that it was four o'clock, and time to get ready for my journey. I did not lose any time, and after a hot cup of tea, which the cheery Mrs. Keating had herself prepared for me, was on my way under Andy's care to Recess, where we were to meet the "long car" to Galway.

Andy was, for a wonder, silent, and as I myself felt in a most active frame of mind, this rather gave me an opportunity for some amusement. I waited for a while to see if he would suggest any topic in his usual style; but as there was no sign of a change, I began:—

"You are very silent today, Andy. You are sad! What is it?"

"I'm thinkin'!"

"So I thought, Andy. But who are you thinking of?"

"Faix, I'm thinkin' iv poor Miss Norah there wid ne'er a bhoy on the flure at all, at all; an' iv the fairy girrul at Knocknacar—the poor craythur waitin' for some kind iv a leprachaun to come back to her. They do say, yer 'an'r, that the fairies is mighty fond iv thim leprachauns intirely. Musha! but it's a quare thing that weemen of all natures thinks a power more iv minkind what is hard to be caught nor iv thim that follys thim an' is had aisy!"

"Indeed! Andy." I felt he was getting on dangerous ground, and thought it would be as well to keep him to generalities if I could.

"Shure they do tell me so; that the girruls, whether fairies or weemen, is more fond iv lukin' out fur leprachauns, or min if that's their kind, than the clargy is iv killin' the divil—an' they've bin at him fur thousands iv years, an' him not turned a hair."

"Well! Andy, isn't it only natural, too? If we look at the girls and make love to them, why shouldn't they have a turn too, poor things, and make love to us? Now you would like to have a wife, I know; only that you're too much afraid of any woman."

"Thrue for ye! But shure an' how could I go dhrivin' about the counthry av I had a wife iv me own in wan place? It's meself that's welkim everywhere, jist because any wan iv the weemen might fear I'd turn the laugh on her whin I got her home; but a car-dhriver can no more shpake soft to only wan girrul nor he can dhrive his car in his own shanty."

"Well! but Andy, what would you do if you were to get married?"

"Faix, surr, an' the woman must settle that whin she comes. But, begor! it's not for a poor man like me—nor for the likes iv me—that the fairies does be keepin' their eyes out. I tell yer 'an'r that poor min isn't iv much account anyhow! Shure poverty is the worst iv crimes; an' there's no hidin' it like th' others. Patches is saw a mighty far way off; and shure enough they're more frightfuller nor even the polis!"

"By George! Andy," said I, "I'm afraid you're a cynic."

"A cynic, sir; an', faix, what sin am I up to now?"

"You say poverty is a crime."

"Begor! but it's worse! Most crimes is forgave afther a bit; an' the law is done wid ye whin ye're atin' yer skilly. But there's some people—aye! an' lashins iv thim too—what 'd rather see ye in a good shute iv coffin than in a bad shute iv clothes!"

"Why, Andy, you're quite a philosopher!"

"Bedad, that's quare; but whisper me now, surr, what kind iv a thing's that?"

"Well! it's a very wise man—one who loves wisdom."

"Begor! yer 'an'r, lovin' girruls is more in my shtyle; but I thought maybe it was some new kind iv a Protestan'."

"Why a Protestant?"

"Sorra wan iv me knows! I thought maybe they can believe even less nor the ould wans."

Andy's method of theological argument was quite too difficult for me, so I was silent; but my companion was not. He, however, evidently felt that theological disquisition was no more his *forte* than my own, for he instantly changed to another topic:—

"I'll be goin' back to Knockcalltecrore to-morra, yer 'an'r. I've been tould to call fur Mr. Caicy, th' attorney—savin' yer prisence—to take him back to Carnaclif. Is there any missage ye'd like to send to any wan?" He looked at me so slyly that his meaning was quite obvious.

"Thanks, Andy, but I think not; unless you tell Mr. Dick that we have had a pleasant journey this morning."

"Nothin' but that?—to nobody?"

"Who to, for instance, Andy?"

"There's Miss Norah, now! Shure girruls is always fond iv gettin' missages, an' most iv all from people what they're not fond iv!"

"Meaning me?"

"Oh, yis! oh, yis! if there's wan more nor another what she hates the sight iv, it's yer 'an'r! Shure didn't I notice it in her eye ere yistherday night, beyant at the boreen gate? Faix! but it's a nice eye Miss Norah has! Now, yer 'an'r, wouldn't an eye like that be betther for a young gintleman to luk into, than the quare eye iv yer fairy girrul—the wan that ye wor lukin' for, an' didn't find!"

The sly way in which Andy looked at me as he said this was quite indescribable. I have seen sly humour in the looks of children where the transparent simplicity of their purpose was a foil to their manifest intention to pretend to deceive. I have seen the arch glances of pretty young women when their eyes contradicted with resistless force the apparent meaning of their words; but I have never seen any slyness which could rival that of Andy. However, when he had spoken as above, he seemed to have spent the last bolt in his armoury; and for the remainder of the drive to Recess he did not touch again on the topic, or on a kindred one.

When I was in the hotel porch waiting the arrival of the long car, Andy came up to me:—

"What day will I be in Galway for yer 'an'r?"

"How do you mean, Andy? I didn't tell you I was coming back."

Andy laughed a merry, ringing laugh:—

"Begor! yer 'an'r, d'ye think there's only wan way iv tellin' things? Musha! but spache 'd be a mighty precious kind iv a thing if that was the way!"

"But, Andy, is not speech the way to make known what you wish other people to know?"

"Ah, go to God! I'd like to know if ye take it for granted whin ye ask a girrul a question an' she says 'no,' that she manes it—or that she intends ayther that ye should think she manes it. Faix! it 'd be a harrd wurrld to live in, if that was so; an' there 'd be mighty few widdys in it ayther!"

"Why widows, Andy?"

"Shure, isn't wives the shtuff that widdys is made iv!"

"Oh! I see. I'm learning, Andy—I'm getting on!"

"Yis! yer 'an'r. Ye haven't got on the long cap now; but I'm afeerd it's only a leather medal ye'd get as yit. Niver mind! surr. Here's the long car comin'; an' whin ye tellygraph to Misther Dick to sind me over to Galway fur to bring ye back, I'll luk up Miss Norah an' ax her to condescind to give ye some lessons in the differ betwixt 'yes' an' 'no' as shpoke by girruls. I'm tould now, it's a mighty intherestin' kind iv a shtudy for a young gintleman!"

There was no answering this Parthian shaft.

"Good-bye! Andy," I said, as I left a sovereign in his hand.

"Good luck! yer 'an'r; though what's the use iv wishin' luck to a man, whin the fairies is wid him!"

The last thing I saw was Andy waving his ragged hat as we passed the curve of the road round the lake before Recess was hidden from our view.

When I got to Galway I found Mr. Caicy waiting for me. He was most hearty in his welcome; and told me that as there was nearly an hour to wait before the starting of the Dublin express, he had luncheon on the table, and that we could discuss our business over it. We accordingly adjourned to his house, and after explaining to him what I wanted done with regard to the purchase of the property at Knockcalltecrore, I told him that Dick knew all the details, and would talk them over with him when he saw him on the next evening.

I began my eastward journey with my inner man in a most comfortable condition. Indeed, I concluded that there was no preparation for a journey like a bottle of 'Sneyd's 47' between two. I got to Dublin in time for the night mail, and on the following morning walked into Mr. Chapman's office at half-past ten o'clock.

He had all the necessary information for me; indeed, his zeal and his kindness were such that then and there I opened my heart to him, and was right glad that I had done so when I felt the hearty grasp of his hand as he wished me joy and and all good fortune. He was, of course, on the side of prudence. He was my own lawyer and my father's friend; and it was right and fitting that he should be. But it was quite evident that in the background of his musty life there was some old romance—musty old attorneys always have romances—so at least say the books. He entered heartily into my plan; and suggested that, if I chose, he would come with me to see the school and the schoolmistress in Paris.

"It will be better, I am sure," he said, "to have an old man like myself with you, and who can in our negotiations speak for her father. Indeed, my dear boy, from being so old a friend of your father's, and having no children of my own, I have almost come to look on you as my son, so it will not be much of an effort to regard Miss Norah as my daughter. The schoolmistress will, in the long run, be better satisfied with my standing *in loco parentis* than with your's." It was a great relief to me to find my way thus smoothed, for I had half expected some objection or remonstrance on his part. His kind offer was, of course, accepted; and the next morning found us in Paris.

We went to see the school and the schoolmistress. All was arranged as we wished. Mr. Chapman did not forget that Norah wished to have all the extra branches of study, or that I wished to add all that could give a charm to her life. The schoolmistress opened her eyes at the total of Norah's requirements, which Mr. Chapman summed up as "all extras"— the same including the use of a saddle-horse, and visits to the opera and such performances as should be approved of, under the special care and with the special accompaniment of Madame herself.

I could see that for the coming year Norah's lines would lie in pleasant places in so far as Madame Lepecheaux could accomplish it. The date of her coming was to be fixed by letter, and as soon as possible.

Mr. Chapman had suggested that it might be well to arrange with Madame Lepecheaux that Norah should be able to get what clothes she might require, and such matters as are wanted by young ladies of the position which she was entering. The genial French woman quite entered into the idea, but insisted that the representative of Norah's father should come with her to the various *magasins* and himself make arrangements. He could not refuse; and as I was not forbidden by the unsuspecting lady, I came too.

These matters took up some time, and it was not until the fifth day after I had left Connemara that we were able to start on our return journey. We left at night, and after our arrival in the early morning went, as soon as we had breakfasted, to Mr. Chapman's office to get our letters.

I found two. The first I took to the window to read, where I was hidden behind a curtain, and where I might kiss it without being seen; for, although the writing was strange to me—for I had never seen her handwriting—I knew that it was from Norah.

Do any of us who arrive at middle life ever attempt to remember our feelings on receiving the first letter from the woman or the man of our love? Can there come across the long expanse of commonplace life, strewn as it is with lost beliefs and shattered hopes, any echo—any after-glow—of that time, any dim recollection of the thrill of pride and joy that flashed through us at such a moment? Can we rouse ourselves from the creeping lethargy of the contented acceptance of things, and feel the generous life-blood flowing through us once again?

I held Norah's letter in my hand, and it seemed as though with but one more step, I should hold my darling herself in my arms. I opened her letter most carefully; anything that her hands had touched was sacred to me. And then her message—the message of her heart to mine—sent direct and without intermediary, reached me:—

My dear Arthur,

"I hope you had a good journey, and that you enjoyed your trip to Paris. Father and I are both well; and we have had excellent news of Eugene, who has been promoted to more important work. We have seen Mr. Sutherland every day. He says that everything is going just as you wish it. Mr. Murdock has taken old Bat Moynahan to live with him since you went; they are always together, and Moynahan seems to be always drunk. Father thinks that Mr. Murdock has some purpose on foot, and that it cannot be a good one. We shall all be glad to see you soon again. I am afraid this letter must seem very odd to you; but you know I am not accustomed to writing letters. You must believe one thing—that whatever I say to you, I feel and believe with all my heart. I got your letters, and I cannot tell you what pleasure they gave me, or how I treasure them. Father sends his love and duty. What could I send that words could carry? I may not try yet. Perhaps I shall be more able to do what I wish, when I know more.

Norah

The letter disappointed me! Was any young man ever yet satisfied with written words, when his medium had hitherto been rosy lips, with the added commentary of loving eyes? And yet when I look back on that letter from a peasant girl, without high education or knowledge of the world, and who had possibly never written a letter before except to her father or brother, or a girl friend, and but few even of these—when I read in every word its simplicity and truth, and recognise the *arrière pensée* of that simple phrase, "whatever I say to you I feel and think with all my heart," I find it hard to think that any other letter that she or anyone else could have written, could have been more suitable, or could have meant more.

When I had read Norah's letter over a few times, and feared that Mr. Chapman would take humorous notice of my absorbtion, I turned to the other letter, which I knew was from Dick. I brought this from the window to the table, beside which I sat to read it, Mr. Chapman being still deep in his own neglected correspondence.

I need not give his letter in detail. It was long and exhaustive, and told me accurately of every step taken and everything accomplished since I had seen him. Mr. Caicy had made his appearance, as arranged, and the two had talked over and settled affairs. Mr. Caicy had lost no time, and fortune had so favoured him that he found that nearly all the tenants on the east side of the hill wished to emigrate, and so were anxious to realize on their holdings. The estate from which they held was in bankruptcy; and as a sale was then being effected, Mr. Caicy had purchased the estate, and then made arrangements for all who wished to purchase to do so on easy terms from me. The nett result was, that when certain formalities should be complied with, and certain moneys paid, I should own the whole of Knockcalltecrore and the land immediately adjoining it, together with certain other parcels of land in the neighbourhood. There were other matters of interest also inhis letter. He told me that Murdock, in order to spite and injure Joyce, had completed the damming up of the stream which ran from his land into the Cliff Fields by blocking with great stones the narrow chine in the rocks through which it fell; that this, coupled with the continuous rains had made the bog rise enormously, and that he feared much there would be some disaster. His fear was increased by what had taken place at Knocknacar. Even here the cuttings had shown some direful effects of the rain; the openings, made with so much trouble, had become choked, and as a consequence the bog had risen again, and had even spread downwards on its original course. Alarmed by these things, Dick had again warned Murdock of the danger in which he stood from the position of his house; and further, from tampering with the solid bounds of the bog itself. Murdock had not taken his warnings in good part—not any better than usual—and the interview had, as usual, ended in a row. Murdock had made the quarrel the occasion of ventilating his grievance against me for buying the whole mountain, for by this time it had leaked out that I was the purchaser. His language, Dick said, was awful. He cursed me and all belonging to me. He cursed Joyce and Norah, and Dick himself, and swore to be revenged on us all, and told Dick that he would balk me of finding the treasure—even if I were to buy up all Ireland, and if he had to peril his soul to forestall me. Dick ended his description of his proceedings characteristically:—"In fact, he grew so violent, and said such insulting things of you and others, that I had to give him a good sound thrashing."

"Others"—that meant Norah, of course—good old Dick! It was just as well for Mr. Murdock's physical comfort, and for the peace of the neighbourhood, that I did not meet him then and there; for, under these favouring conditions, there would have been a continuance of his experiences under the hands of Dick Sutherland.

Then Dick went on to tell me at greater length what Norah had conveyed in her letter—that, since I had left, Murdock had taken Bat Moynahan to live with him, and kept him continually drunk; that the two of them were evidently trying to locate the whereabouts of the treasure; and that, whenever they thought they were not watched, they trespassed on Joyce's land, to get near a certain part of the bog.

"I mean to watch them the first dark night," wrote Dick, at the close of his letter; "for I cannot help thinking that there is some devilment on foot. I don't suppose you care much for the treasure—you've got a bigger treasure from Knockcalltecrore than ever was hidden in it by men— but, all the same, it is yours after Murdock's time is up; and, as the guardian of your interest, I feel that I have a right to do whatever may be necessary to protect you. I have seen, at times, Murdock give such a look at Moynahan out of the corners of his eyes—when he thought no one was looking—that, upon my soul, I am afraid he means—if he gets the chance—to murder the old man, after he has pumped him of all he knows. I don't want to accuse a man of such an intention, without being able to prove it, and of course have said nothing to a soul; but I shall be really more comfortable in my mind when the man has gone away."

By the time I had finished the letter, Mr. Chapman had run through his correspondence—vacation business was not much in his way—and we discussed affairs.

The settlement of matters connected with my estate, and the purchase of Knockcalltecrore, together with the making of certain purchases— including a ring for Norah—kept me a few days in London; but at length all was complete, and I started on my trip to the West of Ireland. Before leaving, I wrote to Norah that I would be at Knockcalltecrore on the morning of the 20th October; and also to Dick, asking him to see that Andy was sent to meet me at Galway on the morning of the 19th— for I preferred rather to have the drive in solitude, than to be subjected to the interruptions of chance fellow-passengers.

At Dublin Mr. Caicy met me, as agreed; and together we went to various courts, chambers, offices, and banks—completing the purchase with all the endless official formalities and eccentricities habitual to a country whose administration has traditionally adopted and adapted every possible development of all belonging to red-tape.

At last, however, all was completed; and very early the next morning Mr. Caicy took his seat in the Galway express, in a carriage with the owner of Knockcalltecrore, to whom he had been formally appointed Irish law agent.

The journey was not a long one, and it was only twelve o'clock when we steamed into Galway. As we drew up at the platform, I saw Dick, who had come over to meet me. He was, I thought, looking a little pale and anxious; but as he did not say anything containing the slightest hint of any cause for such a thing, I concluded that he wished to wait until we were alone. This, however, was not to be for a little while; for Mr. Caicy had telegraphed to order lunch at his house, and thither we had to repair. We walked over; although Andy, who was in waiting outside the station, grinning from ear to ear, offered to "rowl our 'an 'rs over in half a jiffey."

Lunch over, and our bodies the richer for some of Mr. Caicy's excellent port, we prepared to start. Dick took occasion to whisper to me:—

"Some time on the road propose to walk for a bit, and send on the car. I want a talk with you alone, without making a mystery!"

"All right, Dick. Is it a serious matter?"

"Very serious!"

XV

A Midnight Treasure Hunt

When, some miles on our road, we came to a long stretch of moorland, I told Andy to stop till we got off. This being done, I told him to go on and wait for us at the next house, as we wished to have a walk.

"The nixt house?" queried Andy, "the very nixt house? Must it be that same?"

"No, Andy!" I answered, "the next after that will do equally well, or the third if it is not too far off. Why do you want to change?"

"Well, yer 'an'r, to tell ye the thruth there's a girrul at the house beyant what thinks it's a long time on the road I am widout doin' anythin' about settlin' down, an' that its time I asked her fortin, anyhow. Musha! but it's afeerd I am to shtop there, fur maybe she'd take advantage iv me whin she got me all alone, an' me havin' to wait there till yez come. An' me so softhearted, that maybe I'd say too much or too little."

"Why too much or too little?"

"Faix! if I said too much I might be settled down before the month was out; an' if I said too little I might have a girrul lukin' black at me iv'ry time I dhruv by. The house beyant it is a public, an' shure I know I'm safe there anyhow—if me dhrouth'll only hould out!"

I took the hint, and Andy spun my shilling in the air as he drove off. Dick and I walked together, and when he was out of earshot I said:—

"Now, old fellow, we are alone! What is it?"

"It's about Murdock."

"Not more than you told me in your letter, I hope. I owe you a good turn for that thrashing you gave him!"

"Oh, that was nothing; it was a labour of love! What I want to speak of is a much more serious affair."

"Nothing to touch Norah, I hope?" I said anxiously.

"This individual thing is not, thank God! but everything which that ruffian can do to worry her or any of us will be done. We'll have to watch him closely."

"What is this new thing?"

"It is about old Moynahan. I am in serious doubt and anxiety as to what I should do. At present I have only suspicion to go on, and not the faintest shadow of proof, and I really want help and advice."

"Tell me all about it."

"I shall! exactly as I remember it; and when I have told you, you may be able to draw some conclusion which can help us."

"Go on! but remember I am, as yet, in ignorance of what it is all about. You must not take any knowledge on my part for granted."

"I'll bear it in mind. Well! you remember what I said in my letter, that I had a suspicion of Murdock, and intended watching him?" I nodded. "Two nights after I had written that, the evening was dark and wet—just the weather I would have chosen myself had I had any mysterious purpose on hand. As soon as it got dark I put on my black waterproof and fishing boots and a sou'wester, and then felt armed for any crouching or lying down that might be required. I waited outside Murdock's house in the laneway, where I could see from the shadows on the window that both men were in the house. I told you that old Bat Moynahan had taken up his residence entirely with the Gombeen Man——"

"And that he was always drunk!"

"Exactly! I see you understand the situation. Presently I heard a stumble on the stone outside the porch, and peeping in through the hedge I saw Murdock holding up old Moynahan. Then he shut the door and they came down the path. The wind was by this time blowing pretty strongly, and made a loud noise in the hedgerows, and bore in the roar of the surf. Neither of the men could hear me, for I took care as I followed them to keep on the leeward side, and always with something between us. Murdock did not seem to have the slightest suspicion that any one was even on the hill side, let alone listening, and he did not even lower his tone as he spoke. Moynahan was too drunk to either know or care how loud he spoke, and indeed both had to speak pretty loud in order to be heard through the sound of the growing storm. The rain fell in torrents, and the men passed down the boreen stumbling and slipping. I followed on the other side of the hedge, and I can tell you I felt grateful to the original Mackintosh, or Golosh, or whatever was the name of the Johnny who invented waterproof. When they had reached the foot of the hill, they went on the road which curves round by the south-east, and I managed to scramble through the fir wood without losing sight of them. When they came to the bridge over the stream," where it runs out on the north side of the Peninsula, they turned up on the far bank. I slipped over the bridge behind them, and got on the far side of the fringe of alders. Here they stopped and sheltered for a while, and as I was but a few feet from them I heard every word which passed. Murdock began by saying to Moynahan:—

"'Now, keep yer wits about ye, if ye can. Ye'll get lashins iv dhrink whin we get back, but remember ye promised to go over the ground where yer father showed ye that the Frinchmin wint wid the gun carriage an' the horses. Where was it now that he tuk ye?' Moynahan evidently made an effort to think and speak:—

"'It was just about this shpot wheer he seen thim first. They crast over the sthrame—there wor no bridge thin nigher nor Galway—an' wint up the side iv the hill sthraight up.'

"'Now, couldn't ye folla the way yer father showed ye? Jist think. It's all dark, and there's nothin' that ye know to confuse ye—no threes what has growed up since thin. Thry an' remember, an' ye'll have lashins iv dhrink this night, an' half the goold whin we find it.'"

"'I can go! I can show the shpot! Come on.' He made a sudden bolt down into the river, which was running unusually high. The current almost swept him away; but Murdock was beside him in a moment, crying out:—

"'Go an! the wather isn't deep! don't be afeerd! I'm wid ye.' When I heard this I ran round and across the bridge, and was waiting behind the hedge on the road when they came up again. The two men went up the hill straight for perhaps a hundred yards, I still close to them; then Moynahan stopped:—

"'Here's about the shpot me father told me that he seen the min whin the moon shone out. Thin they went aff beyant,' and he pointed to the south. The struggle through the stream had evidently sobered him somewhat, for he spoke much more clearly.

"'Come on thin,' cried Murdock, and they moved off.

"'Here's wheer they wint to, thin,' said Moynahan, as he stopped on the south side of the hill—as I knew it to be from the louder sound of the surf which was borne in by the western gale. 'Here they wor, jist about here, an' me father wint away to hide from thim beside the big shtone at the Shleenanaher so that they wouldn't see him.' Then he paused, and went on in quite a different voice:—

"There, now I've tould ye enough for wan night. Come home! for it's chilled to the harrt I am, an' shtarved wid the cowld. Come home! I'll tell no more this night.' The next sound I heard was the popping of a cork, and then the voice of Murdock in a cheery tone:—

"'Here, take a sup of this, ould man. It's chilled we both are, an' cramped wid cowld. Take a good dhraw, ye must want it if ye're as bad as I am!' The gurgle that followed showed that he had obeyed orders; this was confirmed within an incredibly short time by his voice as he spoke again.

"'Me father hid there beyant. Come on!' We all, each in his own way, moved down to the Shleenanaher, and stood there. Moynahan spoke first.

"'From here, he seen them jist over the ridge iv the hill. I can go there now; come on!' He hurried up the slope, Murdock holding on to him. I followed, now crouching low, for there was but little shelter here. Moynahan stopped and said:—

"'It was just here!'

"'How do ye know?' asked Murdock doubtfully.

"'How do I know! Hasn't me father been over the shpot wid me a score iv times; aye, an' a hundhred times afore that be himself. It was here, I tell ye, that he seen the min wid the gun carriage for the last time. Do ye want to arguey it?'

"'Not me!' said Murdock, and as he spoke I saw him stoop—for as I was at the time lying on the ground I could see his outline against the dark sky. He was looking away from me, and as I looked too I could see him start as he whispered to himself:—

"'Be God! but it's thrue! there's the gun carriage!' There it was! Art, true enough before my eyes, not ten feet away on the edge of the bog! Moynahan went on:—

"'Me father tould me that the mountain was different at that time; the bog only kem down about as low as this. Musha! but its the quare lot it has shifted since thin!' There was a pause, broken by Murdock, who spoke in a hoarse, hard voice:—

"'An' where did he see them nixt?' Moynahan seemed to be getting drunker and drunker, as was manifest in his later speech; his dose of whiskey had no doubt been a good one.

"'He seen them next to the north beyant—higher up towards Murdock's house.'

"'Towards Murdock's house! Ye mane Joyce's?'

"'No, I mane Black Murdock's; the wan he had before he robbed Joyce. But begor! he done himself! It's on Joyce's ground the money is! He's a nagur, anyhow—Black Murdock the Gombeen—bloody end to him!' and he relapsed into silence. I could hear Murdock grind his teeth; then after a pause he spoke as the bottle popped again.

"'Have a sup; it'll kape out the cowld.' Moynahan took the bottle.

"'Here's death and damnation to Black Gombeen!' and the gurgling was heard again.

"'Come! now, show me the shpot where yer father last saw the min!' Murdock spoke authoritatively, and the other responded mechanically, and ran rather than walked along the side of the hill. Suddenly he stopped.

"'Here's the shpot!' he said, and incontinently tumbled down.

"'Git up! Wake up!' shouted Murdock in his ear. But the whiskey had done its work; the man slept, breathing heavily and stentoriously, heedless of the storm and the drenching rain. Murdock gathered a few stones and placed them together—I could hear the sound as they touched each other. Then he, too, took a pull at the bottle, and sat down beside Moynahan. I moved off a little, and when I came to a whin bush got behind it for a little shelter, and raising myself looked round. We were quite close to the edge of the bog, about half way between Joyce's house and Murdock's, and well in on Joyce's land. I was not satisfied as to what Murdock would do, so I waited.

"Fully an hour went by without any stir, and then I heard Murdock trying to awaken old Moynahan. I got down on the ground again and crawled over close to them. I heard Murdock shake the old man, and shout in his ear; presently the latter awoke, and the Gombeen Man gave him another dose of whiskey. This seemed to revive him a little as well as to complete his awakening.

"'Musha! but it's cowld I am!' he shivered.

"'Begor it is—git up and come home!' said Murdock, and he dragged the old man to his feet.

"'Hould me up, Murtagh,' said the latter, 'I'm that cowld I can't shtand, an' me legs is like shtones—I can't feel them at all, at all!'

"'All right!' said the other, 'walk on a little bit—sthraight—as ye're goin' now—I'll just shtop to cork the bottle.'

"From my position I could see their movements, and as I am a living man, Art! I saw Murdock turn him with his face to the bog, and send him to walk straight to his death!"

"Good God! Dick—are you quite certain?"

"I haven't the smallest doubt on my mind. I wish I could have, for it's a terrible thing to remember! That attempt to murder in the dark and the storm, comes between me and sleep! Moreover, Murdoch's action the instant after showed only too clearly what he intended. He turned quickly away, and I could hear him mutter as he moved past me on his way down the hill:—

"'He'll not throuble me now—curse him! an' his share won't be required,' and then he laughed a low horrible laugh, slow and harsh, and as though to himself; and I heard him say:—

"'An' whin I do get the chist, Miss Norah, ye'll be the nixt!'"

My blood began to boil as I heard of the villain's threat:—"Where is he Dick? He must deal with me for that."

"Steady, Art! steady!" and Dick laid his hand on me.

"Go on!" I said.

"I couldn't go after him, for I had to watch Moynahan, whom I followed close, and I caught hold of as soon as I thought Murdock was too far to see me. I was only just in time, for as I touched him he staggered, lurched forward, and was actually beginning to sink in the bog. It was at one of those spots where the rock runs sheer down into the morass. It took all my strength to pull him out, and when I did get him on the rock he sank down again into his drunken sleep. I thought the wisest thing I could do was to go to Joyce's for help; and as, thanks to my experiments with the magnets all those weeks, I knew the ground fairly well, I was able to find my way—although the task was a slow and difficult one.

When I got near I saw a light at the window. My rubber boots, I suppose, and the plash of the falling rain dulled my footsteps, for as I drew near I could see that a man was looking in at the window, but he did not hear me. I crept up behind the hedge and watched him. He went to the door and knocked—evidently net for the first time; then the door was opened, and I could see Joyce's figure against the light that came from the kitchen.

"'Who's there? What is it?' he asked. Then I heard Murdock's voice:—

"'I'm lookin' for poor ould Moynahan. He was out on the hill in the evenin', but he hasn't kem home, an' I'm anxious about him, for he had a sup in him, an' I fear he may have fallen into the bog. I've been out lukin' for him, but I can't find him. I thought he might have kem in here.'

"'No, he has not been here. Are you sure he was on the hill?'

"'Well, I thought so—but what ought I to do? I'd be thankful if ye'd advise me. Be the way, what o'clock might it be now?'

"Norah, who had joined her father, ran in and looked at the clock.

"'It is just ten minutes past twelve,' she said.

"'I don't know what's' to be done,' said Joyce. 'Could he have got to the shebeen?'

"'That's a good idea! I suppose I'd betther go there an' luk afther him. Ye see, I'm anxious about him, for he's been livin' wid me, an' if anythin' happened to him, people might say I done it!'

"'That's a queer thing for him to say!' said Norah to her father.

"Murdock turned on her at once.

"'Quare thing—no more quare than the things they'll be sayin' about you before long.'

"'What do you mean?' said Joyce, coming out.

"'Oh, nawthin', nawthin'! I must look for Moynahan.' And without a word he turned and ran. Joyce and Norah went into the house. When Murdock had quite gone I knocked at the door, and Joyce came out like a thunderbolt.

"'I've got ye now ye ruffian'—he shouted—'what did ye mean to say to me daughter?' but by this time I stood in the light, and he recognized me.

"'Hush!' I said, 'let me in quietly'—and when I passed in we shut the door. Then I told them that I had been out on the mountain, and had found Moynahan. I told them both that they must not ask me any questions, or let on to a soul that I had told them anything—that much might depend on it—for I thought, Art, old chap, that they had better not be mixed up in it, however the matter might end. So we all three went out with a lantern, and I brought them to where the old man was asleep. We lifted him, and between us carried him to the house; Joyce and I undressed him and put him in bed, between warm blankets. Then I came away and went over to Mrs. Kelligan's, where I slept in a chair before the fire.

"The next morning when I went up to Joyce's I found that Moynahan was all right—that he hadn't even got a cold, but that he remembered nothing whatever about his walking into the bog. He had even expressed his wonder at seeing the state his clothes were in. When I went into the village I found that Murdock had been everywhere and had told everyone of his fears about Moynahan. I said nothing of his being safe, but tried quietly to arrange matters so that I might be present when Murdock should set his eyes for the first time on the man he had tried to murder. I left him with a number of others in the shebeen, and went back to bring Moynahan, but found, when I got to Joyce's that he had already gone back to Murdock's house. Joyce had told him, as we had arranged, that when Murdock had come asking for him he had been alarmed, and had gone out to look for him; had found him asleep on the hill-side, and had brought him home with him. As I found that my scheme of facing Murdock with his victim was frustrated, I took advantage of Murdock's absence to remove the stones which he had placed to mark the spot where the treasure was last seen. I found them in the form of a cross, and moving them, replaced them at a spot some distance lower down the line of the bog. I marked the place, however, with a mark of my own—four stones put widely apart at the points of a letter Y—the centre marking the spot where the cross had been. Murdock returned to his house not long after, and within a short time ran down to tell that Moynahan had found his way home, and was all safe. They told me that he was then white and scared-looking." Here Dick paused:—

"Now, my difficulty is this. I know he tried to murder the man, but I am not in a position to prove it. No man could expect his word to be taken in such a matter and under such circumstances. And yet I am morally certain that he intends to murder him still. What should I do? To take any preventive steps would involve making the charge which I cannot prove. As yet neither of the men has the slightest suspicion that I am concerned in the matter in any way—or that I even know of it. Now may I not be most useful by keeping a watch and biding my time?"

I thought a moment, but there seemed to be only one answer:—

"You are quite right, Dick! We can do nothing just at present. We must keep a sharp look out, and get some tangible evidence of his intention—something that we can support—and then we can take steps against him. As to the matter of his threat to harm Norah, I shall certainly try to bring that out in a way we can prove, and then he shall have the hottest corner he ever thought of in his life."

"Quite right that he should have it, Art; but we must think of her too. It would not do to have her name mixed up with any gossip. She will be going away very shortly, I suppose, and then his power to hurt her will be nil. In the mean time everything must be done to guard her."

"I shall get a dog—a good savage one—this very day; that ruffian must not be able to even get near the house again——" Dick interrupted me:—

"Oh, I quite forgot to tell you about that. The very day after that night I got a dog and sent it up. It is the great mastiff that Meldon, the dispensary doctor, had—the one that you admired so much. I specially asked Norah to keep it for you, and train it to be always with her. She promised that she would always feed him herself and take him about with her. I am quite sure she understood that he was to be her protector."

"Thank you, Dick," I said, and I am sure he knew I was grateful.

By this time we had come near the house, outside which the car stood. Andy was inside, and evidently did not expect our coming so soon, for he sat with a measure of stout half emptied before him on the table, and on each of his knees sat a lady—one evidently the mother of the other. As we appeared in the doorway he started up.

"Be the powdhers, there's the masther! Git up, acushla!"—this to the younger woman, for the elder had already jumped up. Then to me:—

"Won't ye sit down, yer 'an'r—there's only the wan chair, so ye see the shifts we're dhruv to, whin there's three iv us. I couldn't put Mrs. Dempsey from off iv her own shtool, an' she wouldn't sit on me knee alone—the dacent woman!—so we had to take the girrul on too. They all sit that way in these parts!" The latter statement was made with brazen openness and shameless effrontery. I shook my finger at him:—

"Take care, Andy. You'll get into trouble one of these days!"

"Into throuble! for a girrul sittin' on me knee! Begor! the Govermint'll have to get up more coorts and more polis if they want to shtop that ould custom. An' more betoken, they'll have to purvide more shtools, too. Mrs. Dempsey, whin I come round agin, mind ye kape a govermint shtool for me! Here's the masther wouldn't let any girrul sit on any wan's knee. Begor! not even the quality nor the fairies! All right, yer 'an'r, the mare's quite ready. Good-bye, Mrs. Dempsey. Don't forgit the shtool—an' wan too for Biddy! Gee up, ye ould corncrake!" and so we resumed our journey.

As we went along Dick gave me all details regarding the property which he and Mr. Caicy had bought for me. Although I had signed deeds and papers without number, and was owner in the present or in future of the whole hill, I had not the least idea of either the size or disposition of the estate. Dick had been all over it, and was able to supply me with every detail. As he went on he grew quite enthusiastic—everything seemed to be even more favourable than he had at first supposed. There was plenty of clay; and he suspected that in two or three places there was pottery clay, such as is found chiefly in Cornwall. There was any amount of water; and when we should be able to control the whole hill and regulate matters as we wished, the supply would enable us to do anything in the way of either irrigation or ornamental development. The only thing we lacked, he said, was limestone, and he had a suspicion that limestone was to be found somewhere on the hill.

"I cannot but think," said he, "that there must be a streak of limestone somewhere. I cannot otherwise account for the subsidence of the lake on the top of the hill. I almost begin to think that that formation of rock to which the Snake's Pass is due runs right through the hill, and that we shall find that the whole top of it has similar granite cliffs, with the hollow between them possibly filled in with some rock of one of the later formations. However, when we get possession I shall make accurate search. I tell you, Art, it will well repay the trouble if we can find it. A limestone quarry here would be pretty well as valuable as a gold mine. Nearly all these promontories on the western coast of Ireland are of slate or granite, and here we have not got lime within thirty miles. With a quarry on the spot, we can not only build cheap and reclaim our own bog, but we can supply five hundred square miles of country with the rudiments of prosperity, and at a nominal price compared with what they pay now!"

Then he went on to tell me of the various arrangements effected—how those who wished to emigrate were about to do so, and how others who wished to stay were to have better farms given them on what we called "the mainland"; and how he had devised a plan for building houses for them—good solid stone houses, with proper offices and farmyards. He concluded what seemed to me like a somewhat modified day-dream:—

"And if we can find the limestone—well! the improvements can all be done without costing you a penny; and you can have around you the most prosperous set of people to be found in the country."

In such talk as this the journey wore on till the evening came upon us. The day had been a fine one—one of those rare sunny days in a wet autumn. As we went I could see everywhere the signs of the continuous rains. The fields were sloppy and sodden, and the bottoms were flooded; the bogs were teeming with water; the roads were washed clean—not only the mud but even the sand having been swept away, and the road metal was everywhere exposed. Often, as we went along, Dick took occasion to illustrate his views as to the danger of the shifting of the bog at Knockalltecrore by the evidence around us of the destructive power of the continuous rain.

When we came to the mountain gap where we got our first and only view of Knockalltecrore from the Galway road, Andy reined in the mare, and turned to me, pointing with his whip:—

"'There beyant, yer 'an'r, is Knockalltecrore—the hill where the threasure is. They do say that a young English gintleman has bought up the hill, an' manes to git the threasure for himself. Begor! perhaps he has found it already. Here! Gee up! ye ould corncrake! What the divil are ye kapin' the quality waitin' for?" and we sped down the road.

The sight of the hill filled me with glad emotion, and I do not think that it is to be wondered at. And yet my gladness was followed by an unutterable gloom—a gloom that fell over me the instant after my eyes took in the well-known hill struck by the falling sunset from the west. It seemed to me that all had been so happy and so bright and so easy for me, that there must be in store some terrible shock or loss to make the balance even, and, to reduce my satisfaction with life to the level above which man's happiness may not pass.

There was a curse on the hill! I felt it and realized it at that moment for the first time. I suppose I must have shown something of my brooding fear in my face, for Dick, looking round at me after a period of silence, said suddenly:—

"Cheer up Art, old chap! Surely you, at any rate, have no cause to be down on your luck! Of all men that live, I should think you ought to be about the very happiest!"

"That's it, old fellow," I answered. "I fear that there must be something terrible coming. I shall never be quite happy till Norah and all of us are quite away from the Hill."

"What on earth do you mean? Why, you have just bought the whole place!"

"It may seem foolish, Dick; but the words come back to me and keep ringing in my ears—'The Mountain holds—and it holds tight.'" Dick laughed:—

"Well, Art, it is not my fault, or Mr. Caicy's, if you don't hold it tight. It is yours now, every acre of it; and, if I don't mistake, you are going to make it in time—and not a long time either—into the fairest bower to which the best fellow ever brought the fairest lady! There now, Art, isn't that a pretty speech?"

Dick's words made me feel ashamed of myself, and I made an effort to pull myself together, which lasted until Dick and I said good-night.

XVI

A Grim Warning

I cannot say the night was a happy one. There were moments when I seemed to lose myself and my own anxieties in thoughts of Norah and the future, and such moments were sweet to look back on—then as they are now; but I slept only fitfully and dreamt frightfully.

It was natural enough that my dreams should centre around Knockcalltecrore; but there was no good reason why they should all be miserable or terrible. The Hill seemed to be ever under some uncomfortable or unnatural condition. When my dreams began, it was bathed in a flood of yellow moonlight, and at its summit was the giant Snake, the jewel of whose crown threw out an unholy glare of yellow light, and whose face and form kept perpetually changing to those of Murtagh Murdock.

I can now, with comparatively an easy effort, look back on it all, and disentangle or give a reason for all the phases of my thought. The snake "wid side whiskers" was distinctly suggested the first night I heard the legend at Mrs. Kelligan's; the light from the jewel was a part of the legend itself; and so on with every fact and incident. Presently, as I dreamt, the whole Mountain seemed to writhe and shake as though the great Snake was circling round it, deep under the earth; and again this movement changed into the shifting of the bog. Then through dark shadows that lay athwart the hill I could see the French soldiers, with their treasure-chest, pass along in dusky, mysterious silence, and vanish in the hill side. I saw Murdock track them; and, when they were gone, he and old Moynahan—who suddenly and mysteriously appeared beside him—struggled on the edge of the bog, and, with a shuddering wail, the latter threw up his arms and sank slowly into the depths of the morass. Again Norah and I were wandering together, when suddenly Murdock's evil face, borne on a huge serpent body, writhed up beside us; and in an instant Norah was whirled from my side and swept into the bog, I being powerless to save her or even help her.

The last of all my dreams was as follows:—Norah and I were sitting on the table rock in the Cliff Fields; all was happy and smiling around us. The sun shone and the birds sang, and as we sat hand in hand, the beating of our hearts seemed a song also. Suddenly there was a terrible sound—half a roar, as of an avalanche, and half a fluttering sound, as of many great wings. We clung together in terror, waiting for the portent which was at hand. And then over the cliff poured the whole mass of the bog, foul-smelling, fœtid, terrible, and of endless might. Just as it was about to touch us, and as I clasped Norah to me, so that we might die together, and whilst her despairing cry was in my ear, the whole mighty mass turned into loathsome, writhing snakes, sweeping into the sea!

I awoke with a scream which brought nearly every one in the hotel into my bedroom. Dick was first, and found me standing on the floor, white and drunk with terror.

"What is it, old fellow?—oh! I see, only a nightmare! Come on! he's all right; it's only a dream!" and almost before I had realized that the waking world and not the world of shadows was around me, the room was cleared and I was alone. I lit a candle and put on some clothes; as it was of no use trying to sleep again after such an experience, I got a book and resolutely set to reading. The effort was successful, as such efforts always are, and I quite forgot the cause of my disturbance in what I read. Then the matter itself grew less interesting. . .

There was a tap at my door. I started awake—it was broad daylight, and the book lay with crumpled leaves beside me on the floor. It was a message to tell me that Mr. Sutherland was waiting breakfast for me. I called out that I would be down in a few minutes, which promise I carried out as nearly as was commensurate with the requirements of the tub and the toilet. I found Dick awaiting me; he looked at me keenly as I came in, and then said heartily:—

"I see your nightmare has not left any ill-effects. I say! old chap, it must have been a whopper—a regular Derby winner among nightmares—worse than Andy's old corncrake. You yelled fit to wake the dead. I would have thought the contrast between an ordinary night and the day you are going to have would have been sufficient to satisfy anyone without such an addition to its blackness." Then he sung out in his rich voice:—

> "Och, Jewel, kape dhramin' that same till ye die,
> For bright mornin' will give dirty night the black lie."

We sat down to breakfast, and I am bound to say, from the trencher experience of that meal, that there is nothing so fine as an appetiser for breakfast, as a good preliminary nightmare.

We drove off to Knockcalltecrore. When we got to the foot of the hill we stopped as usual. Andy gave me a look which spoke a lot, but he did not say a single word—for which forbearance I owed him a good turn. Dick said:—

"I want to go round to the other side of the hill, and shall cross over the top. I shall look you up, if I may, at Joyce's about two o'clock."

"All right," I said; "we shall expect you," and I started up the hill.

When I got to the gate, and opened it, there was a loud, deep barking, which, however, was instantly stilled. I knew that Norah had tied up the mastiff, and I went to the door. I had no need to knock; for as I came near, it opened, and in another instant Norah was in my arms. She whispered in my ear when I had kissed her:—

"I would like to have come out to meet you, but I thought you would rather meet me here!" Then, as we went into the sitting-room, hand-in-hand, she whispered again:—

"Aunt has gone to buy groceries, so we are all alone. You must tell me all about everything."

We sat down close together, still hand-in-hand, and I told her all that we had done since I had left. When I had finished the Paris part of the story, she put up her hands before her face, and I could see the tears drop through her fingers.

"Norah! Norah! Don't cry, my darling! What is it?"

"Oh, Arthur, I can't help it! It is so wonderful—more than all I ever longed or wished for!" Then she took her hands away, and put them in mine, and looked me bravely in the face, with her eyes half-laughing and half-crying, and her cheeks wet, and said:—

"Arthur, you are the Fairy Prince! There is nothing that I can wish for that you have not done—even my dresses are ready by your sweet thoughtfulness. It needs an effort, dear, to let you do all this—but I see it is quite right—I must be dressed like one who is to be your wife. I shall think I am pleasing you afresh, every time I put one of them on; but I must pay for them myself. You know I am quite rich now. I have all the money you paid for the Cliff Fields; father says it ought to go in such things as will fit me for my new position, and will not hear of taking any of it."

"He is quite right, Norah, my darling—and you are quite right, too— all shall be just as you wish. Now tell me all about everything since I went away."

"May I bring in Turco? he is so quiet with me; and he must learn to know you and love you, or he wouldn't be any friend of mine." She looked at me lovingly, and went and brought in the mastiff, by whom I was forthwith received into friendship.

That was indeed a happy day! We had a family consultation about the school; the time of beginning was arranged, and there was perfect accord amongst us. As Dick and I drove back through the darkness, I could not but feel that, even if evil were looming ahead of us, at least some of us had experienced what it is to be happy.

It had been decided that after a week's time—on the 28th October—Norah was to leave for school. Her father was to bring her as far as London, and Mr. Chapman was to take her over to Paris. This was Joyce's own wish; he said:—

"'Twill be betther for ye, darlin', to go widout me. Ye'll have quite enough to do for a bit, to keep even wid the girls that have been reared in betther ways nor you, widout me there to make little iv ye."

"But, father," she remonstrated, "I don't want to appear any different from what I am! And I am too fond of you, and too proud of you, not to want to appear as your daughter."

Her father stroked her hair gently as he answered:—

"Norah! my darlin', it isn't that. Ye've always been the good and dutiful daughter to me; an' in all your pretty life there's not wan thing I wish undone or unsaid. But I'm older than you, daughter, an' I know more iv the world; an' what I say, is best for ye—now, and in yer future. I'm goin' to live wid Eugene; an' afther a while I suppose I, too, 'll be somethin' different from what I am. An' thin, whin I've lived awhile in a city, and got somethin' of city ways, I'll come an' see ye, maybe. Ye must remimber, that it's not only of you we've to think, but of th' other girls in the school. I don't want to have any of them turnin' up their noses at ye—that's not the way to get the best out iv school, me dear; for I suppose school is like everywhere else in the world—the higher ye're able to hould yer head, the more others'll look up to ye!"

His words were so obviously true, that not one of us had a word to say, and the matter was acquiesced in *nem. con.* I myself got leave to accompany the party as far as London—but not beyond. It was further arranged that Joyce should take his daughter to Galway, to get some clothes for her—just enough to take her to Paris—and that when in Paris she should have a full outfit under the direction of Madame Lepechaux. They were to leave on Friday, so as to have the Saturday in Galway; and as Norah wanted to say good-bye on the Sunday to old schoolfellows and friends in the convent, they would return on Monday, the 25th October. Accordingly, on the morning after next, Joyce took a letter for me to Mr. Caicy, who was to pay to him whatever portion of the purchase-money of his land he should require, and whom I asked to give all possible assistance in whatever matters either he or Norah might desire. I would have dearly liked to have gone myself with them, but the purpose and the occasion were such that I could not think of offering to go. On the day fixed they left on the long car from Carnaclif. They started in torrents of rain, but were as well wrapped up as the resources of Dick and myself would allow.

When they had gone, Dick and I drove over to Knockcalltecrore. Dick wished to have an interview with Murdock, regarding his giving up possession of the land on the 27th, as arranged.

We left Andy as usual at the foot of the hill, and went up to Murdock's house. The door was locked; and although we knocked several times, we could get no answer. We came away, therefore, and went up the hill, as Dick wished me to see where, according to old Moynahan, was the last place at which the Frenchmen had been seen. As we went on and turned the brow of the mound, which lay straight up—for the bog-land lay in a curve round its southern side—we saw before us two figures at the edge of the bog. They were those of Murdock and old Moynahan. When we saw who they were, Dick whispered to me:—

"They are at the place to which I changed the mark, but are still on Joyce's land."

They were working just as Dick and I had worked with Murdock, when we had recovered the gun-carriage, and were so intent on the work at which they toiled with feverish eagerness, that they did not see us coming; and it was only when we stood close beside them that they were conscious of our presence. Murdock turned at once with a scowl and a sort of snarl. When he saw who it was, he became positively livid with passion, and at once began to bombard us with the foulest vituperation. Dick pressed my arm, as a hint to keep quiet and leave the talking to him, and I did nothing; but he opposed the Gombeen Man's passion with an unruffled calm. Indeed, he seemed to me to want even to exasperate Murdock to the last degree. When the latter paused for a second for breath, he quietly said:—

"Keep your hair on, Murdock! and just tell me quietly why you are trespassing; and why, and what, you are trying to steal from this property?"

Murdock made no answer, so Dick went on:—

"Let me tell you that I act for the owner of this land, who bought it as it is, and I shall hold you responsible for your conduct. I don't want to have a row needlessly, so if you go away quietly, and promise to not either trespass here again, or try to steal anything, I shall not take any steps. If not, I shall do as the occasion demands."

Murdock answered him with the most manifestly intentional insolence:—

"You! ye tell me to go away! I don't ricognize ye at all. This land belongs to me frind, Mr. Joyce, an' I shall come on it whin I like, and do as I like. Whin me frind tells me not to come here, I shall shtay away. Till then I shall do as I like!"

Said Dick:—

"You think that will do to bluff me because you know Joyce is away for the day, and that, in the meantime, you can do what you want, and perhaps get out of the bog some property that does not belong to you. I shall not argue with you any more; but I warn you that you will have to answer for your conduct."

Murdock and Moynahan continued their pulling at the rope. We waited till the haul was over, and saw that the spoil on this occasion was a part of the root of a tree. Then, when both men were sitting exhausted beside it, Dick took out his notebook, and began to make notes of everything. Presently he turned to Murdock, and said:—

"Have you been fishing, Mr. Murdock? What a strange booty you have brought up! It is really most kind of you to be aiding to secure the winter firing for Mr. Joyce and my friend. Is there anything but bogwood to be found here?"

Murdock's reply was a curse and a savage scowl; but old Moynahan joined in the conversation:—

"Now, I tould ye, Murtagh, that we wur too low down!"

"Shut up!" shouted the other, and the old man shrank back as if he had been struck. Dick looked down, and seemed to be struck by the cross of loose stones at his feet, and said:—

"Dear me! that is very strange—a cross of stones. It would almost seem as if it were made here to mark something; but yet"—here he lifted one of the stones—"it cannot have been long here; the grass is fresh under the stones." Murdock said nothing, but clenched his hands and ground his teeth. Presently, however, he sent Moynahan back to his house to get some whiskey. When the latter was out of earshot, Murdock turned to us, and said:—

"An' so ye think to baffle me! do ye? Well! I'll have that money out—if I have to wade in yer blood. I will, by the livin' God!" and he burst into a string of profanities that made us shudder.

He was in such deadly earnest that I felt a pity for him, and said impulsively:—

"Look here! if you want to get it out, you can have a little more time if you like, if only you will conduct yourself properly. I don't want to be bothered looking for it. Now, if you'll only behave decently, and be something like a civilized being, I'll give you another month if you want it!"

Again he burst out at me with still more awful profanities. He didn't want any of my time! He'd take what time he liked! God Himself—and he particularized the persons of the Trinity—couldn't balk him, and he'd do what he liked; and if I crossed his path it would be the worse for me! And, as for others, that he would send the hard word round the country about me and my leman!—I couldn't be always knocking the ruffian down, so I turned away and called to Dick:—

"Coming!" said Dick, and he walked up to Murdock and knocked him down. Then, as the latter lay dazed on the grass, he followed me.

"Really," he said, apologetically, "the man wants it. It will do him good!"

Then we went back to Carnaclif.

These three days were very dreary ones for me: we spent most of the time walking over Knockcalltecrore and making plans for the future. But, without Norah, the place seemed very dreary!

We did not go over on the Monday, as we knew that Joyce and Norah would not get home until late in the evening, and would be tired. Early, however, on the day after—Tuesday—we drove over. Joyce was out, and Dick left me at the foot of the boreen, so when I got to the house I found Norah alone.

The dear girl showed me her new dresses with much pride; and presently going to her room put on one of them, and came back to let me see how she looked. Her face was covered with blushes. Needless to say that I admired the new dress, as did her father, who just then came in.

When she went away to take off the dress Joyce beckoned me outside. When we got away from the house he turned to me; his face was very grave, and he seemed even more frightened than angry.

"There's somethin' I was tould while I was away, that I think ye ought to know."

"Go on, Mr. Joyce!"

"Somebody has been sayin' hard things about Norah!"

"About Norah! Surely there is nobody mad enough or bad enough to speak evil of her."

"There's wan!" He turned as he spoke, and looked instinctively in the direction of Murdock's house.

"Oh, Murdock! as he threatened—what did he say?"

"Well, I don't know. I could only get it that somebody was sayin' somethin', an' that it would be well to have things so that no wan could say anythin' that we couldn't prove. It was a frind tould me—and that's all he would tell! Mayhap he didn't know any more himself; but I knew him to be a frind!"

"And it was a friendly act, Mr. Joyce. I have no doubt that Murdock has been sending round wicked lies about us all! But thank God! in a few days we will be all moving, and it doesn't matter much what he can do."

"No! it won't matter much in wan way, but he's not goin', all the same, to throw dirt on me child. If he goes on I'll folly him up!"

"He won't go on, Mr. Joyce. Before long, he'll be out of the neighbourhood altogether. To tell you the truth, I have bought the whole of his land, and I get possession of it tomorrow; and then I'll never let him set foot here again. When once he is out of this, he will have too much other wickedness on hand to have time to meddle with us!"

"That's thrue enough! Well! we'll wait an' see what happens—but we'll be mighty careful all the same."

"Quite right," I said, "we cannot be too careful in such a matter!" Then we went back to the house, and met Norah coming into the room in her red petticoat, which she knew I liked. She whispered to me! oh so sweetly:—

"I thought, dear, you would like me to be the old Norah, today. It is our last day together in the old way." Then hand-in-hand we went down to the Cliff Fields, and sat on the table-rock for the last time, and feasted our eyes on the glorious prospect, whilst we told each other our bright dreams of the future.

In the autumn twilight we came back to the house; Dick had, in the meantime, come in, and we both stayed for tea. I saw that Dick had something to tell me, but he waited until we were going home before he spoke.

It was a sad parting with Norah that night; for it was the last day together before she went off to school. For myself, I felt that whatever might be in the future—and I hoped for much—it was the last time that I might sit by the firelight with the old Norah. She, too, was sad, and when she told me the cause of her sadness, I found that it was the same as my own.

"But oh! Arthur, my darling, I shall try—I shall try to be worthy of my great good fortune—and of you!" she said, as she put her arms round my neck, and leaning her head on my bosom, began to cry.

"Hush! Norah. Hush, my darling!" I said, "you must not say such things to me. You, who are worthy of all the good gifts of life. Oh, my dear! my dear! I am only fearful that you may be snatched away from me by some terrible misfortune—I shall not be happy till you are safely away from the shadow of this fateful mountain and are beginning your new life."

"Only one more day!" she said. "Tomorrow we must settle up everything—and I have much to do for father—poor father! how good he is to me. Please God! Arthur, we shall be able some day to repay him for all his goodness to me!" How inexpressibly sweet it was to me to hear her say "we" shall be able, as she nestled up close to me.

Ah! that night! Ah! that night!—the end of the day when, for the last time, I sat on the table-rock with the old Norah that I loved so well. It almost seemed as if Fate, who loves the keen contrasts of glare and gloom, had made on purpose that day so bright, and of such flawless happiness!

As we went back to Carnaclif Dick told me what had been exercising his mind all the afternoon. When he had got to the bog he found that it had risen so much that he thought it well to seek the cause. He had gone at once to the place where Murdock had dammed up the stream that ran over into the Cliff Fields, and had found that the natural position of the ground had so far aided his efforts that the great stones thrown into the chine had become solidified with the rubbish by the new weight of the risen bog into a compact mass, and unless some heroic measure, such as blowing up the dam, should be taken, the bog would continue to rise until it should flow over the lowest part of the solid banks containing it.

"As sure as we are here, Art," he said, "that man will do himself to death. I am convinced that if the present state of things goes on, with the bog at its present height, and with this terrible rainfall, there will be another shifting of the bog—and then, God help him, and perhaps others too! I told him of the danger, and explained it to him—but he only laughed at me and called me a fool and a traitor—that I was doing it to prevent him getting his treasure—his treasure, forsooth!—and then he went again into those terrible blasphemies—so I came away; but he is a lost man, and I don't see how we can stop him." I said earnestly:—

"Dick, there's no danger to them—the Joyces—is there?"

"No!" be answered, "not the slightest—their house is on the rock, high over the spot, and quite away from any possible danger."

Then we relapsed into silence, as we each tried to think out a solution.

That night it rained more heavily than ever. The downfall was almost tropical—as it can be on the West Coast—and the rain on the iron roof of the stable behind the hotel sounded like thunder; it was the last thing in my ears before I went to sleep.

That night again I kept dreaming—dreaming in the same nightmare fashion as before. But although the working of my imagination centred round Knockcalltecrore and all it contained, and although I suffered dismal tortures from the hideous dreams of ruin and disaster which afflicted me, I did not on this occasion arouse the household. In the morning when we met, Dick looked at my pale face and said:—

"Dreaming again, Art! Well, please God, it's all nearly over now. One more day, and Norah will be away from Knockcalltecrore."

The thought gave me much relief. The next morning—on Thursday, 28th of October—we should be on our way to Galway *en route* for London, whilst Dick would receive on my behalf possession of the property which I had purchased from Murdock. Indeed his tenure ended at noon this very day; but we thought it wiser to postpone taking possession until after Norah had left. Although Norah's departure meant a long absence from the woman I loved, I could not regret it, for it was after all but a long road to the end I wished for. The two years would soon be over. And then!—and then life would begin in real earnest, and along its paths of sorrow as of joy Norah and I should walk with equal steps.

Alas! for dreaming! The dreams of the daylight are often more delusive than even those born of the glamour of moonlight or starlight, or of the pitchy darkness of the night!

It had been arranged that we were not on this day to go over to Knockcalltecrore, as Norah and her father wanted the day together. Miss Joyce, Norah's aunt, who usually had lived with them, was coming back to look after the house. So after breakfast Dick and I smoked and lounged about, and went over some business matters, and we arranged many things to be done during my absence. The rain still continued to pour down in a perfect deluge—the roadway outside the hotel was running like a river, and the wind swept the rain-clouds so that the drops struck like hail. Every now and again, as the gusts gathered in force, the rain seemed to drive past like a sheet of water; and looking out of the window, we could see dripping men and women trying to make headway against the storm. Dick said to me:—

"If this rain holds on much longer it will be a bad job for Murdock. There is every fear that if the bog should break under the flooding he will suffer at once. What an obstinate fool he is—he won't take any warning! I almost feel like a criminal in letting him go to his death—ruffian though he is; and yet what can one do? We are all powerless if anything should happen." After this we were silent. I spoke the next:—

"Tell me, Dick, is there any earthly possibility of any harm coming to Joyce's house in case the bog should shift again? Is it quite certain that they are all safe?"

"Quite certain, old fellow. You may set your mind at rest on that score. In so far as the bog is concerned, she and her father are in no danger. The only way they could run any risk of danger would be by their going to Murdock's house, or by being by chance lower down on the hill, and I do not think that such a thing is likely to happen."

This set my mind more at ease, and while Dick sat down to write some letters I continued to look at the rain.

By-and-by I went down to the tap-room, where there were always a lot of peasants, whose quaint speech amused and interested me. When I came in one of them, whom I recognized as one of our navvies at Knocknacar, was telling something, for the others all stood round him. Andy was the first to see me, and said as I entered:—

"Ye'll have to go over it all agin, Mike. Here's his 'an'r, that is just death on to bogs—an' the like," he added, looking at me slyly.

"What is it?" I asked.

"Oh, not much, yer 'an'r, except that the bog up at Knocknacar has run away intirely. Whin the wather rose in it, the big cuttin' we med tuk it all out, like butthermilk out iv a jug. Begor! there never was seen such a flittin' since the wurrld begun. An' more betoken, the quare part iv it is that it hasn't left the bit iv a hole behind it at all, but it's all mud an' wather at the prisint minit."

I knew this would interest Dick exceedingly, so I went for him. When he heard it he got quite excited, and insisted that we should go off to Knocknacar at once. Accordingly Andy was summoned, the mare was harnessed, and with what protection we could get in the way of wraps, we went off to Knocknacar through the rain storm.

As we went along we got some idea of the damage done—and being done—by the wonderful rainfall. Not only the road was like a river, and the mountain streams were roaring torrents, but in places the road was flooded to such a dangerous depth that we dared not have attempted the passage only that, through our repeated journeys, we all knew the road so well.

However, we got at last to Knocknacar, and there found that the statement we heard was quite true. The bog had been flooded to such a degree that it had burst out through the cutting which we had made, and had poured in a great stream over all the sloping moorland on which we had opened it. The brown bog and black mud lying all over the stony space looked like one of the lava streams which mark the northern side of Vesuvius. Dick went most carefully all over the ground wherever we could venture, and took a number of notes. Indeed. the day was beginning to draw in, when, dripping and chilled, we prepared for our return journey through the rain. Andy had not been wasting his time in the sheebeen, and was in one of his most jocular humours; and when we too were fortified with steaming hot punch we were able to listen to his fun without wanting to kill him.

On the journey back, Dick—when Andy allowed him speech— explained to me the various phenomena which we had noticed. When we got back to the hotel it was night. Had the weather been fine we might have expected a couple more hours of twilight; but with the mass of driving clouds overhead, and the steady downpour of rain, and the fierce rush of the wind, there was left to us not the slightest suggestion of day.

We went to bed early, for I had to rise by daylight for our journey on the morrow. After lying awake for some time listening to the roar of the storm and the dash of the rain, and wondering if it were to go on for ever, I sank into a troubled sleep.

It seemed to me that all the nightmares which had individually afflicted me during the last week returned to assail me collectively on the present occasion. I was a sort of Mazeppa in the world of dreams. Again and again the fatal hill and all its mystic and terrible associations haunted me!—Again the snakes writhed around and took terrible forms! Again she I loved was in peril! Again Murdock seemed to arise in new forms of terror and wickedness! Again the lost treasure was sought under terrible conditions; and once again I seemed to sit on the table-rock with Norah, and to see the whole mountain rush down on us in a dread avalanche, and turn to myriad snakes as it came! And again Norah seemed to call to me, "Help! help! Arthur! Save me! Save me!" And again, as was most natural, I found myself awake on the floor of my room—though this time I did not scream—wet and quivering with some nameless terror, and with Norah's despairing cry in my ears.

But even in the first instant of my awakening I had taken a resolution which forthwith I proceeded to carry into effect. These terrible dreams—whencesoever they came—must not have come in vain! The grim warning must not be despised! Norah was in danger, and I must go to her at all hazards!

I threw on my clothes and went and woke Dick. When I told him my intention he jumped up at once and began to dress, whilst I ran downstairs and found Andy, and set him to get out the car at once.

"Is it goin' out agin in the shtorm ye are? Begor! ye'd not go widout some rayson, an' I'm not the bhoy to be behind whin ye want me. I'll be ready, yer 'an'r, in two skips iv a dead salmon!" and Andy proceeded to make, or rather complete, his toilet, and hurried out to the stable to get the car ready. In the mean time Dick had got two lanterns and a flask, and showed them to me.

"We may as well have them with us. We do not know what we may want in this storm."

It was now past one o'clock, and the night was pitchy dark. The rain still fell, and high overhead we could hear the ceaseless rushing of the wind. It was a lucky thing that both Andy and the mare knew the road thoroughly, for otherwise we never could have got on that night. As it was, we had to go much more slowly than we had ever gone before.

I was in a perfect fever. Every second's delay seemed to me like an hour. I feared—nay more, I had a deep conviction—that some dreadful thing was happening, and I had over me a terrible dread that we should arrive too late.

XVII

The Catastrophe

As we drew closer to the mountain, and recognized our whereabouts by the various landmarks, my dread seemed to grow. The night was now well on, and there were signs of the storm abating; occasionally the wind would fall off a little, and the rain beat with less dreadful violence. In such moments some kind of light would be seen in the sky—or, to speak more correctly, the darkness would be less complete—and then the new squall which followed would seem by contrast with the calm to smite us with renewed violence. In one of these lulls we saw for an instant the mountain rise before us, its bold outline being shown darkly against a sky less black. But the vision was swept away an instant after by a squall and a cloud of blinding rain, leaving only a dreadful memory of some field for grim disaster. Then we went on our way even more hopelessly; for earth and sky, which in that brief instant we had been able to distinguish, were now hidden under one unutterable pall of gloom.

On we went slowly. There was now in the air a thunderous feeling, and we expected each moment to be startled by the lightning's flash or the roar of Heaven's artillery. Masses of mist or sea fog now began to be borne landward by the passing squalls. In the time that elapsed between that one momentary glimpse of Knockcalltecrore and our arrival at the foot of the boreen a whole lifetime seemed to me to have elapsed, and in my thoughts and harrowing anxieties I recalled—as drowning men are said to do before death—every moment, every experience since I had first come within sight of the western sea. The blackness of my fears seemed only a carrying inward of the surrounding darkness, which was made more pronounced by the flickering of our lanterns, and more dread by the sounds of the tempest with which it was laden.

When we stopped in the boreen, Dick and I hurried up the hill, whilst Andy, with whom we left one of the lanterns, drew the horse under the comparative shelter of the wind-swept alders, which lined the entrance to the lane. He wanted a short rest before proceeding to Mrs. Kelligan's, where he was to stop the remainder of the night, so as to be able to come for us in the morning.

As we came near Murdock's cottage Dick pressed my arm.

"Look!" he called to me, putting his mouth to my ear so that I could hear him, for the storm swept the hill fiercely here, and a special current of wind came whirling up through the Shleenanaher. "Look!" he is up even at this hour. There must be some villainy afloat!"

When we got up a little farther he called to me again in the same way.

"The nearest point of the bog is here; let us look at it." We diverged to the left, and in a few minutes were down at the edge of the bog.

It seemed to us to be different from what it had been. It was raised considerably above its normal height, and seemed quivering all over in a very strange way. Dick said to me very gravely:—

"We are just in time. There's something going to happen here."

"Let us hurry to Joyce's," I said, "and see if all is safe there."

"We should warn them first at Murdock's," he said. "There may not be a moment to lose." We hurried back to the boreen and ran on to Murdock's, opened the gate, and ran up the path. We knocked at the door, but there was no answer. We knocked more loudly still, but there came no reply.

"We had better make certain," said Dick, and I could hear him more easily now, for we were in the shelter of the porch. We opened the door, which was only on the latch, and went in. In the kitchen a candle was burning, and the fire on the hearth was blazing, so that it could not have been long since the inmates had left. Dick wrote a line of warning in his pocket-book, tore out the leaf, and placed it on the table where it could not fail to be seen by anyone entering the room. We then hurried out, and up the lane to Joyce's.

As we drew near we were surprised to find a light in Joyce's window also. I got to the windward side of Dick, and shouted to him:—

"A light here also! there must be something strange going on." We hurried as fast as we could up to the house. As we drew close the door was opened, and through a momentary lull we heard the voice of Miss Joyce, Norah's aunt:—

"Is that you, Norah?"

"No!" I answered.

"Oh! is it you, Mr. Arthur? Thank God ye've come! I'm in such terror about Phelim an' Norah. They're both out in the shtorm, an' I'm nigh disthracted about them."

By this time we were in the house, and could hear each other speak, although not too well even here, for again the whole force of the gale struck the front of the house, and the noise was great.

"Where is Norah? Is she not here?"

"Oh no! God help us! Wirrastru! wirrastru!" The poor woman was in such a state of agitation and abject terror that it was with some difficulty we could learn from her enough to understand what had occurred. The suspense of trying to get her to speak intelligibly was agonizing, for now every moment was precious; but we could not do anything or make any effort whatever until we had learned all that had occurred. At last, however, it was conveyed to us that early in the evening Joyce had gone out to look after the cattle, and had not since returned. Late at night old Moynahan had come to the door half drunk, and had hiccoughed a message that Joyce had met with an accident and was then in Murdock's house. He wanted Norah to go to him there, but Norah only was to go and no one else. She had at once suspected that it was some trap of Murdock's for some evil purpose, but still she thought it better to go, and accordingly called to Hector, the mastiff, to come with her, she remarking to her aunt "I am safe with him, at any rate." But Hector did not come. He had been restless, and groaning for an hour before, and now on looking for him they had found him dead. This helped to confirm Norah's suspicions, and the two poor women were in an agony of doubt as to what they should do. Whilst they were discussing the matter Moynahan had returned—this time even drunker than before—and repeated his message, but with evident reluctance. Norah had accordingly set to work to cross-examine him, and after a while he admitted that Joyce was not in Murdock's house at all—that he had been sent with the message and told when he had delivered it to go away to mother Kelligan's and not to ever tell anything whatever of the night's proceedings—no matter what might happen or what might be said. When he had admitted this much he had been so overcome with fright at what he had done that he began to cry and moan, and say that Murdock would kill him for telling on him. Norah had told him he could remain in the cottage where he was, if he would tell her where her father was, so that she could go to look for him; but that he had sworn most solemnly that he did not know, but that Murdock knew, for he told him that there would be no chance of seeing him at his own house for hours yet that night. This had determined Norah that she would go out herself, although the storm was raging wildly, to look for her father. Moynahan, however, would not stay in the cottage, as he said he would be afraid to, unless Joyce himself were there to protect him; for if there were no one but women in the house Murdock would come and murder him and throw his body into the bog, as he had often threatened. So Moynahan had gone out into the night by himself, and Norah had shortly after gone out also, and from that moment she—Miss Joyce—had not set eyes on her, and feared that some harm had happened.

This the poor soul told us in such an agony of dread and grief that it was pitiful to hear her, and we could not but forgive the terrible delay. I was myself in deadly fear, for every kind of harrowing possibility rose before me as the tale was told. It was quite evident that Murdock was bent on some desperate scheme of evil; he either intended to murder Norah or to compromise her in some terrible way. I was almost afraid to think of the subject. It was plain to me that by this means he hoped, not only to gratify his revenge, but to get some lever to use against us, one and all, so as to secure his efforts in searching for the treasure. In my rage against the cowardly hound, I almost lost sight of the need of thankfulness for one great peril avoided.

However, there was no time at present for further thought—action, prompt and decisive, was vitally necessary. Joyce was absent—we had no clue to where he could be. Norah was alone on the mountain, and with the possibility of Murdock assailing her, for he, too, was abroad—as we knew from the fact of his being away from his house.

We lost not a moment, but went out again into the storm. We did not, however, take the lantern with us, as we found by experience that its occasional light was in the long run an evil, as we could not by its light see any distance, and the grey of the coming dawn was beginning to show through the abating storm, with a' faint indication that before long we should have some light.

We went down the hill westward until we came near the bog, for we had determined to make a circuit of it as our first piece of exploration, since we thought that here lay the most imminent danger. Then we separated, Dick following the line of the bog downward whilst I went north, intending to cross at the top and proceed down the farther side. We had agreed on a signal, if such could be heard through the storm, choosing the Australian "coo-ee," which is the best sound to travel known.

I hurried along as fast as I dared, for I was occasionally in utter darkness. Although the morning was coming with promise of light, the sea-wind swept inland masses of swiftly-driving mist, which, whilst they encompassed me, made movement not only difficult and dangerous, but at times almost impossible. The electric feeling in the air had become intensified, and each moment I expected the thunderstorm to burst.

Every little while I called, "Norah! Norah!" in the vain hope that, whilst returning from her search for her father, she might come within the sound of my voice. But no answering sound came back to me, except the fierce roar of the storm laden with the wild dash of the breakers hurled against the cliffs and the rocks below.

Even then, so strangely does the mind work, the words of the old song, "The Pilgrim of Love," came mechanically to my memory, as though I had called "Orinthia" instead of "Norah:"—

"Till with 'Orinthia' all the rocks resound."

On, on I went, following the line of the bog, till I had reached the northern point, where the ground rose and began to become solid. I found the bog here so swollen with rain that I had to make a long detour so as to get round to the western side. High up on the hill there was, I knew, a rough shelter for the cattle; and as it struck me that Joyce might have gone here to look after his stock, and that Norah had gone hither to search for him, I ran up to it. The cattle were there, huddled together in a solid mass behind the sheltering wall of sods and stones. I cried out as loudly as I could from the windward side, so that my voice would carry:—

"Norah! Norah! Joyce! Joyce! Are you there? Is anyone there?"

There was a stir amongst the cattle and one or two low "moos" as they heard the human voice, but no sound from either of those I sought; so I ran down again to the further side of the bog. I knew now that neither Norah nor her father could be on this point of the hill, or they would have heard my voice; and as the storm came from the west, I made a zigzag line going east to west as I followed down the bog so that I might have a chance of being heard—should there be anyone to hear. When I got near to the entrance to the Cliff Fields I shouted as loudly as I could, "Norah! Norah!" but the wind took my voice away as it would sweep thistles down, and it was as though I made the effort but no voice came, and I felt awfully alone in the midst of a thick pall of mist.

On, on I went, following the line of the bog. Lower down there was some shelter from the storm, for the great ridge of rocks here rose between me and the sea, and I felt that my voice could be heard further off. I was sick at heart and chilled with despair, till I felt as if the chill of my soul had extended even to my blood; but on I went with set purpose, the true doggedness of despair.

As I went I thought I heard a cry through the mist—Norah's voice! It was but an instant, and I could not be sure whether my ears indeed heard, or if the anguish of my heart had created the phantom of a voice to deceive me. However, be it what it might, it awoke me like a clarion; my heart leaped and the blood surged in my brain till I almost became dizzy. I listened to try if I could distinguish from what direction the voice had come.

I waited in agony. Each second seemed a century, and my heart beat like a trip-hammer. Then again I heard the sound—faint, but still clear enough to hear. I shouted with all my power, but once again the roar of the wind overpowered me; however, I ran on towards the voice.

There was a sudden lull in the wind—a blaze of lightning lit up the whole scene, and, some fifty yards before me, I saw two figures struggling at the edge of the rocks. In that welcome glance, infinitesimal though it was, I recognized the red petticoat which, in that place and at that time, could be none other than Norah's. I shouted as I leapt forward; but just then the thunder broke overhead, and in the mighty and prolonged roll every other sound faded into nothingness, as though the thunderclap had come on a primeval stillness. As I drew near to where I had seen the figures, the thunder rolled away, and through its vanishing sound I heard distinctly Norah's voice:—

"Help! Help! Arthur! Father! Help! Help!" Even in that wild moment my heart leaped, that of all names, she called on mine the first.—Whatever men may say, Love and Jealousy are near kinsmen!

I shouted in return, as I ran, but the wind took my voice away—and then I heard her voice again, but fainter than before:—

"Help! Arthur—Father! Is there no one to help me now!" And then the lightning flashed again, and in the long jagged flash we saw each other, and I heard her glad cry before the thunderclap drowned all else. I had seen that her assailant was Murdock, and I rushed at him, but he had seen me too, and before I could lay hands on him he had let her go, and with a mighty oath which the roll of the thunder drowned, he struck her to the earth and ran.

I raised my poor darling, and, carrying her a little distance, placed her on the edge of the ridge of rocks beside us, for by the light in the sky, which grew paler each second, I saw that a stream of water rising from the bog, was flowing towards us. She was unconscious—so I ran to the stream and dipped my hat full of water to bring to revive her. Then I remembered the signal of finding her, and putting my hands to my lips I sounded the "Coo-ee," once, twice. As I stood I could see Murdock running to his house, for every instant it seemed to grow lighter, and the mist to disperse. The thunder had swept away the rain-clouds, and let in the light of the coming dawn.

But even as I stood there—and I had not delayed an unnecessary second—the ground under me seemed to be giving way. There was a strange shudder or shiver below me, and my feet began to sink. With a wild cry—for I felt that the fatal moment had come—that the bog was moving, and had caught me in its toils, I threw myself forward towards the rock. My cry seemed to arouse Norah like the call of a trumpet. She leaped to her feet, and in an instant seemed to realize my danger, and rushed towards me. When I saw her coming I shouted to her:—

"Keep back! keep back." But she did not pause an instant, and the only words she said were:—

"I am coming, Arthur! I am coming!"

Half way between us there was a flat-topped piece of rock, which raised its head out of the surrounding bog. As she struggled towards it, her feet began to sink, and a new terror for her was added to my own. But she did not falter a moment, and, as her lighter weight was in her favour, with a great effort she gained it. In the meantime I struggled forward. There was between me and the rock a clump of furze bushes; on these I threw myself, and for a second or two they supported me. Then even these began to sink with me, for faster and faster, with each succeeding second, the earth seemed to liquify and melt away.

Up to now I had never realized the fear, or even the possibility, of death to myself—hitherto all my fears had been for Norah. But now came to me the bitter pang which must be for each of the children of men on whom Death has laid his icy hand. That this dread moment had come there was no doubt; nothing short of a miracle could save me!

No language could describe the awful sensation of that melting away of the solid earth—the most dreadful nightmare would be almost a pleasant memory compared with it.

I was now only a few feet from the rock whose very touch meant safety to me—but it was just beyond my reach! I was sinking to my doom!—I could see the horror in Norah's eyes, as she gained the rock and struggled to her feet.

But even Norah's love could not help me—I was beyond the reach of her arms, and she no more than I could keep a foothold on the liquifying earth. Oh! that she had a rope and I might be saved! Alas! she had none—even the shawl that might have aided me had fallen off in her struggle with Murdock.

But Norah had, with her woman's quick instinct, seen a way to help me. In an instant she had had torn off her red petticoat of heavy homespun cloth and thrown one end to me. I clutched and caught it with a despairing grasp—for by this time only my head and hands remained above the surface.

"Now, O God! for strength!" was the earnest prayer of her heart; and my thought was:—

"Now, for the strong hands that that other had despised!"

Norah threw herself backward with her feet against a projecting piece of the rock, and I felt that if we could both hold out long enough I was saved.

Little by little I gained! I drew closer and closer to the rock! Closer! closer still! till with one hand I grasped the rock itself, and hung on, breathless, in blind desperation. I was only just able to support myself, for there was a strange dragging power in the viscous mass that held me, and greatly taxed my strength, already exhausted in the terrible struggle for life. The bog was beginning to move! But Norah bent forward, kneeling on the rock, and grasped my coat collar in her strong hands. Love and despair lent her additional strength, and with one last great effort she pulled me upward—and in an instant more I lay on the rock safe and in her arms.

During this time, short as it was, the morning had advanced, and the cold grey mysterious light disclosed the whole slope before us dim in the shadow of the hill. Opposite to us, across the bog, we saw Joyce and Dick watching us, and between the gusts of wind we faintly heard their shouts.

To our right, far down the hill, the Shleenanaher stood out boldly, its warder rocks struck by the grey light falling over the hill-top. Nearer to us, and something in the same direction, Murdock's house rose a black mass in the centre of the hollow.

But as we looked around us, thankful for our safety, we grasped each other more closely, and a low cry of fear emphasized Norah's shudder—for a terrible thing began to happen.

The whole surface of the bog, as far as we could see it in the dim light, became wrinkled, and then began to move in little eddies, such as one sees in a swollen river. It seemed to rise and rise till it grew almost level with where we were, and instinctively we rose to our feet and stood there awestruck, Norah clinging to me, and with our arms round each other.

The shuddering surface of the bog began to extend on every side to even the solid ground which curbed it, and with relief we saw that Dick and Joyce stood high up on a rock. All things on its surface seemed to melt away and disappear, as though swallowed up. This silent change or demoralization spread down in the direction of Murdock's house—but when it got to the edge of the hollow in which the house stood, it seemed to move as swiftly forward as water leaps down a cataract.

Instinctively we both shouted a warning to Murdock—he, too, villain though he was, had a life to lose. He had evidently felt some kind of shock or change, for he came rushing out of the house full of terror. For an instant he seemed paralyzed with fright as he saw what was happening. And it was little wonder! for in that instant the whole house began to sink into the earth—to sink as a ship founders in a stormy sea, but without the violence and turmoil that marks such a catastrophe. There was something more terrible—more deadly in that silent, causeless destruction than in the devastation of the earthquake or the hurricane.

The wind had now dropped away; the morning light struck full over the hill, and we could see clearly. The sound of the waves dashing on the rocks below, and the booming of the distant breakers filled the air—but through it came another sound, the like of which I had never heard, and the like of which I hope, in God's providence, I shall never hear again—a long, low gurgle, with something of a sucking sound; something terrible—resistless—and with a sort of hiss in it, as of seething waters striving to be free.

Then the convulsion of the bog grew greater; it almost seemed as if some monstrous living thing was deep under the surface and writhing to escape.

By this time Murdock's house had sunk almost level with the bog. He had climbed on the thatched roof, and stood there looking towards us, and stretching forth his hands as though in supplication for help. For a while the superior size and buoyancy of the roof sustained it, but then it too began slowly to sink. Murdock knelt, and clasped his hands in a frenzy of prayer.

And then came a mighty roar and a gathering rush. The side of the hill below us seemed to burst. Murdock threw up his arms—we heard his wild cry as the roof of the house, and he with it, was in an instant sucked below the surface of the heaving mass.

Then came the end of the terrible convulsion. With a rushing sound, and the noise of a thousand waters falling, the whole bog swept, in waves of gathering size, and with a hideous writhing, down the mountain-side to the entrance of the Shleenanaher—struck the portals with a sound like thunder, and piled up to a vast height. And then the millions of tons of slime and ooze, and bog and earth, and broken rock swept through the Pass into the sea.

Norah and I knelt down, hand-in-hand, and with full hearts thanked God for having saved us from so terrible a doom.

The waves of the torrent rushing by us at first came almost level with us; but the stream diminished so quickly, that in an incredibly short time we found ourselves perched on the top of a high jutting rock, standing sharply up from the sloping sides of a deep ravine, where but a few minutes before the bog had been. Carefully we climbed down, and sought a more secure place on the base of the ridge of rocks behind us. The deep ravine lay below us, down whose sides began to rattle ominously, here and there, masses of earth and stones deprived of their support below where the torrent had scoured their base.

Lighter and lighter grew the sky over the mountain, till at last one red ray shot up like a crack in the vault of heaven, and a great light seemed to smite the rocks that glistened in their coat of wet. Across the ravine we saw Joyce and Dick beginning to descend, so as to come over to us. This aroused us, and we shouted to them to keep back, and waved our arms to them in signal; for we feared that some landslip or some new outpouring of the bog might sweep them away, or that the bottom of the ravine might be still only treacherous slime. They saw our gesticulations, if they did not hear our voices, and held back. Then we pointed up the ravine, and signalled them that we would move up the edge of the rocks. This we proceeded to do, and they followed on the other side, watching us intently. Our progress was slow, for the rocks were steep and difficult, and we had to keep eternally climbing up and descending the serrated edges, where the strata lapped over each other; and besides we were chilled and numbed with cold.

At last, however, we passed the corner where was the path down to the Cliff Fields, and turned eastwards up the hill. Then in a little while we got well above the ravine, which here grew shallower, and could walk on more level ground. Here we saw that the ravine ended in a deep cleft, whence issued a stream of water. And then we saw hurrying up over the top of the cleft Joyce and Dick.

Up to now, Norah and I had hardly spoken a word. Our hearts were too full for speech; and, indeed, we understood each other, and could interpret our thoughts by a subtler language than that formulated by man.

In another minute Norah was clasped in her father's arms. He held her close, and kissed her, and cried over her; whilst Dick wrung my hand hard. Then Joyce left his daughter, and came and flung his arms round me, and thanked God that I had escaped; whilst Norah went up to Dick, and put her arms round him, and kissed him as a sister might.

We all went back together as fast as we could; and the sun that rose that morning rose on no happier group—despite the terror and the trouble of the night. Norah walked between her father and me, holding us both tightly, and Dick walked on my other side with his arm in mine. As we came within sight of the house, we met Miss Joyce—her face grey with anxiety. She rushed towards us, and flung her arms round Norah, and the two women rocked each other in their arms; and then we all kissed her—even Dick, to her surprise. His kiss was the last, and it seemed to pull her together; for she perked up, and put her cap straight—a thing which she had not done for the rest of us. Then she walked beside us, holding her brother's hand.

We all talked at once and told the story over and over again of the deadly peril I had been in, and how Norah had saved my life; and here the brave girl's fortitude gave way. She seemed to realize all at once the terror and the danger of the long night, and suddenly her lips grew white, and she would have sunk down to the ground only that I had seen her faint coming and had caught her and held her tight. Her dear head fell over on my shoulder, but her hands never lost their grasp of my arm.

We carried her down toward the house as quickly as we could; but before we had got to the door she had recovered from her swoon, and her first look when her eyes opened was for me, and the first word she said was—

"Arthur! Is he safe"

And then I laid her in the old arm-chair by the hearth-place, and took her cold hands in mine, and kissed them and cried over them—which I hoped vainly that no one saw.

Then Miss Joyce, like a true housekeeper, stirred herself, and the flames roared up the chimney, and the slumbering kettle on the chain over the fire woke and sang again; and it seemed like magic, for all at once we were all sipping hot whiskey punch, and beginning to feel the good effects of it.

Then Miss Joyce hurried away Norah to change her clothes, and Dick and I went with Joyce, and we all rigged ourselves out with whatever came to hand; and then we came back to the kitchen and laughed at each other's appearance. We found Miss Joyce already making preparations for breakfast, and succeeding pretty well, too.

And then Norah joined us, but she was not the least grotesque; she seemed as though she had just stepped out of a band-box—she seemed so trim and neat, with her grey jacket and her Sunday red petticoat. Her black hair was coiled in one glorious roll round her noble head, and there was but one thing which I did not like, and which sent a pang through my heart—a blue and swollen bruise on her ivory forehead where Murdock had struck her that dastard blow! She saw my look and her eyes fell, and when I went to her and kissed the wound and whispered to her how it pained me, she looked up at me and whispered so that none of the others could hear:—

"Hush! hush! Poor soul, he has paid a terrible penalty; let us forget as we forgive!" And then I took her hands in mine and stooped to kiss them, whilst the others all smiled happily as they looked on; but she tried to draw them away, and a bright blush dyed her cheeks as she murmured to me:—

"No! no, Arthur! Arthur dear, not now! I only did what anyone would do for you!" and the tears rushed to her eyes.

"I must! Norah," said I, "I must! for I owe these brave hands my life!" and I kissed them and she made no more resistance. Her father's voice and words sounded very true as he said:—

"Nay, daughter, it is right that he should kiss those hands this blessed mornin', for they took a true man out of the darkness of the grave!"

And then my noble old Dick came over too, and he raised those dear hands reverently to his lips, and said very softly:—

"For he is dear to us all!"

By this time Miss Joyce had breakfast well under weigh, and one and all we thought that it was time we should let the brightness of the day and the lightness of our hearts have a turn; and Joyce said heartily:—

"Come now! Come now! Let us sit down to breakfast; but first let us give thanks to Almighty God that has been so good to us, and let us forgive that poor wretch that met such a horrible death. Rest to his soul!"

We were all silent for a little bit, for the great gladness of our hearts, that came through the terrible remembrance thus brought home to us, was too deep for words. Norah and I sat hand in hand, and between us was but one heart, and one soul, and one thought—and all were filled with gratitude.

When once we had begun breakfast in earnest a miniature babel broke out. We had each something to tell and much to hear; and for the latter reason we tacitly arranged, after the first outbreak, that each should speak in turn.

Miss Joyce told us of the terrible anxiety she had been in ever since she had seen us depart, and how every sound, great or small—even the gusts of wind that howled down the chimney and made the casements rattle—had made her heart jump into her mouth, and brought her out to the door to see if we or any of us were coming. Then Dick told us how, on proceeding down the eastern side of the bog, he had diverged so as to look in at Murdock's house to see if he were there, but had found only old Moynahan lying on the floor in a state of speechless drunkenness, and so wet that the water running from his clothes had formed a pool of water on the floor. He had evidently only lately returned from wandering on the hill-side. Then as he was about to go on his way he had heard, as he thought, a noise lower down the hill, and on going towards it had met Joyce carrying a sheep which had its leg broken, and which he told him had been blown off a steep rock on the south side of the hill. Then they two had kept together after Dick had told him of our search for Norah, until we had seen them in the coming grey of the dawn.

Next Joyce took up the running, and told us how he had been working on the top of the mountain when he saw the signs of the storm coming so fast that he thought it would be well to look after the sheep and cattle, and see them in some kind of shelter before the morning. He had driven all the cattle which were up high on the hill into the shelter where I had found them, and then had gone down the southern shoulder of the hill, placing all the sheep and cattle in places of shelter as well as he could, until he had come across the wounded one, which he took on his shoulders to bring it home, but which had since been carried away in the bursting of the bog. He finished by reminding me jocularly that I owed him something for his night's work, for the stock was now all mine.

"No!" said I, "not for another day. My purchase of your ground and stock was only to take effect from after noon of the 28th, and we are now only at the early morning of that day; but at any rate I must thank you for the others," for I had a number of sheep and cattle which Dick had taken over from the other farmers whose land I had bought.

Then I told over again all that had happened to me. I had to touch on the blow which Norah had received, but I did so as lightly as I could; and when I said "God forgive him!" they all added softly, "Amen!"

Then Dick put in a word about poor old Moynahan:—

"Poor old fellow, he is gone also. He was a drunkard, but he wasn't all bad. Perhaps he saved Norah last night from a terrible danger. His life mayhap may leaven the whole lump of filth and wickedness that went through the Shleenanaher into the sea last night!"

We all said "Amen" again, and I have no doubt that we all meant it with all our hearts.

Then I told again of Norah's brave struggle and how, by her courage and her strength, she took me out of the very jaws of a terrible death. She put one hand before her eyes—for I held the other close in mine—and through her fingers dropped her welling tears.

We sat silent for a while, and we felt that it was only right and fitting when Joyce came round to her and laid his hand on her head and stroked her hair as he said:—

"Ye have done well, daughter—ye have done well!"

XVIII

The Fulfilment

When breakfast was finished, Dick proposed that we should go now and look in the full daylight at the effect of the shifting of the bog. I suggested to Norah that perhaps she had better not come as the sight might harrow her feelings, and, besides, that she would want some rest and sleep after her long night of terror and effort. She point blank refused to stay behind, and accordingly we all set out, having now had our clothes dried and changed, leaving only Miss Joyce to take care of the house.

The morning was beautiful and fresh after the storm. The deluge of rain had washed everything so clean that already the ground was beginning to dry, and as the morning sun shone hotly there was in the air that murmurous hum that follows rain when the air is still. And the air was now still—the storm seemed to have spent itself, and away to the West there was no sign of its track, except that the great Atlantic rollers were heavier and the surf on the rocks rose higher than usual.

We took our way first down the hill, and then westward to the Shleenanaher, for we intended, under Dick's advice, to follow, if possible, up to its source the ravine made by the bog. When we got to the entrance of the Pass we were struck with the vast height to which the bog had risen when its mass first struck the portals. A hundred feet overhead there was the great brown mark, and on the sides of the Pass the same mark was visible, declining quickly as it got seaward and the Pass widened, showing the track of its passage to the sea.

We climbed the rocks and looked over. Norah clung close to me, and my arm went round her and held her tight as we peered over and saw where the great waves of the Atlantic struck the rocks three hundred feet below us, and were for a quarter of a mile away still tinged with the brown slime of the bog.

We then crossed over the ravine, for the rocky bottom was here laid bare, and so we had no reason to fear waterholes or pitfalls. A small stream still ran down the ravine and, shallowing out over the shelf of rock, spread all across the bottom of the Pass, and fell into the sea—

something like a miniature of the Staubach Fall, as the water whitened in the falling.

We then passed up on the west side of the ravine, and saw that the stream which ran down the centre was perpetual—a live stream, and not merely the drainage of the ground where the bog had saturated the earth. As we passed up the hill we saw where the side of the slope had been torn bodily away, and the great chasm where once the house had been which Murdock took from Joyce, and so met his doom. Here there was a great pool of water—and indeed all throughout the ravine were places where the stream broadened into deep pools, and again into shallow pools where it ran over the solid bed of rock. As we passed up, Dick hazarded an explanation or a theory:—

"Do you know it seems to me that this ravine or valley was once before just as it is now. The stream ran down it and out at the Shleenanaher just as it does now. Then by some landslips, or a series of them, or by a falling tree, the passage became blocked, and the hollow became a lake, and its edges grew rank with boggy growth; and then, from one cause and another—the falling in of the sides, or the rush of rain storms carrying down the detritus of the mountain, and perpetually washing down particles of clay from the higher levels—the lake became choked up; and then the lighter matter floated to the top, and by time and vegetable growth became combined. And so the whole mass grew cohesive and floated on the water and slime below. This may have occurred more than once. Nay, moreover, sections of the bog may have become segregated or separated by some similarity of condition affecting its parts, or by some formation of the ground, as by the valley narrowing in parts between walls of rock so that the passage could be easily choked. And so, solid earth formed to be again softened and demoralized by the later mingling with the less solid mass above it. It is possible, if not probable, that more than once, in the countless ages that have passed, this ravine has been as we see it—and again as it was but a few hours ago!"

No one had anything to urge against this theory, and we all proceeded on our way.

When we came to the place where Norah had rescued me, we examined the spot most carefully, and again went over the scene and the exploit. It was almost impossible to realize that this great rock, towering straight up from the bottom of the ravine, had, at the fatal hour, seemed only like a tussock rising from the bog. When I had climbed to the top

I took my knife and cut a cross on the rock, where my brave girl's feet had rested, to mark the spot.

Then we went on again. Higher up the hill we came to a place, where, on each side a rocky promontory, with straight deep walls, jutted into the ravine, making a sort of narrow gateway or gorge in the valley. Dick pointed it out:—

"See! here is one of the very things I spoke of, that made the bog into sections or chambers, or tanks, or whatever we should call them. More than that, here is an instance of the very thing I hinted at before—that the peculiar formation of the Snake's Pass runs right through the hill! If this be so!—but we shall see later on."

On the other side was, we agreed, the place where old Moynahan had said the Frenchmen had last been seen. Dick and I were both curious about the matter, and we agreed to cross the ravine and make certain, for, if it were the spot, Dick's mark of the stones in the Y shape would be a proof. Joyce and Norah both refused to let us go alone, so we all went up a little further, where the sides of the rock sloped on each side, and where we could pass safely, as the bed was rock and quite smooth with the stream flowing over it in a thin sheet.

When we got to the bottom, Joyce, who was looking round, said suddenly:—

"What is that like a square block behind the high rock on the other side?" He went over to it, and an instant after, gave a great cry and turned and beckoned to us. We all ran over—and there before us, in a crescent-shaped nook, at the base of the lofty rock, lay a wooden chest. The top was intact, but one of the lower corners was broken, as though with a fall; and from the broken aperture had fallen out a number of coins, which we soon found to be of gold.

On the top of the chest we could make out the letters R. F. in some metal, discoloured and corroded with a century of slime, and on its ends were great metal handles—to each of which something white was attached. We stooped to look at them, and then Norah, with a low cry, turned to me, and laid her head on my breast, as though to shut out some horrid sight. Then we investigated the mass that lay there.

At each end of the chest lay a skeleton—the fleshless fingers grasping the metal handle. We recognized the whole story at a glance, and our hats came off.

"Poor fellows!" said Dick, "they did their duty nobly. They guarded their treasure to the last." Then he went on. "See! they evidently stepped into the bog, straight off the rock, and were borne down at once, holding tight to the handles of the chest they carried—or stay"—and he stooped lower and caught hold of something:—

"See how the bog can preserve! this leather strap attached to the handles of the chest each had round his shoulder, and so, willy nilly, they were dragged to their doom. Never mind! they were brave fellows all the same, and faithful ones—they never let go the handles—look! their dead hands clasp them still. France should be proud of such sons! It would make a noble coat of arms, this treasure chest sent by freemen to aid others—and with two such supporters!"

We looked at the chest and the skeletons for a while, and then Dick said:—

"Joyce, this is on your land—for it is yours till tomorrow—and you may as well keep it—possession is nine points of the law—and if we take the gold out, the government can only try to claim it. But if they take it, we may ask in vain!" Joyce answered:—

"Take it I will, an' gladly; but not for meself. The money was sent for Ireland's good—to help them that wanted help, an' plase God! I'll see it does'nt go asthray now!"

Dick's argument was a sensible one, and straightway we wrenched the top off the chest, and began to remove the gold; but we never stirred the chest or took away those skeleton hands from the handles which they grasped.

It took us all, carrying a good load each, to bring the money to Joyce's cottage. We locked it in a great oak chest, and warned Miss Joyce not to say a word about it. I told Miss Joyce that if Andy came for me he was to be sent on to us, explaining that we were going back to the top of the new ravine.

We followed it up further, till we reached a point much higher up on the hill, and at last came to the cleft in the rock whence the stream issued. The floor here was rocky, and it being so, we did not hesitate to descend, and even to enter the chine. As we did so, Dick turned to me:—

"Well! it seems to me that the mountain is giving up its secrets today. We have found the Frenchmen's treasure, and now we may expect, I suppose, to find the lost crown! By George! though, it is strange! they said the Snake became the Shifting Bog, and that it went out, by the Shleenanaher!—as we saw the bog did."

When we got well into the chine, we began to look about us curiously. There was something odd—something which we did not expect. Dick was the most prying, and certainly the most excited of us all. He touched some of the rock, and then almost shouted:—

"Hurrah! this a day of discoveries.—Hurrah! hurrah!"

"Now, Dick, what is it?" I asked—myself in a tumult, for his enthusiasm, although we did not know the cause, excited as all.

"Why! man, don't you see! this is what we have wanted all along,"

"What is? Speak out, man dear! We are all in ignorance!" Dick laid his hand impressively on the rock:—

"Limestone! There is a streak of it here, right through the mountain—and, moreover, look! look!—this is not all nature's work—these rocks have been cut in places by the hands of men!" We all got very excited, and hurried up the chine; but the rocks now joined over our heads, and all was dark beyond, and the chine became a cave.

"Has anyone a match—we must have a light of some kind here," said Joyce.

"There is the lantern in the house. I shall run for it. Don't stir until I get back," I cried; and I ran out and climbed the side of the ravine, and got to Joyce's house as soon as I could. My haste and impetuosity frightened Miss Joyce, who called in terror:—

"Is there anything wrong—not an accident I hope?"

"No! no! we only want to examine a rock, and the place is dark. Give us the lantern quick, and some matches."

"Aisy! aisy, alanna!" she said. "The rock won't run away!"

I took the lantern and matches and ran back. When we had lit the lantern, Norah suggested that we should be very careful, as there might be foul air about. Dick laughed at the idea.

"No foul air here, Norah; it was full of water a few hours ago," and taking the lantern, he went into the narrow opening. We all followed, Norah clinging tightly to me. The cave widened as we entered, and we stood in a moderate sized cavern, partly natural and partly hollowed out by rough tools. Here and there, were inscriptions in strange character, formed by straight vertical lines something like the old telegraph signs, but placed differently.

"Ogham!—one of the oldest and least known of writings," said Dick, when the light fell on them as he raised the lantern.

At the far end of the cave was a sort of slab or bracket, formed of a part of the rock carven out. Norah went towards it, and called us to her with a loud cry. We all rushed over, and Dick threw the light of the lantern on her; and then exclamations of wonder burst from us also.

In her hand she held an ancient crown of strange form. It was composed of three pieces of flat gold joined all along one edge, like angle iron, and twisted delicately. The gold was wider and the curves bolder in the centre, from which they were fined away to the ends and then curved into a sort of hook. In the centre was set a great stone, that shone with the yellow light of a topaz, but with a fire all its own!

Dick was the first to regain his composure and, as usual, to speak:—

"The Lost Crown of Gold!—the crown that gave the hill its name, and was the genesis of the story of St. Patrick and the King of the Snakes! Moreover, see, there is a scientific basis for the legend. Before this stream cut its way out through the limestone, and made this cavern, the waters were forced upwards to the lake at the top of the hill, and so kept it supplied; but when its channel was cut here—or a way opened for it by some convulsion of nature, or the rending asunder of these rocks—the lake fell away."

He stopped, and I went on:—

"And so, ladies and gentlemen, the legend is true, that the Lost Crown would be discovered when the water of the lake was found again."

"Begor! that's thrue, anyhow!" said the voice of Andy in the entrance. "Well, yer 'an'r, iv all the sthrange things what iver happened, this is the most sthrangest! Fairies isn't in it this time, at all, at all!"

I told Andy something of what had happened, including the terrible deaths of Murdock and Moynahan, and sent him off to tell the head constable of police, and any one else he might see. I told him also of the two skeletons found beside the chest.

Andy was off like a rocket. Such news as he had to tell would not come twice in a man's lifetime, and would make him famous through all the country-side. When he was gone, we decided that we had seen all that was worth while, and agreed to go back to the house, where we might be on hand to answer all queries regarding the terrible occurrences of the night. When we got outside the cave, and had ascended the ravine, I noticed that the crown in Norah's hands had now none of the yellow glare of the jewel, and feared the latter had been lost. I said to her:—

"Norah, dear! have you dropped the jewel from the crown?"

She held it up, startled, to see; and then we all wondered again—for the jewel was still there, but it had lost its yellow colour, and shone with a white light, something like the lustre of a pearl seen in the midst of the flash of diamonds. It looked like some kind of uncut crystal, but none of us had ever seen anything like it.

We had hardly got back to the house when the result of Andy's mission began to be manifested. Every soul in the country-side seemed to come pouring in to see the strange sights at Knockcalltecrore. There was a perfect babel of sounds; and every possible and impossible story, and theory, and conjecture was ventilated at the top of the voice of every one, male and female.

The head constable was one of the first to arrive. He came into the cottage, and we gave him all the required details of Murdock's and Moynahan's death, which he duly wrote down, and then went off with Dick to go over the ground.

Presently there was a sudden silence amongst the crowd outside, the general body of which seemed to continue as great as ever from the number of new arrivals—despite the fact that a large number of those present had followed Dick and the head constable in their investigation of the scene of the catastrophe. The silence was as odd as noise would have been under ordinary circustances, so I went to the door to see what it meant. In the porch I met Father Ryan, who had just come from the scene of the disaster. He shook me warmly by the hand, and said loudly, so that all those around might hear:—

"Mr. Severn, I'm real glad and thankful to see ye this day. Praise be to God, that watched over ye last night, and strengthened the arms of that brave girl to hold ye up." Here Norah came to join us; and he took her warmly by both hands, whilst the people cheered:—

"My! but we're all proud of ye! Remember that God has given a great mercy through your hands—and ye both must thank Him all the days of your life! And those poor men that met their death so horribly—poor Moynahan, in his drunken slumber! Men! it's a warning to ye all! Whenever ye may be tempted to take a glass too much, let the fate of that poor soul rise up before ye and forbid ye to go too far. As for that unhappy Murdock, may God forgive him and look lightly on his sins! I told him what he should expect—that the fate of Ahab and Jezebel would be his. For as Ahab coveted the vineyard of his neighbour Naboth, and as Jezebel wrought evil to aid him to his desire, so this man hath coveted his neighbour's goods and wrought evil to ruin him. And now behold his fate, even as the fate of Ahab and Jezebel! He went without warning and without rites—and no man knows where his body lies. The fishes of the sea have preyed on him, even as the dogs on Jezebel." Here Joyce joined us, and he turned to him:—

"And do you, Michael Joyce, take to heart the lesson of God's goodness! Ye thought when yer land and yer house was taken that a great wrong was done ye, and that God had deserted ye; and yet so inscrutable are His ways that these very things were the salvation of ye and all belonging to ye. For in his stead you and yours would have been swept in that awful avalanche into the sea!"

And now the head constable returned with Dick, and the priest went out. I took the former aside and asked him if there would be any need for Norah to remain, as there were other witnesses to all that had occurred. He told me that there was not the slightest need. Then he went away after telling the people that we all had had a long spell of trouble and labour, and would want to be quiet and have some rest. And so, with a good feeling and kindness of heart which I have never seen lacking in this people, they melted away; and we all came within the house, and shut the door, and sat round the fire to discuss what should be done. Then and there we decided that the very next day Norah should start with her father, for the change of scene would do her good, and take her mind off the terrible experiences of last night.

So that day we rested. The next morning Andy was to drive Joyce and Norah and myself off to Galway, en route for London and Paris.

In the afternoon Norah and I strolled out together for one last look at the beautiful scene from our tablerock in the Cliff Fields. Close as we had been hitherto, there was now a new bond between us; and when we were out of sight of prying eyes—on the spot where we had first told our loves, I told her of my idea of the new bond. She hung down her head, but drew closer to me as I told her how much more I valued my life since she had saved it for me—and how I should in all the two years that were to come try hard that every hour should be such as she would like me to have passed.

"Norah, dear!" I said, "the bar you place on our seeing each other in all that long time will be hard to bear, but I shall know that I am enduring for your sake." She turned to me, and with earnest eyes looked lovingly into mine as she said:—

"Arthur! dear Arthur, God knows I love you! I love you so well that I want to come to you, if I can, in such a way that I may never do you discredit; and I am sure that when the two years are over—and, indeed, they will not go lightly for me—you will not be sorry that you have made the sacrifice for me. Dear! I shall ask you when we meet on our wedding morning if you are satisfied."

When it was time to go home we rose up, and—it might have been that the evening was chilly—a cold feeling came over me, as though I still stood in the shadow of the fateful hill. And there in the Cliff Fields I kissed Norah Joyce for the last time!

THE TWO YEARS SPED QUICKLY enough, although my not being able to see Norah at all was a great trial to me. Often and often I felt tempted almost beyond endurance to go quietly and hang round where she was so that I might get even a passing glimpse of her; but I felt that such would not be loyal to my dear girl. It was hard not to be able to tell her, even now and again, how I loved her, but it had been expressly arranged—and wisely enough too—that I should only write in such a manner as would pass, if necessary, the censorship of the schoolmistress. "I must be," said Norah to me, "exactly as the other girls are—and, of course, I must be subject to the same rules." And so it was that my letters had to be of a tempered warmth, which caused me now and again considerable pain.

My dear girl wrote to me regularly, and although there was not any of what her schoolmistress would call "love" in her letters, she always kept me posted in all her doings; and with every letter it was borne in on me that her heart and feelings were unchanged.

I had certain duties to attend to with regard to my English property, and this kept me fairly occupied.

Each few months I ran over to the Knockcalltecrore, which Dick was transforming into a fairyland. The discovery of the limestone had, as he had conjectured, created possibilities in the way of building and of waterworks of which at first we had not dreamed. The new house rose on the table-rock in the Cliff Fields. A beautiful house it was, of red sandstone with red tiled roof and quaint gables, and jutting windows and balustrades of carven stone. The whole Cliff Fields were laid out as exquisite gardens, and the murmur of water was everywhere. None of this I ever told Norah in my letters, as it was to be a surprise to her.

On the spot where she had rescued me we had reared a great stone—a monolith whereon a simple legend told the story of a woman's strength and bravery. Round its base were sculptured the history of the mountain from its legend of the King of Snakes down to the lost treasure and the rescue of myself. This was all carried out under Dick's eye. The legend on the stone was:—

NORAH JOYCE
a Brave Woman
on this spot
by her Courage and Devotion
saved a man's life.

At the end of the first year Norah went to another school at Dresden for six months; and then, by her own request to Mr. Chapman, was transferred to an English school at Brighton, one justly celebrated amongst Englishwomen.

These last six months were very, very long to me; for as the time drew near when I might claim my darling the suspense grew very great, and I began to have harrowing fears lest her love might not have survived the long separation and the altered circumstances.

I heard regularly from Joyce. He had gone to live with his son Eugene, who was getting along well, and was already beginning to make a name for himself as an engineer. By his advice his father had taken a sub-section of the great Ship Canal, then in progress of construction, and with the son's knowledge and his own shrewdness and energy was beginning to realize what to him was a fortune. So that the purchase-money of Shleenanaher, which formed his capital, was used to a good purpose.

At last the long period of waiting came to an end. A month before Norah's school was finished, Joyce went to Brighton to see her, having come to visit me beforehand. His purpose and mine was to arrange all about the wedding, which we wanted to be exactly as she wished. She asked her father to let it be as quiet as possible, with absolutely no fuss— no publicity, and in some quiet place where no one knew us.

"Tell Arthur," she said, "that I should like it to be somewhere near the sea, and where we can get easily on the Continent."

I fixed on Hythe, which I had been in the habit of visiting occasionally, as the place where we were to be married. Here, high over the sea level, rises the grand old church where the bones of so many brave old Norsemen rest after a thousand years. The place was so near to Folkestone that after the wedding and an informal breakfast we could drive over to catch the mid-day boat. I lived the requisite time in Hythe, and complied with all the formalities.

I did not see my darling until we met in the churchporch, and then I gazed on her with unstinted admiration. Oh! what a peerless beauty she was! Every natural grace and quality seemed developed to the full. Every single grace of womanhood was there—every subtle manifestation of high breeding—every stamp of the highest culture. There was no one in the porch—for those with me delicately remained in the church when they saw me go out to meet my bride—and I met her with a joy unspeakable. Joyce went in and left her with me a moment—they had evidently arranged to do so—but when we were quite alone she said to me with a very serious look:—

"Mr. Severn, before we go into the church answer me one question— answer me truthfully, I implore you!" A great fear came upon me that at the last I was to suffer the loss of her I loved—that at the moment when the cup of happiness was at my lips it was to be dashed aside—and it was with a hoarse voice and a beating heart I answered:—

"I shall speak truly, Norah! What is it?" She said very demurely:—

"Mr. Severn! are you satisfied with me?" I looked up and caught the happy smile in her eyes, and for answer took her in my arms to kiss her: but she said:—

"Not yet, Arthur! not yet! What would they say? And besides, it would be unlucky." So I released her, and she took my arm, and as we came up the aisle together I whispered to her:—

"Yes, my darling! Yes! yes! a thousand times. The time has been long, long; but the days were well spent!" She looked at me with a glad, happy look as she murmured in my ear:—

"We shall see Italy soon, dear, together. I am so happy!" and she pinched my arm.

That was a very happy wedding, and as informal as it was happy. As Norah had no bridesmaid, Dick, who was to have been my best man, was not going to act; but when Norah knew this she insisted on it, and said sweetly:—

"I should not feel I was married properly unless Dick took his place. And as to my having no bridesmaid, all I can say is, if we had half so good a girl friend, she would be here, of course!"

This settled the matter, and Dick with his usual grace and energy carried out the best man's chief duty of taking care of his principal's hat.

There were only our immediate circle present, Joyce and Eugene, Miss Joyce—who had come all the way from Knocknacar, Mr. Chapman, and Mr. Caicy—who had also come over from Galway specially. There was one other old friend also present, but I did not know it until I came out of the vestry, after signing the register, with my wife on my arm.

There, standing modestly in the background, and with a smile as manifest as a ten acre field, was none other than Andy—Andy so well dressed and smart that there was really nothing to distinguish him from any other man in Hythe. Norah saw him first, and said heartily:—

"Why, there is Andy! How are you, Andy?" and held out her hand. Andy took it in his great fist, and stooped and kissed it as if it had been a saint's hand and not a woman's:—

"God bless and keep ye, Miss Norah darlin'—an' the Virgin and the saints watch over ye both." Then he shook hands with me.

"Thank you, Andy!" we said both together, and then I beckoned Dick and whispered to him.

We went back to breakfast in my rooms, and sat down as happy a party as could be—the only one not quite comfortable at first being Andy. He and Dick both came in quite hot and flushed. Dick pointed to him:—

"He's an obstinate, truculent villain, is Andy. Why, I had to almost fight him to make him come in. Now, Andy, no running away—it is Miss Norah's will!" and Andy subsided bashfully into a seat. It was fully several minutes before he either smiled or winked. We had a couple of hours to pass before it became time to leave for Folkestone; and when breakfast was over, one and then another said a few kindly words. Dick opened the ball by speaking most beautifully of our own worthiness, and of how honestly and honourably each had won the other, and of the long life and happiness that lay, he hoped and believed, before us. Then Joyce spoke a few manly words of his love for his daughter and his pride in her. The tears were in his eyes when he said how his one regret in life was that her dear mother had to look down from Heaven her approval on this day, instead of sharing it amongst us as the best of mothers and the best of women. Then Norah turned to him and laid her head on his breast and cried a little—not unhappily, but happily, as a bride should cry at leaving those she loves for one she loves better still.

Of course both the lawyers spoke, and Eugene said a few words bashfully. I was about to reply to them all, when Andy got up and crystallized the situation in a few words:—

"Miss Norah an' yer 'an'r, I'd like, if I might make so bould, to say a wurrd fur all the men and weemen in Ireland that ayther iv yez iver kem across. I often heerd iv fairies, an' Masther Art knows well how he hunted wan from the top iv Knocknacar to the top iv Knockcalltecrore, and I won't say a wurrd about the kind iv a fairy he wanted to find—not even in her quare kind iv an eye—bekase I might be overlooked, as the masther was; and more betoken, since I kem here Masther Dick has tould me that I'm to be yer 'an'r's Irish coachman. Hurroo! an' I might get evicted from that same houldin' fur me impidence in tellin' tales iv the Masther before he was married; but I'll promise yez both that there'll be no man from the Giant's Causeway to Cape Clear what'll thry, an' thry hardher, to make yer feet walk an' yer wheels rowl in aisy ways than meself. I'm takin' a liberty, I know, be sayin' so much, but plase God! ye'll walk yer. ways wid honour an' wid peace, believin' in aich other an' in God—an' may He bless ye both, an' yer childher, and yer childher's childher to folly ye. An' if iver ayther iv yez wants to shtep into glory over a man's body, I hope ye'll not look past poor ould Andy Sullivan!"

Andy's speech was quaint, but it was truly meant, for his heart was full of quick sympathy, and the honest fellow's eyes were full of tears as he concluded.

Then Miss Joyce's health was neatly proposed by Mr. Chapman and responded to in such a way by Mr. Caicy that Norah whispered me that she would not be surprised if Aunt took up her residence in Galway before long.

And now the hour was come to say good-bye to all friends. We entered our carriage and rolled away, leaving behind us waving hands, loving eyes, and hearts that beat most truly.

And the great world lay before us with all the possibilities of happiness that men and women may win for themselves. There was never a cloud to shadow our sunlit way; and we felt that we were one.

A Note About the Author

Bram Stoker (1847–1912) was an Irish novelist. Born in Dublin, Stoker suffered from an unknown illness as a young boy before entering school at the age of seven. He would later remark that the time he spent bedridden enabled him to cultivate his imagination, contributing to his later success as a writer. He attended Trinity College, Dublin from 1864, graduating with a BA before returning to obtain an MA in 1875. After university, he worked as a theatre critic, writing a positive review of acclaimed Victorian actor Henry Irving's production of *Hamlet* that would spark a lifelong friendship and working relationship between them. In 1878, Stoker married Florence Balcombe before moving to London, where he would work for the next 27 years as business manager of Irving's influential Lyceum Theatre. Between his work in London and travels abroad with Irving, Stoker befriended such artists as Oscar Wilde, Walt Whitman, Hall Caine, James Abbott McNeill Whistler, and Sir Arthur Conan Doyle. In 1895, having published several works of fiction and nonfiction, Stoker began writing his masterpiece *Dracula* (1897) while vacationing at the Kilmarnock Arms Hotel in Cruden Bay, Scotland. Stoker continued to write fiction for the rest of his life, achieving moderate success as a novelist. Known more for his association with London theatre during his life, his reputation as an artist has grown since his death, aided in part by film and television adaptations of *Dracula*, the enduring popularity of the horror genre, and abundant interest in his work from readers and scholars around the world.

A Note from the Publisher

Spanning many genres, from non-fiction essays to literature classics to children's books and lyric poetry, Mint Edition books showcase the master works of our time in a modern new package. The text is freshly typeset, is clean and easy to read, and features a new note about the author in each volume. Many books also include exclusive new introductory material. Every book boasts a striking new cover, which makes it as appropriate for collecting as it is for gift giving. Mint Edition books are only printed when a reader orders them, so natural resources are not wasted. We're proud that our books are never manufactured in excess and exist only in the exact quantity they need to be read and enjoyed.

Discover more of your favorite classics with Bookfinity™.

- Track your reading with custom book lists.
- Get great book recommendations for your personalized Reader Type.
- Add reviews for your favorite books.
- AND MUCH MORE!

Visit **bookfinity.com** and take the fun Reader Type quiz to get started.

Enjoy our classic and modern companion pairings!